Obsidian

2

Obsidian

A Novel By
Sam Rogers

Gowen Place Press
Bainbridge Island, Washington

Also by Sam Rogers:

The Fulcrum: Selected Poems 2000 - 2010

The Suicide Diversion

Epistle Paternal: A Letter To Our Sons

Beagle's Noose

Cover design by Chris Peters, chrispeters.com

ISBN: 978-0-9847183-6-8
Gowen Place Press
Bainbridge Island, Wa 98110
Samrogers2000@yahoo.com
samrogersbooks.com

Non ducor, duca

I am not led, I lead

1

EMPTY

July, 1972

Erica didn't sleep all night. Instead, she sat up in bed, supported by pillows, listening to coyotes sing across the valley, memories flowing through the ragged sphere of her awareness. When dawn finally came, she went to her studio and began to work, as she had on twenty thousand other mornings. The light in the space was diffuse across her vision. She sat cross-legged on the floor, reminding herself as always of when she'd been a child at play with her toys. A chunk of sandstone was cool and rough in her hands. She was surrounded by objects she'd collected during her forty years in the desert: a variety of rocks chosen not for rarity but for colors and shapes appealing to her, along with sticks of piñon, cholla, and juniper, metal from abandoned equipment and vehicles, wood from structures that had long ago fallen down and been blown by the winds across the sand.

She spread rocks out on the tan woven blanket she used for composition, placing them first into a circle. Sticks became the spokes of a wheel. After some consideration, she arranged the rocks into a square and assembled a latticework of wood to join the corners. Her fingers, the skin tough at the tips, were as deft as ever, sorting and placing the materials with intuitive abandon.

However, as the morning went on, she became frustrated. She could arrange things but wasn't able to see them distinctly. Without good visual feedback, she had little sense of where she was going in the process. Clarity of sight had become increasingly elusive over the past year but now she felt she was losing it for good. Turning her head to peer out with her peripheral vision didn't help much. The world in front of her had been swallowed up in a drifting glow that offered no consolation whatsoever.

She stood abruptly, her knees cracking, and lifted the edge of the blanket. With a swift jerk of her wrists, she sent her materials flying across the room. She fled the studio, moving across the courtyard and through the house by memory. In the living room, she threw herself down into the ancient and malodorous armchair. Just as she had tried in the past to use her sheer mental energy to will lovers to come to her or to bring destruction upon her enemies (with varying degrees of success), she tried as she sat through the afternoon into the night to will, without hope, for something to happen, whether it would be the return of her sight, her death, or some event she couldn't imagine, a surprise that would change everything.

2

ARRIVAL

The way ran in thick darkness below the cottonwood trees, past the pool and the kitchen, away from the center of the ranch, back into the mesas. Moving quickly to avoid early risers, following the beam of his flashlight, Michael followed the path along a meandering arroyo. Cliffs loomed on either side, narrowing to a box canyon whose jagged outline above cut the teeming stars into a wedge. The splash of a waterfall signaled the location of a side trail that he climbed in darkness to the top of the mesa. He jogged past what he knew was a small Anasazi site, across a cactus-filled plain, then over a ridge to a campsite with fire rings.

He rested a few minutes, ignoring his thirst, watching the stars dissolve in a deep blue growing steadily brighter. The camp, set among boulders and low gnarled trees, was poised in the ebb of night. He'd been there before to help out with a burro trip for the senior high kids. The teenagers and the burros turned out to be kindred spirits - staying up late, braying loudly, kicking at restrictions. He'd wanted to come back to this place with Sheila. Thinking of her sent him stumbling ahead with a fiery pressure inside his skull. He feared he was doomed to have his heart crushed in every relationship he had. As if to confound the cliche, his heart beat steadily and strongly even as he gained altitude, suggesting that his brain was likely to break long before his heart gave way.

As the day expanded around him, the path formed a broad ascending curve that passed near the mouth of an abandoned uranium mine where he found the undiluted gloom inside compelling in contrast to the ever-brightening light of morning. The trail led him past watering stations and salt licks for cattle, through miles of scrub brush, gradually gaining altitude until he scrambled to the summit crest of Mesa Montejo towering over the broad basin of the Valle Luminoso.

He stood on the edge of a five hundred foot drop. Spread out before him, undulating in the rising heat, were mountains, mesas, canyons, arroyos, plains, and a river turned back by an earthen dam to form a sprawling lake. The focal point in this composition was Obsidian, the ridge-topped peak that was the remnant of a volcano that had erupted in prehistory, propelling its lava out in a thousand mile radius.

Below him, about a mile away, at the near edge of the vast plain, was an adobe house: a flat-roofed structure with two wings, built around a courtyard open on one side to the view. A swallow emerging from its aerie in the rock was taken aback by his human presence and immediately transformed itself into a whistling blur accelerating straight up. When he tilted his head back to follow it, the sky was so vast and empty he felt he was being pulled to the zenith. He closed his eyes and shook his head. Inside his eyelids, neon shards of color floated, in the same shades as the paint in the bedroom of his childhood home in Greenwich Village, New York City. That home was gone now, his parents were dead, and he'd been cast out to the world like an orphan in a Dickens novel, at least in his own estimation.

Was the house below him a place of refuge or another false anchorage that would cut him adrift? He'd come this far so he might as well find out. Without reflection, he found himself descending the steep escarpment although no obvious route presented itself. Moving carelessly and rapidly, he soon slipped on a scree of loose pebbles. His feet were propelled out toward the void. As he fell, he slammed repeatedly into the sandstone, each impact creating a momentary tableau of earth and sky framed in pain.

He landed hard on his tailbone and came to rest sitting on a large flat boulder, part of the talus slope at the base of the cliff. Dust swirled in spiral vapors around his head. Small fragments of stone, set in motion by his descent, continued to fall for several minutes. The sun had crossed over the mesas and pressed its glare down on his scalp. In his haste to leave during the night, he'd neglected to bring his Yankees cap. He lowered his head to his knees for relief from the blast of light.

Between his shoes, a black ant worked its way across the pitted surface of the rock in search of sustenance in this barren terrain. His ridiculous good fortune at falling so far without breaking anything did not relieve the pressure in his head or the pain, emotional more than physical, he carried in his chest. He looked forward about three hundred yards to the adobe house that presented a blank impassive face, its stark right angles broken only by a wooden ladder leaning against the side.

His jeans had been stained in rust and tan by the fall. When he stood to brush them, a surge of dizziness made him stumble. The momentum of his staggering carried him down the slope and across the desert. Wary of rattlesnakes, he tripped heavily between the piñon trees and juniper bushes. A sudden pattern in the ground made him stop, one boot raised in the air. Rocks the size of a fist had been set into the shape of an hourglass. Sticks of cholla cactus in descending height had been placed upright in the ground along one of the interior edges of the design. The colors and angles of the elements echoed each other in a way he couldn't quite define but found pleasing. This was obviously a human production yet conveyed the same natural elegance displayed in the petroglyphs on the sides of the mesas above the ranch. He set his foot down to the side so as not to disturb the art and continued on.

After crossing the dirt road, he stood for a moment looking at the front of the house, an expanse of dried mud with lightning-shaped cracks descending from roof to ground. A black Mercedes and a battered red pickup truck waited under a frame structure to the side. A whisper of air stirred the dust in the yard. The windows were shuttered against the heat whose shimmerings he parted as he approached the house. The front door was composed of ancient weathered wood, the grain so deep it stood out in relief. Standing on the low stone sill, he lifted his hand and rapped his knuckles lightly on the door. What followed was a long silence in the still afternoon.

The door opened. Wearing a black dress with velvet buttons down its front, a woman he knew to be Erica Hanlon stood cloaked in the shadows of the house, radiating smooth cool air out to him. Her head was thrust slightly forward and to the side. Her filmy blue eyes moved down and then up, surveying him from head to foot and back again, seeming to break him down into his component shapes and colors. With her aquiline nose and erect posture, she carried an air of imperious self-possession. Although she didn't utter a word, he realized she was waiting, so he said the first words that came to him:

"I'm Michael Spielman. Do you need any help with the chores?"

She looked at him intently, without blinking. Then she stepped back and turned to the side, offering the profile made famous by her husband, a sculptor equally renowned. Michael took this as an invitation and walked in. She closed the door and moved past him, brushing his shoulder, striding into the courtyard where Obsidian was on full display, the distinctive ridged summit placed to the left of center in the composition. She stood in her ankle-length dress, her hands folded at her waist, her gray hair pulled back tightly to the base of her skull and tied off with a piece of white yarn. Her body was square to him but her head was turned toward the mountain, as if waiting to hear what it might say. Her face held an intricate network of lines and folds yet a youthful force emanated from her.

"Where were you born?" she asked abruptly, as if this was the automatic first question she put to everyone she met.

"New York City."

"I lived there. What do your parents do?"

"My mother died three years ago. She was an accountant. My father was a teacher and a poet, too, I guess. He died, before her."

This was the minimal version. He hoped she wouldn't press him.

"You have brothers and sisters?"

"No. I'm not aware of any."

Her face was turned away from him and her eyes looked askance.

"Humph. You've been working for the church people, I suppose."

The thirty thousand acres surrounding Erica's land was called Ranch of the Spirits and was owned by the Protestant Conference of the West Coast. Michael had, indeed, been part of the Ranch's summer college staff, at least until that morning.

"Yes, but not any more."

"Are you religious?"

He was unnerved that she wasn't looking directly at him but she was obviously paying attention.

"I don't know what to believe."

She made an affirmative grunt.

"That's right. We don't have evidence for the absurd lies the churches try to foist upon us. This is my religion."

She thrust her chin toward the landscape with its interdependent elements of basin and mountains and sky, Obsidian

Peak presiding over this very particular world. Following her gaze, Michael was lost for a few seconds in the miles of space before him. His East Coast eyes, raised on near horizons, had only recently adjusted to how far he could see out here.

"Are you handy?"

At first he thought she was asking him if he lived nearby and he couldn't figure out what to say. He didn't really live anywhere at the moment. Then he realized she was talking about his manual dexterity.

"Sure, a little, I guess. During college, I was an assistant apartment manager and had to make repairs around the building."

"What did you study in college?"

"I went to Pratt Institute for Art in Brooklyn, but I left in my senior year."

She swung her head suddenly around and stared directly at him. Beneath the clouded surface of her eyes, her pupils were expanding. He took a step back from the impact of this intense regard.

"What medium?"

"Painting."

"Is that right?"

"I never did any sculpture." He said this as if it would somehow allay her fears.

"Whose work do you like?"

He considered for a moment and thought of the pattern of rocks he'd seen out in the desert. But something about the way she was waiting made him feel that mentioning her work would get him shown to the door. So he told another part of the truth.

"Cezanne?"

"Complex architecture and good color. Well, you could do worse."

She cocked her head and peered into his face in a way that made him feel like potential prey. The muscles in his back were clenched tight and radiated pain from the fall. He shrugged his shoulders but that just rearranged the tension. After a long moment, she came to a decision.

"You can assist me with chores for now but strictly on a trial basis. If you want to stay, there's a room you can use."

He was surprised, shocked even, that she'd let a stranger into her house so quickly but she gave the impression of someone who made snap decisions based on intuition. He wondered whether he'd be paid and how much, and he wasn't sure he ever actually agreed to the arrangement but he found himself following her along the interior porch of the courtyard down to the end of the wing where she opened a door. The room was sparsely decorated with a thin mattress on a metal cot, a rickety wooden table, a battered folding chair, and a chest of drawers. A small engraving on the wall was a Picasso, numbered thirteen of one hundred, depicting a laughing goat's head. Erica gestured toward the open door of the bathroom before turning away as if to avoid dwelling on his needs in that area.

She said, "I sleep with a Colt revolver under my pillow and I know how to use it."

She didn't add to this information so he said, "Okay?"

She turned and left the room, closing the door behind her.

He immediately went in to the sink, dipped his head to the silvered tap, and drank what felt like gallons of water. He removed his clothes and showered off the dust of the day's journey, finding his body covered with scrapes and bruises from his fall. Afterward, even though it was barely four p.m., he collapsed heavily onto the bed in his underwear and plummeted into sleep.

3

DEFENSE

She walked quickly to her bedroom, shut the door, and locked it. She sat on the bed and pulled the Colt from under the pillow. It was a gift from her father when she'd first moved away from the farm to take art classes in New York City some fifty years before. She'd only used it once, when a drunk was banging on the door of her apartment in Hell's Kitchen and yelled he was going to break it down. She took the Colt from the mantel of the fireplace and, dressed in her flannel nightgown with a faded roses print, threw open the door, pointing the pistol directly between the eyes of the flushed-face stevedore who stood with his hammy fist hanging in the air. She cocked back the hammer with her left hand and said, with a coolness she didn't feel, "I believe you have the wrong apartment."

His eyes had been closed to mere slits but the dark circle of the Colt's barrel opened his lids wide so she could see the network of red veins across his irises.

"Yes, ma'am. Many apologies to you."

With his hand still in the air, he pivoted on a heel and stumbled down the hall. She slammed the door with force, loud enough to make him think it was a shot, eliciting a high-pitched squeal followed by the heavy thump of him falling to the floor. A scrabbling sound indicated he'd stood himself up and she heard his rapid, heavy footfalls going to the stairwell and down the four flights of the walk-up. She was trembling but felt a sense of triumph, knowing she would have shot him if she'd been forced to. She felt the same way about the young man she had recklessly invited into her house. She would shoot him if she had to but realized that killing him was not the deepest impulse she had.

4

WAKING

In the darkness, when he awoke, the rough fiber of the blanket scratched at his cheek. He stood and walked with uncertain steps to the door. He opened it and found the courtyard was lit by a single bulb whose illumination was surpassed by the glow from the stars overhead. In the dim light, he looked at his watch and could see the hour and minute hands indicating two o'clock but the second hand was still. Even shaking his wrist didn't move it. He realized the watch must have broken in his fall. He used the bathroom, returned to bed, and looked up at the swirling colors his eyes imposed on the blackness. He thought, "Now I'll never get back to sleep."

When he returned to awareness, every item in the room was incandescent from the sun. Light even bounced at him from the long-faded varnish of the bureau and desk. He dressed in his dirty clothes and made his way into the kitchen where he found hot coffee on the stove. Bread, butter, jam, a box of Rice Krispies, and milk were laid out on the counter next to a note which read: "Patch adobe outside house. Materials and tools in shed. Extra clothes in dresser." He poured coffee from a battered kettle on the stove, made toast, and found a bowl and spoon for the cereal. Sitting at the wooden kitchen table, he ate quickly and wondered where Erica was.

5

JOB

She hardly talked to him for the first week. His assigned tasks were basic maintenance, well within his capabilities: reinforcing the support beams in the garage, repairing the stone fireplace where the mortar had crumbled, fixing leaks in the plumbing, along with the apparently endless task of keeping the adobe walls intact. He rose early each morning, brought to consciousness by the first light. His watch never did start again so he always checked the time on the stove clock as he entered the kitchen.

A woman named Lupe from the village would arrive around nine to clean house and make lunch. She smiled at him but they were mutually shy and didn't converse. At lunch he ate her sandwiches while sitting on an ancient bench in the shade at the side of the courtyard. Flitting between the pillars, hummingbirds made the loudest noise around the house just from the vibrations of their wings. Lupe cleaned through the afternoon and cooked dinner before going home at five p.m.

Throughout the day, he'd catch glimpses of Erica sitting in the living room as he passed by the window, or she'd be walking slowly through the desert outside the house as he slapped adobe on the wall. Lupe would sometimes drive her away in the Mercedes after lunch but he had no idea what they did on those trips. He'd heard that Erica owned a house in Chamisa, the nearby village, so he assumed she spent at least some of her time there.

In the evening, he ate his meal in the kitchen while Erica ate hers in the dining room. She wasn't avoiding him, he thought. She just didn't seem interested. While he was at the table, she would come into the kitchen and leave her dirty dishes by the sink, but with no more acknowledgement than a simple nod. She made long phone calls in the living room but he couldn't hear what she said.

While he was eating his meals, his eyes moved up from his plate to the ancient porcelain sink and then down again to the food. He tried not to think about the past, whether in recent, middle, or distant history. He felt as if his emotions and creativity had been hollowed out and might never again be filled. The spartan house with its carefully chosen furnishings and art pieces exactly reflected his state of mind. Rejecting internal muddle, he wanted to look at one thing at a time, to find rest in the mere act of perception. After he ate, without receiving any instructions, he did the dishes so they wouldn't sit out all night and lure the ants. He was careful only to run the tap when necessary, the desert having already taught him how precious the water was.

6

FINE

After he'd been working there for several weeks, he was brushing tar on the roof in the heat of the sun when he heard the screech of brakes. He looked down to see his previous employer, Jed Mills, the director of Spirit Ranch, stepping from his truck as a plume of dust drifted up and over the house. Jed ascended the ladder, his lean frame unfolding like a collapsible yard stick as he climbed onto the roof. He gave Michael a thin smile and lit his pipe, sending blue smoke into the air to mingle with the dust particles gleaming in the light.

"So," he said, "We've been wondering where you were. How's it going?"

Michael leaned on the pole handle of his tar-soaked brush and kept his gaze fixed on the clouds rushing over the top of the mesa he had so suddenly descended. He thought about the question. Finally, the answer came to him.

"Just fine."

Jed calmly puffed on the pipe. The smoke rose up slowly, twisted in a current of air, and then drifted across the valley.

"We were worried about you, leaving like you did, without a word to anyone. Not that you didn't have cause, of course."

Michael noticed how the granite cap on top of the mesa stood out sharply against the clouds emerging above the etched rim. He remembered the axiom from William Blake, that the definite line was the necessary component of any art work, generating the energy of opposition. He wanted to assert the boundary between who he was at Erica's house and who he'd been at the Ranch. He could feel stubbornness churning in his stomach and rising up.

Jed took the pipe from his mouth and examined the contents of the bowl.

"Made any plans?"

"All I know is that I'm definitely not going back to the Ranch."

Jed nodded and again drew on his pipe. The ascending smoke was the same shade of gray as his close-cropped hair. He pulled the pipe from his mouth and tamped down on the coals with his callused thumb.

"Talked to Sheila. Said she was sorry about what happened."

Michael looked down between his feet and examined the whorled patterns on the tar. He didn't say a word and didn't plan to. These damn cowboys had been driving him crazy with their taciturn ways ever since he'd arrived. Now it was his turn to keep his mouth shut. Jed puffed awhile more. Conversation with him often involved uncomfortable silences but Jed's style was to wait as long as it took for the right words to come.

Finally he moved toward the ladder. He climbed down until his legs disappeared, stopped, and pointed his pipe at Michael.

"Erica is a friend of ours so we want her treated right."

Michael was surprised by this.

"I have every intention of doing a good job here," he replied.

"That's okay then."

Jed went down the ladder with a goodbye wave. Michael noticed he didn't go to his truck but knocked on the front door and went inside to talk to Erica. Michael didn't really care. Jed didn't know anything bad about him except that he was foolish in love. He dipped his brush in the tar and went back to spreading it in long, even strokes. Every so often, he stopped, straightened his back, and looked over toward Obsidian. The mountain was becoming his talisman in the distance, a constant uncritical companion.

That night, after dinner, Jed stopped by and dropped off the gear Michael had left in the bunkhouse at the ranch. He was happy to get his backpack as it contained his clothes (including his beloved Yankees cap), his camping gear, and his art supplies. At the bottom of the load were a hawk's feather and an ojo de dios, both gifts from Sheila. He stuck the feather into the yarn of the ojo, took it to the courtyard, and threw it so it spun like a Frisbee far out into the desert.

The shelf in his room held a solid assortment of books: Rex Stout, Dorothy Sayers, Willa Cather, Edith Wharton, George Eliot, Dickens, Twain, Jane Austen, the poetry of Yeats and Hardy and Dickinson. Evenings he spent in his room reading as he'd never read before, slowly, savoring each sentence, wanting not to run out of books too fast. One night, as he began to doze off, an image came to him, as clearly as if he were actually out in the desert: he was lying quietly on the ground, looking up at the sky, an obsidian-tipped arrow sticking out of his chest, the point just rising into his field of vision. He sat up in bed and looked wildly around the room, searching in vain for something familiar, holding his chest where the dream arrow had emerged.

7

DINNER

Erica had guests over for dinner one night. In the dining room were two men and two women, all middle-aged but much younger than Erica. The men, both gray-haired, one with a precise Van Dyke beard, wore bolo ties with turquoise stones. The women clutched the edges of black lace shawls draped over their shoulders. Erica herself wore a mantilla so red that Michael couldn't help but think of blood. The table was set with tall candles and elegant china. In the kitchen, Lupe, who'd stayed late for the occasion, smiled at him enigmatically as she washed the dishes and pots. He sat and ate his meal, listening avidly to their conversation about the art world in New York and the eccentric behavior of various artists and gallery owners and patrons. The great city in this year of 1972 was electric with upheaval both culturally and in people's lives. Erica was eager to hear what was going on in Manhattan, where she'd lived for so long.

After washing his plate and cup in the sink, Michael went directly back to his room. He felt both upset that he hadn't been invited and unclear on how one might go about talking to people over a meal. What could he say? How could he make conversation and explain who he was when he wasn't sure himself?

8

HIKE

One morning, he found a note on the kitchen counter with the words: "Sunday. No chores." At first, he was happy for the orientation as he'd lost track of what day it was. However, after breakfast, he wasn't sure what to do. He'd never been invited to relax in the living room although he'd been intrigued by its book collection. In the course of his work, he occasionally looked through the window into Erica's studio at the opposite end of the courtyard from his room. An assortment of potential sculpture materials, mostly found objects from the desert, filled the space. One wall was lined with metal shelving full of tools and cans of paint and thinner. However, he'd never seen Erica working there.

Thinking of that studio, he found himself with a desire to put images on paper, something he hadn't done since he'd drawn sketches of Sheila during the period in which he deluded himself into thinking they were in love. He decided to spend his day off hiking in the desert and trying to do some watercolors. He pulled his paint box out of his large pack along with his brushes, a water jar, paper, sponges, rags, and a pair of boards for mounting. These supplies went into his day pack along with a sandwich, a canteen, and a jar full of water. When he stepped into the front hallway, all was quiet. Although he shared a house with Erica, he usually had no idea what she was doing. He walked out the front door and crossed the road he'd last crossed on the day he arrived at the house.

He didn't want to run into any of the people he knew from the Ranch so he headed off for the empty terrain to the north. He also wanted to stay clear of Jed Mills' house because he knew from working there that Jed's German Shepherds were far-roaming and exuberant in their greeting of anyone who approached. To avoid them, he walked along the edge of the talus slopes skirting the mesas. This meant negotiating the frequent arroyos cut by the intermittent rains over the centuries but he preferred this particular land anyway. He'd found arrowheads and pottery shards in similar places so he walked with his head down, lightly scanning the earth.

The morning sun had not yet crossed over the mesas but the air around him was rosy with suffused light softening the edges of the rock and sending streams of reflective particles flowing around him. The clouds were high and scattered, a display with the unsystematic beauty only nature and, occasionally, art could provide. After the cramped, patterned movements of his daily chores, he felt tremendous relief in the varied motions of hiking over rough ground.

His eyes captured sudden perspectives: a block of orange stone, monumental yet shaped with no similar angles; a fringe of sandy grass gently arcing over a pyramid of pebbles; a low piñon tree with branches forming an ascending spiral. The mesa loomed over him, the empyrean framed at its edge so precisely it hurt him to look at it for long. The fullness of the landscape reminded him of the immensity of feeling he was keeping at bay inside.

Thoughts of Sheila intruded on his awareness, giving him unwanted memories of her above him at night in the bunk house, her wild black hair framed by the rough planks of the ceiling. He forced the images away with a surge of anger. Even if he had put more than he should have into the relationship, she shouldn't have lied to him about what was going on with her.

He really didn't want to think about all that crap. He wanted simply to be out here at the edge of the world, looking on these colors and shapes with a pure eye, registering what was present without the messiness of emotion. Now he had to hike through this most radiant of landscapes with dark roiling thoughts disturbing his awareness. Above all, he wanted not to feel the way he felt.

He decided to concentrate on what was directly ahead of him in his field of vision. Here every edge and surface had been shaped by geologic processes that had, with excruciating slowness, eroded the edges of this high table land into the piles of rubble at his feet. A large brown beetle crested the top of the rock in front of him and waved his antennae at the gargantuan shape of Michael suddenly looming over it. The bug was apparently not at all daunted by his approach. It cocked its head, as if taking a survey sighting of his dimensions, and then casually proceeded over the edge of the rock and down the vertical face.

Ascending the next ridge, Michael looked ahead to a curling line of outthrusts and escarpments. The heat was rising around him, steady, pervasive, dry, almost holding him upright with its pressure. To his left, the terrain descended over several miles to the highway angling down from the north on a grade blasted by dynamite into the mesa formation. If he kept on this path and followed the general bend of the terrain, he'd eventually end up at the road so he only continued on for another mile as the cliffs curved back into a hollow. There he stopped, took a long sip of water, and wiped the sweat from his head. The sandstone loomed over him as if about to fall and crush him under tons of rock. The sun had crossed the top of the mesa and rendered the area around him so bright the rocks looked as if they were glowing from within.

Following an intuition, he climbed up the scree until he reached a narrow ledge clinging to the vertical face of the mesa. A faint track, perhaps a deer path, continued along the ledge, disappearing around the corner. He followed it into a shaded canyon curving so far back it edged out of sight of the highway. Clouds streamed into the kidney-shaped pocket of blue above him. He scanned the vast wall of the cliff, admiring the texture of the surface and the harmony of desert tints.

An odd pattern of striation on the rock caught his attention. At first he saw only a jumble of lines until his eyes refocused and he suddenly realized he was looking at a petroglyph. A figure drawn into the soft rock depicted an elongated being with short legs and a bulbous head, on top of which sat a sort of headdress with wavy rays. Below this central figure was the outline of an animal with antlers, an antelope perhaps, its body a wide oval, the horns freely sketched above an exaggerated head. Other smaller drawings had been placed next to these main ones: a circle with curved extensions, parallel undulations, zig-zags, meandering doodles, all positioned with an artful disregard for overall design, a disregard constituting a pattern in itself.

On the face of a mesa directly behind the ranch, he'd seen another set of petroglyphs placed to look across the broad expanse of the basin to the setting sun, but this place carried with it an air of privacy. The ancient people must have come back here, into this fold of the cliffs, so they could work without being seen by anyone moving along the mesas or across the plains below. Michael knew from Will Sprawlins, the head wrangler at the Ranch, that the basin had been a cauldron of battle and contention for centuries so he wasn't surprised that the artists who worked on this might have wanted to avoid the gaze of passing marauders.

Michael stared up at the figures for a long time before he sat on the ground, opened his pack, and took out his paint box, the jar of water, and a pad of thick paper. The paint box was decorated with his own rough copy of Botticelli's Venus. With a click of the latch, he displayed the paints and mixing surface inside. He placed the box, jar, and brushes in a row on a level rock. A sheet of rough-textured paper went on a mounting board. Dipping a wide brush first into the jar of water and then into the burnt umber, he laid a smear of the yellow-brown paint across the mixing surface and then used it to cover the entire sheet with a light wash.

With a narrow brush poised, he looked up at the ancient designs, trying to emblazon their details in his mind. He began to copy them quickly onto paper, using a lighter ocher to make them stand out, filling page after page with different versions of what he saw. Because of the dryness of the air, he found he had to work twice as fast as he did in the humidity back east. He became absorbed in the process, enjoying the fast flow of paint on paper and the intuitive decisions he had to be make. When he felt he'd done all he could, he carefully stacked the paintings, putting a clean sheet between each one, and placed them between two mounting boards. He positioned the paint box and water jar on top of the stack and carried them gingerly forward on the trail, around the hollow to the outside of the mesa.

When he reached a place with an expansive view of the basin and the mountains beyond, he sat on the trail with his legs on the downward slope and began to paint what was before him. Not bothering to mix colors much, he used primary tones in various concentrations of wash, letting his fingers and eyes guide him. In the past, he'd sometimes overworked a painting until it was a thick muddy mess. Better now, he thought, to let the mistakes happen in plain sight. He sometimes discovered that what he thought were mistakes actually turned out to have an integrity of their own.

As he contemplated the landscape, he began to see more detail. He tried to capture the soft tint of green from the spare vegetation on the plains and the silvery blue of water in the reservoir, a blue edged by the thick brown of mud flats. He painted the clouds in the lightest of grays and captured not so much their exact shapes and sizes as their spirit of swift eager movement above the landscape. He painted happily through the day, slowing down as the hours went on, taking his time about each movement with his brush, each addition of water to the paint. The sun came further over the mesa and beat down on the top of his head, his Yankees cap sparing his eyes a little from the intrusive light. He let himself play with the shapes and colors and depths until he ran out of paper. He finished by cleaning the brushes with water and placing the lids back tightly on the jars. He lay down with his head on the pack, using his cap to shade his face, and fell asleep in the warm air.

When he awoke, the sun was moving down toward the far horizon. He thought hours must have passed. A few flies examined him in the heat of the afternoon. He looked at the paintings and saw that even now, after they'd dried, they held something pleasing to him. He didn't think they'd be hanging in a gallery but they were a start. Every external circumstance, including his disastrous love life and a turbulent upbringing, seemed irrelevant to his happiness as long as he could paint. He carefully placed everything in his pack and started back.

9

EYE

His pupils expanded and contracted painfully as he walked into the darkness of the hallway and out again to the light of the courtyard. Erica sat in a straight-backed chair at the center of the flagstones. Below the brim of her straw cowboy hat, her face in profile had an eagle's sternness as she stared toward Obsidian. When he reached the door of his room, he heard her say, simply, "Come here." He felt afraid and also felt he should face this, whatever it was. If she told him to leave, he was going to pack his gear as fast as he could and start hitchhiking north on the highway. Maybe he'd see if he could get as far as Alaska and find work before the cold set in.

About ten feet away from her, he stopped. She looked up at him, the setting sun reaching under the brim of her hat to illuminate her eyes. Parallel lines ran across her brow, supported by splayed furrows falling along either side of her nose. She had a look he hadn't seen in her face before but could only be described as interest.

"What did you do today?"

He had a momentary urge to consider this direct question to be rude but that didn't quite fit with her intonation. She was curious and wanted to know.

"I went hiking back toward the mesa."

"The mesa behind the house." This was a statement and not a question but he answered it anyway.

"Yes."

"What did you see?"

This felt crucial somehow so he took a moment to consider.

"I saw the cliffs, of course, and the sky. Then I found some petroglyphs in a canyon."

"You saw them."

"Well, yes. They were beautiful."

"I wouldn't say that."

He looked at her and waited for elaboration but she remained silent so he had to ask.

"Why not?"

"Because beauty is a word intended to separate what touches our vanity from the rest of life. No, the point about those cliff drawings is that they *are*."

He felt confused. "They *are*?"

"Those who made them didn't put them on the rock for entertainment, at least not in the way we think of it. They were working from a complete connection with everything around them. People don't know anything about that anymore."

"I'm not sure I understand."

"I wouldn't think so."

This insult was so blatant he couldn't protest. She folded her hands in her lap and looked out to the mountain. Not knowing where to gaze and feeling uncomfortable standing in front of her, Michael looked above the house to the mesa whose colors in the low angle of the sun's rays had become more saturated. Erica sighed and stretched her arms out in front of her.

"What else did you do out there?"

"Nothing. I mean, I hiked, like I said, sat for awhile, fell asleep, did a few water colors, stuff like that." As soon as the words were out of his mouth, he felt he'd made a mistake.

"Let me see them."

His throat thickened so the air was difficult to force through. He could feel a drip of sweat searching for a way down his back.

"I couldn't... My own work... Don't usually... Let people see..."

She held out her hand. He looked down at it with apprehension. Her skin was lined, freckled with age. Her fingers were long and slender but the joints were large and looked strong. He wanted to turn to run but again felt he'd been led to this moment. Kneeling down on the paving stones, he opened his pack, pulled out the stack of watercolors and handed it to her with a hesitant motion, immediately contrasted by her sudden grasp of the paintings. He didn't stand up again but sat cross-legged on the bare stone of the patio so he could see the mountain but didn't have to look directly at her. She slowly turned the pages over, her head tilted, giving her the physical appearance of looking skeptically at his work. He stared down between his knees and noticed a weed emerging from the dirt between two flagstones. He pulled it out with a tug and rolled it between his palms. She closed the book and handed it back to him.

"You have an eye."

He felt as if he'd been told that his illness wasn't actually fatal.

"Thank you," he said.

"You also know when to stop."

"Is that good?"

She fixed him with a gaze from the edge of her vision, giving him a sense of dislocation as if she were both making and not making eye contact simultaneously.

"However, you've been painting too many pretty pictures, haven't you?"

Michael shook his head. "That's what they kept telling me in art school. What do you think? Should I be turning out those ugly abstractions and conceptual pieces just to be modern?"

"You said you went to art school but left."

"I had a huge fight with my senior project advisor. He was one of those far-out guys, making ugly installation pieces he thought were so clever. He hated my work, hated it with a passion, but I can't see what's so wrong about wanting to paint from nature."

She slowly shook her head. "I don't know about that. What I see here is someone who knows how to make pretty pictures, postcard pictures. You might be able to make a living as an illustrator but it's not art."

A surge of energy pushed Michael to his feet. Erica thrust her chin at him to indicate she was willing to take him on.

"I've seen your work in New York. Don't people buy your pieces because they're pretty? Because they're reminded of the desert and want some cactus and weathered wood in their houses?"

Her response was surprisingly temperate. "I don't know why people buy my work. I don't really care. I was just trying to see, as clearly as I could, and respond to what I saw. All I know about your work is from these watercolors. Sometimes you see and sometimes you just fall back on ideas someone else gave you of what's pretty."

As he paced back and forth in the courtyard, a thousand arguments came back to him.

"I've never understood why everyone dismisses my work as being "just" pretty. The head of the department even said it was cartoonish. When I was in high school, I spent summers out on Long Island and made paintings of people's houses and boats for money. What's wrong with that? They're part of the world, aren't they?"

Erica calmly considered this question.

"Back in New York, the rich people would sometimes ask me to make installations designed especially for their walls or gardens or entryways but I didn't do them. They didn't want what I saw. They wanted decoration, and reassurance, and an artist can't worry about making the rich feel better. Did you paint a lot of those houses and boats?"

"I averaged about two a week. Made what I needed for school."

"And did people like them?"

"Yeah. They usually said they were quite pleased."

"In that case, you have to fight their influence. You were illustrating ownership and that's dangerous. It makes you work as a servant and you should only serve what's in front of your eye and what comes from inside you. If you do that, and you're lucky, the rich people might come to you and ask to buy. But don't knock on their doors and beg."

Michael kept pacing with his arms folded, but his anger had subsided. He felt trapped by the truth of what she said.

He turned to Erica. "So what do you think I should do?"

"I can show you."

10

BREAKFAST

Michael dreamt that night of wandering in dense brush on steep slopes in alien terrain. He struggled with and was bloodied by malevolent thorns. Large animals hidden by the darkness came snuffling close to him. He knew if they found him, he'd be eaten. A woman appeared in the forest, her pale form moving at great speed through the trees. He tried to follow her but she kept racing ahead, his glimpses of her giving way to occasional distant flashes of brightness that eventually disappeared altogether.

He woke up to a chilly breeze across his legs and found he'd fallen asleep on top of the covers in just his underwear. He drew his legs up and thrust them under the sheet and blanket. Turning on his side, he curled inward to warm himself. Light flowed in from all four sides of the door as well as through the keyhole and several cracks in the wood. The dark curtain at the single window allowed only a faint glow from the dawn. He was on the verge of going back to sleep. A great lassitude hung suspended in his head and chest. He could have followed it back down to unconsciousness but something kept hovering at the edge of awareness, something he was going to do that day, something that would make it worthwhile for him to rise.

Suddenly he knew. If Erica Hanlon saw in his paintings that at least he had an eye, maybe there was a reason to keep on. The keyhole in front of him was emitting more light by the second, creating a fuzzy halo around the doorknob. He closed his eyes and watched the light show on his eyelids. How strange: to be alive, in New Mexico, in Erica's house, in this body. Ever since his mother's suffering and death, the reality around him was as difficult to grasp as this morning's dream had been. He didn't know what the alternative was but everything seemed odd, including the expanding light pouring through the keyhole, bright enough now to coat the inside of the room with a dim radiance.

What he wanted in his art was to indicate simultaneously the sheer reality and the utter weirdness of it all, to convey his sense of a mysterious presence living within all phenomena. He believed Erica's work achieved that end with her selection of objects from nature and their re-composition, forcing the viewer to stop and look in a different way. She had something to teach him; he was sure of it.

What finally moved him to sit upright in bed and place his bare feet on the cold planks of the floor was a fresh influx of the seemingly infinite reservoir of grief he was usually able to keep below the threshold of consciousness. A variety of strategies were necessary to keep it at bay: He whistled, counted to ten repeatedly, jiggled his legs. He made mental lists of what he wanted to do that day. He did push-ups on the cold wood floor.

In the kitchen, he'd started to assemble breakfast when he glanced through the door to the dining room. Erica was sitting at the table, her face set like a prow into the flow of light. He'd never before seen her there in the morning so he stood for a moment. She angled her head to catch sight of him and motioned him to enter.

As he walked in, the light was so strong that the colors of the dishes, the table, even the dark wooden floor, were washed out in its glow. He sat down and placed the napkin in his lap. He poured himself coffee from a glass pot and orange juice from a silver carafe. Erica took a bite from a piece of dry toast with the crusts cut off. On the heavy antique plate before him was a pile of scrambled eggs, bacon, and sausage.

"Who made breakfast?" he asked.

"Go ahead and eat," replied Erica.

"Did you cook this?"

"I'm not totally unable to do things."

Michael ate for awhile. Dust motes floated in the light.

"This is good. Thank you."

"I want to go for a walk today."

"Okay."

"I want to see what you see."

"How can you do that?"

She laughed.

"Try me."

11

PURPLE

As they walked outside, her arm around his elbow felt fragile yet when she wanted him to turn, the clench was fierce. They crossed the road outside the house and walked toward the red hills, a series of ascending humped ridges he hadn't yet explored. Erica steered him with vigor, her feet shuffling to sense the contours of the path. The hills, with their horizontal bands of color, were shining and raw in the morning light.

Walking into the desert with this old woman embarrassed him. A work crew from maintenance could easily drive by on their way to Jed Mills' house and see them arm in arm. People might think he was out to take advantage of her and, of course, he was. The aura of her fame had attracted him as he researched her life story before he came west. He'd heard about the Ranch of the Spirits from his friend Cathy at school who'd been there the summer before. She knew how depressed he was after his mom's painful death from cancer and suggested New Mexico as the place to relieve his mind.

He'd seen Erica's work at a Whitney show during his senior year in high school. She was a very different artist from who he wanted to be but he'd felt an immediate affinity with her work. Photos of her pieces and installations were in his art history books, along with the basics of her career. She was born in rural Maine, the daughter of school teachers, and became a promising young art student in New York, highly original, a rare woman in the male-dominated sculpture world, who found that her private concerns meshed well with the modern art just coming over from France.

Her propulsion into fame came when she met Harold Lander, a monumental sculptor in the Rodin school who saw her potential, encouraged her work, and promoted the sale of her sculptures. Michael associated her with the art scene in France in the twenties because Lander, who made a fortune with New York commissions, moved their studios to the Midi near where Cezanne had painted. Michael seemed to remember that her relationship with Lander had been stormy, with many affairs on both their parts. Had Picasso been one of her lovers? Hard to imagine the slight elderly lady on his arm giving a ride to the bull but anything was possible.

She finally became fed up with Lander and his alcoholism and abuse and moved out permanently to the Southwest, finding new inspiration for her work in the pervasive light and space. Michael knew there was much more to her biography but the past on this brilliant morning seemed as ephemeral as his dream of the night before.

The hills loomed up as they walked into a landscape far different from the open plains around her house. In the dips between the hills, the horizon was restricted. Above them, the sheer cliffs of the mesas appeared disconnected from the surrounding terrain. Here Erica let go of his arm and began leading him through the winding valleys. Her head was in constant motion, her eyes taking in the shapes and colors as best she could given the limited angles of her vision. Michael stayed close behind her, trying to follow the dancing butterfly of her attention, aided by her running commentary and the precise gestures of her bony hands:

"Some blue there. A line of saffron next to the bush. Look at the granules in the surface. That edge. A different reddish brown in the hollow, where the sun hasn't penetrated..."

She described and analyzed as if they were walking through a massively complex work of art, a sculpture with painted surfaces and an intricate lighting system precisely directed for the greatest effect. Michael thought he knew the limitations of her vision but now he was trying to see what she was seeing but couldn't entirely. He knew how he would paint the scene, choosing a composition and creating a dynamic within it but he found himself frustrated that the landscape had so little actual content from his point of view. No houses, artifacts, or people softened the stark lines, the fields of color. He found himself musing that perhaps he could put in a cowboy on a horse as a focal point. When Erica stopped short, he ran into her back with some force. She was able to hold her ground and spoke without turning to look at him.

"Do you see?"

"Um, yes, of course I see."

"What do you see?"

"Right now I'm looking at the back of your head."

"What about over there?"

She pointed to a bare hill, much like all the rest to him, with cracked earth in bands of color across it.

"You mean, what do I see?"

She exhaled sharply.

"Yes."

"I guess I see a curved line up and down defining the hill, slightly elongated on the right. I see that line of purple..."

"Not purple!"

"What?"

"Do you see any red in that blue?"

"Um, well, maybe in the center part of it."

"I don't. I see blue and an edge of silver and green near the top of the arch."

"So, okay, you see blue but it seems purple to me. What's the big deal?"

She shook her head and walked on. His first thought was that this was definitely not going to work so he might as well just leave now, hit the road and act on his plan from yesterday of hitching to Alaska. Although his head was down, he barely noticed his feet moving through the rusty dirt. As he rounded the hooked trail, he found Erica standing directly before him with her hands on her hips. She glared at him.

"What?" He was daunted by her accusing stare.

"It means something to see, if you want to make art."

"Maybe I just don't see the way you do."

"You can't call that purple. That's not seeing."

"Okay, okay. I was just searching for a word. Maybe it wasn't the right one."

She snorted. "Maybe, he says."

"Look, I'm willing to learn from you, but this doesn't help."

"Are you strong enough to do the work?"

"I don't like being criticized."

"You have to be purified in fire to be good."

Purified in fire? Really? This woman was crazy. Who did she think she was, someone out of mythology?

"I'll be honest with you. I don't like being attacked. This just isn't going to work out. I'm going to hit the road, head west or something."

Not caring whether she followed or not, he turned and started walking back to the house, moving swiftly through the rising heat until he emerged from the hills onto the flatland. In just a few minutes, he could pack his gear. In about forty more minutes, he'd reach the highway and be hitching well before noon, enough time to get up to Colorado before dark. Maybe he'd try to go through Las Vegas, see what was going on there. Erica had never paid him anything and only a few hundred dollars remained of what he'd brought to the West, but he didn't care.

His anger barely kept down a primitive yet familiar feeling, a dread that no one cared about him and no one ever would. A vortex of emotion began to spin in his chest. His rejection of Erica had tapped into a reservoir of fear from long ago. A pointed shard of memory brought back his tiny bedroom in the Village apartment where he grew up and the long hours he'd spent alone there.

And what had started all this? She told him he wasn't seeing correctly. How could anyone see the right way or the wrong way, or make judgments about someone else's vision? That didn't make sense. If he saw purple then he saw purple and he didn't need some arrogant old bitch to tell him differently. Who was she to interpret how his own eyeballs operated? His anger grew as he walked. He was even happy she'd be stumbling along behind him. She herself couldn't see for shit. That's why she was always cocking her head like a goddamned parrot. She could barely see the hills in front of her, much less whether something was purple or not. The funny thing was, he could have done a nice little watercolor of the scene. Just before he'd bumped into her, he'd been thinking of painting a tight composition with a cowboy on his horse among the hills, a soft blue sky with clouds, the yellow cliffs topped by gray caps, the rolling hills lined with purple shadows.

Halfway between the hills and the house, the sun burning his scalp at the part in his hair, he stopped. The desert spread silence all around him. That composition was forming in his mind when she'd asked him what he saw. When he replied, he wasn't talking about what was in front of him but about the picture he was concocting internally. He had no idea what the actual color was of that very real pile of dirt. The purple had been entirely of his own devising. So he'd been wrong and she'd been right, even as blind as she was. He took a deep breath, trying to assimilate this realization.

The option of ignoring her and making good his escape was

tempting but he knew her words would eventually return to disturb his sleep. Here was a possible stance: so what if she'd been right? She'd still be impossible to work with, given her air of superiority. He tried that on for a moment and played back the scene in his memory. To his dismay, he found that although she'd been stern, she hadn't been putting him down nearly as much as he'd imagined. She'd just been telling the truth in her own blunt way.

A choice lay before him: he could cling to his own conceptions and continue to make pretty little paintings that went nowhere, or he could engage directly with the physical world and with Erica, not knowing where that would take him. Leaving meant floundering in the chaos of himself. Staying meant fighting to define who he was in relationship with a very strong personality.

What irked him was that he knew what he'd never admit, that he'd been merely operating on the surface up to this point. The answer didn't seem to be either in the trickiness of the conceptual art they'd tried to foist on him back at Pratt or in the tidy but unchallenging compositions he'd mastered on his own. Staying on here meant abandoning both what he'd opposed and what he thought he knew, altogether truly uncomfortable prospects. The one consolation was that he could always leave although he had the sense that if he didn't go now, he wouldn't go anytime soon.

He started back to the hills and took a few steps but felt claustrophobic. Staying on also meant interacting with and probably doing battle with Erica on a daily basis and he knew he wasn't as tough as she was. Was this old woman really the one to teach him?

All he knew for sure was that she'd been right about the purple. He started walking again and this time kept going, back to meet her.

She was sitting quietly on a large rock. She didn't say anything but simply stood up and took his arm.

After lunch, she showed him into her studio where everything had a thin coating of dust. She gestured awkwardly toward the shelves, as if trying to practice being bounteous.

"Help yourself to what's here. If you need easels and canvases, any other supplies, we'll order them for you." He looked around for a moment and nodded his head. She showed him into the living room, another previously forbidden zone.

"You are also welcome to sit here in the evenings and read."

The walls were lined with an eclectic assortment of classics along with a solid core of large-format art books.

"Maybe I could read out loud to you."

She looked startled at this idea, but nodded her head quickly.

"You can have the mornings to paint and save the chores for the afternoon."

She peered at him from the side of her vision.

"I'd be happy to look at your work and tell you what I think."

"That's what I want... I think."

12

TUTORIAL

At the start of each day, when the sky was light but before the sun rose over the mesas, they had breakfast together without much conversation. After piling the dishes for Lupe, he'd go to the courtyard, walk to its open end, and take in what the morning light revealed. Often she would join him and point out some detail he hadn't noticed, even though his own vision was theoretically unimpaired: a wisp of cloud, a texture in the plains, a column of smoke rising from the mountains near Los Lobos. He'd allow himself to be filled by the seemingly infinite visual input.

When he felt saturated, he'd go to the studio to get his supplies, take them outside, within sight of the house, and paint something austere in response to the reality in front of him. His first series was comprised of watercolors studying the various horizontal lines in the basin below Obsidian. He painted the same elements repeatedly over dozens of sheets, not caring about composition or making them pretty, just trying to portray in color and line the subtle undulations that presented themselves.

Erica would approach him before lunch, often so silently he'd jump when he finally noticed her. She'd scrutinize what he'd been doing but didn't always say anything. Sometimes she'd just grunt affirmatively, a response that at least made him feel he was on the right track. To shake up old habits, he'd try different techniques, such as painting with his left hand or not looking at the paper while he worked. He covered many sheets with these exercises, trying to make a connection between his eye and hand so the least detail of the landscape would register through him.

Erica suggested how various shadings and tints could give a sense of depth to the flat field so the eye would follow the two-dimensional as if it were three. This was such an absorbing and complex process that he never felt he was even close to capturing what was out there. The sensory input delivering itself with such regularity seemed to be a mask hiding the unknowable reality in and around him. He knew painting couldn't get him any closer to reality than anything else but at least it was his direct and immediate response to being in such a mysterious situation.

When he stopped working, even for a few minutes, his mind would wander down endlessly proliferating pathways, trudging through painful scenes of the past and fantasizing about the future, pressure building in his chest and forehead. His only relief was to bring himself back to the elements in front of him: paper, water, color, earth, mountains, valley, sparse high clouds, the thin blue of the acreage of water behind the dam. These were the blocks with which he painstakingly built up his world. He was reminded of when he was a kid and spent countless hours drawing what he could see from the apartment window: an angled section of sky, the red brick building across the street, an Italian grocer, and the never ending parade of New York characters passing on the sidewalks below, dispatched directly from planetary central casting for his amusement. Now, in a terrain almost the polar opposite of the city, he felt the same dedicated absorption that had carried him through those long hours.

In the afternoons, when the sun was so intense he became dizzy if he painted outside, the light scorching his head even when he wore his Yankees cap, Erica began to assign him tasks inside the house. She introduced him to her desk, an enormous old roll-top in a small office next to her bedroom. When she raised the wooden shutter that curved up and then hid itself away into the back of the desk, papers spilled out. She received an enormous amount of mail, especially considering how seldom she herself wrote to anyone.

Every week she'd send Lupe to the post office in Chamisa and Lupe would return with a large canvas sack jammed with letters. Some of it was fan mail she ordered Michael to ignore and burn but the bulk of it involved correspondence from museums and galleries both foreign and domestic, along with invoices from various storage facilities that held her work. All the cubbyholes and drawers in her desk and two tall file cabinets were jammed with her business letters. She gave him the task of putting some order to it all.

Through the blazing afternoons, he sat in the coolness of the thick adobe walls and laid out documents until the entire floor was covered with paper. He paid close attention to the letters from storage companies in Paris, New York, and Denver where she had deposited sculptures over the years (and was paying expensive charges). Her work had apparently never been catalogued so he kept a ledger book for that purpose, listing the names and locations of the pieces. Erica had been amazingly prolific throughout her life: producing, by his calculations, an average of an artwork a week for decades. Only in the last years had the numbers dropped drastically.

Her banking correspondence was daunting to Michael who had never dealt with anything more complicated than balancing his mother's checkbook. Even though she was a bookkeeper, the household budget was always in disarray. As a would-be poet, his father had completely transcended the realm of fiscal responsibility. His parents left behind a tidal wave of debts after they were cut adrift from the planet. Part of his reason for leaving New York was to step out from under the crash of that wave. He had no doubt the letters from creditors, increasingly threatening, were piling up at the Post Office as he'd left no forwarding address. None of the debt was in his name anyway and he'd decided he didn't deserve to devote his life to making up for their imprudence and plain bad luck.

He began with sorting Erica's banking materials by date, hoping to go back and eventually bring it all into balance. She had a money manager in New York but Michael found his correspondence very unhelpful in elucidating the current financial status. His only impression was that Erica had hundreds of thousands of dollars, spread out over many accounts, along with the value of her art that was, at this point, anyway, inestimable.

During these afternoons, she sometimes fussed around behind him, not wanting to participate in the great paper chase but unable to stay away. What Erica did all day was a mystery to him. She didn't work in the studio. She didn't sit for long in the library. She did go for short walks around the house, sometimes with him, sometimes with Lupe, often alone. She also spent a lot of time on the phone in the living room, pausing when he passed as if to prevent him from eavesdropping. Occasionally he'd go by her open bedroom door and see her sitting in the armchair staring at the wall with her head tilted slightly, as if listening to music he couldn't hear.

13

ERRAND

About a month after he arrived, he pointed out to Erica that he'd filled the tall filing cabinets but had stacks of paper left over with no place to put them. His plan was to buy two-drawer cabinets for the far corners of the room where their tops could hold assortments of the found objects from the desert that Erica collected. She told him to take the Mercedes into San Juan where the closest office supply store was located. The Mercedes was air conditioned and the back seat was large enough to accommodate the cabinets. However, he felt an enormous reluctance to venture out and changed his mind on a daily basis about whether he would go himself or simply have them delivered.

Finally, after lunch on a Tuesday in August, he turned the ignition key of the sedan and pulled out of the driveway, turning right on the dirt road, with Obsidian gliding along beside him. When he took the dips of the arroyos a little too fast, the undercarriage of the Mercedes scraped bottom. Just past the sewage ponds, a cattle guard marked the real beginning of the ranch as House Mesa loomed over the cottonwood trees. His impulse was to race through the ranch in a cloud of dust but realized he would only make himself more conspicuous that way. Two girls in shorts and loose t-shirts jogged toward him on the road beneath the alfalfa field. He pulled the Yankees cap down to rest upon his sunglasses, hoping not to be spotted by anyone he knew, especially Sheila. The girls waved as they passed but he didn't recognize them.

At the maintenance shed, the old orange cat named Snaplock sat in the open bay doors and washed himself. The crew was probably up at the construction project on the mesa. Even though he wasn't very skilled as a carpenter, he'd enjoyed the rhythm of the work and the process of making something appear where nothing had been before. Although he was somewhat sorry to be missing all that, he didn't feel it was possible just to drop in on the crew and say hello. The locals who worked for the ranch were often profanely critical of Erica for being the rich Anglo who'd bought and renovated the most ancient dwelling in their historic village and hired townspeople to be her servants. Those actually hired, such as Lupe, didn't complain because they were happy to have the work but her neighbors saw it as exploitation. The locals were intrigued that Erica was hiring yet angry when they were excluded. The crew was bound to give him shit about living with Erica.

At the corner of the field, he passed by Tex and Luisa's house and saw their Chihuahua, Shorty, sleeping in the shade from the awning over the patio. Shorty's left hind leg was in rapid motion, indicating he was dreaming of his favorite activity: humping people's shins. Only Tex's broken down truck was in the driveway. The GTO and the pink Pinto were gone so Tex and Luisa had to be away at work.

Something flashed by in the brush of the arroyo, reminding him of an image he couldn't quite place. It may have been one of their kids who tended to run wild when left alone over the long days of summer vacation. As he topped the next hill, one of the ranch vans was moving fast up the other side toward him, raising an extended cloud of dust behind it. Through the van's dusty windshield, Michael could see that the driver, with a distinctive halo of curly red hair, was Chuck Merrill, his best friend from the maintenance crew. In the course of their work together, Michael subjected Chuck to endless ramblings about Sheila and their relationship. Chuck always listened patiently, even though Michael didn't take his reasonable advice about going slow. Michael felt guilty that they hadn't talked since he fled the ranch.

The van seemed to take an enormous amount of time to reach him. Through the dusty windshield, Chuck glanced over at the Mercedes and looked away. He did a double-take when he realized whose car it was and looked closer. Michael waved at him. Chuck lifted his hand in a salute without waving. Their eyes met as the van rolled by and Michael could see by his expression that Chuck was not happy with him. The incoming guests in the back seats stared idly out the windows as the Mercedes was cloaked in the following dust.

Michael gripped the steering wheel, his fingers spread out on the leather cover over the German steel. He didn't like anyone to be mad at him but dealing with Chuck would have to wait. He guided the Mercedes down the last long hill and crossed the cattle guard with a bump, stopping just before the edge of the paved highway. Nothing coming from the north; nothing from the south. Dust and gravel spinning out behind him, he accelerated onto the highway toward San Juan. His immediate impulse was to keep going, drive the car to Los Angeles, and park it by the Pacific Ocean. He felt as if he'd torn himself from a spider's web and was now buzzing away happily in the free air.

The first section of Route 96 heading south from the ranch was like an amusement park ride as Michael followed the twisting roadbed through cutaway sections of mesas displaying the fantastic shapes and colors of the cliffs. He descended from the high country to a flat part of the road that followed the river into Chamisa. He looked out on the adobe houses along the river and wondered what it would be like to live in this wide basin seemingly as haunted as the Ranch itself.

According to Will Sprawlins, this region had been the hunting ground for various tribes for thousands of years. In the early 1800s, Chamisa became the gathering and trading center for the mountain men who trapped beaver from the streams for a hundred miles around. The land was so hotly contested among various factions that no settlers were able to establish homesteads there until the latter part of the 19th century. Some trace of all that bloodshed must remain in the soil and the air and Michael wondered if the dreams of the locals were troubled by that violent history.

As he approached Chamisa, he had a momentary desire to have a cold beer at El Casita, the bar up in the village that at least tolerated white kids from the ranch stopping in. Only a momentary twitch on the steering wheel to the right indicated his impulse to stop in for a cold one. On the way back, he told himself. Then he passed by Angie's bar on the left, a dark den even on the brightest of days, unappreciative of outsiders intruding into its edgy gloom for drinks.

After Chamisa, he continued into an ordinary southwestern landscape, the land without the magic. He settled into New Mexico driving mode: going very fast, edging up close behind cars to pass them, taking chances in the rare passing zones. The sparse clouds passed quickly overhead.

He cranked up the air conditioning, pulled the classical tape out of the 8 track, and put in a Jimi Hendrix tape he'd brought with him from the East. Cruising at about seventy-five, the Mercedes was buffeted by pockets of warm morning air as he pounded the steering wheel to the music. Hendrix repeatedly asked the musical question: "Hey, Joe, where you going with that gun in your hand?"

14

FLAME

Sunlight saturated the plains below Obsidian's dark ridge, piercing the crescents of dimmed clarity at the edges of Erica's vision. She sat by the window in the studio, feeling relieved that Michael was gone and yet missing him, goddamn it. His watercolors were all around her, resting on the easels and taped to the walls. They were childish and unformed but that was their strength as well. The pretty pictures he'd shown her before had been replaced by something looser and less studied.

On that afternoon when he walked away from her out in the hills, she was sure that he was gone for good. After the first rush of anger and contempt had passed, she was staggered by the passionate loss she felt. In the midst of the vast landscape she could barely see, she sat on a stone with no intention of ever moving again. Lupe would probably assume that Erica had gone off on one of her impulsive trips and might not miss her for weeks. Erica had long ago arranged to pay Lupe automatically from a San Juan bank account. Erica's friends from the old days were accustomed to leaving messages on her machine that she sometimes wouldn't answer for months. She thought it unlikely any hiker would find her. She always took her own path through the labyrinth of hills and most people were content to explore the mere edges of the area. A spiral of greedy birds would be the first indication to the people at the ranch that something large had died out there. She felt the heat attempt to penetrate to the cold at her marrow. She expected nothing, and sat in the emptiness, all too familiar to her. But then she heard Michael's loping stride moving swiftly through the desert back to her.

Now she stood up and moved through the house's fog to the kitchen. Looking for what? A cup of tea: the British response to any emotion, a habit she'd picked up during her long stays in London and Edinburgh while Harold worked on public sculpture commissions. The sooty kettle was almost the same color as the stove, blending into its surface so she had to wave her hands over the burners several times, as if making mystical passes, in order to find it at the back. She grasped the worn wooden handle and carried the kettle to the sink, the metal clunking against the side of the basin. She ran the cold water to fill it until her wrist bent from the weight.

After she found Michael could paint a little, she began to develop a fantasy that she could pass on her creativity by taking him in as an apprentice. Her attachment to him surprised her. She supposed he was good looking in a soft and passive way. His mustache and lean frame reminded her of Harold in his younger days, although Michael certainly didn't have the buzzing and annoying energy Harold had possessed in abundance. Michael was taller than Harold and this in itself was an attraction, that in this trivial way, Michael trumped the famous and cantankerous sculptor.

Was she so needy right now that anyone's approach would move her? His evident depression and self-doubt placed him at the opposite extreme from the decisive self-possession that had driven her life. Despite her own episodes of depression and despair, she knew what was necessary to make her way in the world as an artist, the paradoxical combination of willfulness and openness demanded by the vocation, and she wanted to impart this understanding to someone else before she died. The fading of her sight, along with the multitude of pains in her body, indicated that the end of her physical powers was at hand. Michael in his youth and vague talents evoked the dark loss within her she didn't want to examine although it drove so much of her emotional turmoil over the last decade: the fading of her vocation as an artist.

She placed the kettle carefully on a burner, touching the front of the stove with the tips of her fingers to orient herself. She reached on the shelf next to the stove and took down the box of wooden kitchen matches. The striking surface was scarred from frequent use. Inside, the few remaining matches rattled against the sides. She took one out, felt for the rounded end, and drew it sharply along the side of the box.

Scrape and hiss: a lick of flame. She turned on the gas and thrust the match under the kettle. The gas blew a sudden breath of fire, searing her knuckles. She pulled back in a pained spasm, dropping the still burning match to the floor. When she bent over to retrieve it, the flame from the burner caught a lock of her unbound hair. A burst of orange flared next to her eye with an acrid crackling. She slammed her hand against her temple and put the fire out.

She edged slowly toward the table, bumped it with her hip, found the chair by waving her hand, and sat down. She was afraid to move now, a rarity in her life. The burn across her knuckles throbbed. She touched her hair and felt the burned ends crumble against her fingers. The sharp sour odor of burning hair filled her nostrils.

A memory arose of the time when Harold's brood of five immensely demanding children from his first marriage came to visit them in France. Loyal to their Boston Brahmin mother, the quintet of imps seized the opportunity of this first gathering with their father's new wife to attack Erica with gusto, criticizing her least action until all she could do was flee to her studio and lock the door. There she lit a candle (that burning smell) and sat quietly but in great tension for hours, finally falling asleep on the floor with her head on her arm.

She had thought about having a child with Harold but dealing with his children had been daunting. The youngest girl, Catherine, who looked like she'd just stepped out of a pre-Raphaelite painting, was the only one she stayed in touch with. She'd even gone to Catherine's wedding in Portugal where she had to endure again the scorn of the siblings. However, by that time, Erica had become skilled at wielding scorn herself and enjoyed staring daggers right back at them through the ceremony and the reception.

In an attempt to satisfy her maternal drive, she went on to

engage a series of protégés, young men and women, on whom she lavished some measure of the nurturing instinct for which she had no outlet but none of them ever stirred her as Michael did. Perhaps it was because she'd been alone for the past year, at a time when her sight had gone through its most precipitous decline, that she felt so vulnerable to the appeal of someone who was himself almost a child in temperament and understanding.

Yet something mature and erotic was also very much alive in her feelings for him. When Michael talked to her, she could feel his breath moving across her face; her skin warmed from his mere presence. She always reveled in the exercise of her senses when another human being was close. Whether said being was male or female didn't much matter to her although most of her relationships had been with men. The critical factor for her was always beauty: of the spirit, of the intellect, or of the body.

She didn't know whether she and Michael would ever be physically close (she couldn't imagine exactly how that might come about) but his presence in the house, the warm masculine smell of him, his clumsy and careless habits, all reminded her of the intimate part of her life that had been lost for too long. She and Harold had lived separately for ten years before his death in 1950. She found her inspiration (and her houses) in New Mexico while he stayed in the South of France, so tremulous from Parkinsons he used long straws to drink from his bottles of wine. She hired caregivers to look after him and visited every winter for several months, trying to keep up her work despite his endless complaints. Although she brought many lovers into her life, none of them lasted for more than a year or so. After being subservient to a demanding and capricious mate for so long, she wanted to have the upper hand in any relationship and that vexed the egos of the men and women who temporarily shared her life.

However, now that the visual world was fading away and the art that had been her passion was no longer possible for her as a practice, she felt ready to give herself up to something, or someone, else. Was Michael the one? Was he mature enough to live with her and take on the responsibilities associated with being the companion of Erica Hanlon?

For some time, her companions had been middle-aged women worshipful of her art but she'd tired of their crotchety ways, tending to conflict directly with her own crotchets, and had left this job unfilled for the past year. She knew someone as young as Michael was likely to stay for a short while only and then move on to other pursuits and relationships.

But he seemed so lost she wasn't sure he'd be able to go anywhere fast. She might be able to tempt him to stay in order to share in her renown even as his own skills were developing. The main thing was to set him on the path of becoming an artist yet still keep him with her. That balance would be tricky to achieve because every increase in his own powers would mean a lessening of his dependence on hers. He would, of course, leave eventually but she intended to keep him with her for as long as she could. Maybe, although she was ashamed to admit she wanted this, she could keep him with her until the end.

The water was now roaring in the kettle. The day was fiercely hot outside yet no matter how warm it was, she still felt cold at her center. She had tended to be cold-blooded in her youth but the tendency had become extreme over the last decades. Even the scorching desert sun took a long time to warm her bones. She inhaled deeply, stood up, and started the process of making tea. She found the canister in its place on the shelf, located the tea strainer in the drawer, pinched out the amount she liked, and put it all in a cup. She turned off the flame and groped for an oven mitt. She found it in a dangerous position, lying on a back burner, and slipped it on to lift the still vibrating kettle into the air. While pouring, she felt a splash of boiling water on her shoe. The leather was thick so she wasn't burned.

She sat at the table, her hands around the cup, the steam rising up and moistening her face. She thought of Michael and how he would sweat right through his shirt in the course of a day. She knew it would be many hours before his return and all she could do was sit with the memory in her nose of his earthy fragrance.

15

TOWN

San Juan had the feel of a border town even though it was far up river from old Mexico. The town was mostly single story with facades of adobe and vinyl, shaded only by light poles and utility wires. The Sangre de Cristo mountains floated serenely above the exhaust fumes. Traffic was always thick no matter what time of day because the approaching highways funneled down to crowded boulevards with frequent traffic lights. Low riders slid slowly through the streets, hopping intermittently on hydraulic shocks, Spanish rock blasting from huge speakers. Every pickup had a full gun rack across the back window of its cab. Even minor traffic confrontations were known to escalate into lively shooting wars.

As he pulsed forward in the waves of vehicles, Michael glanced at the slip of paper bearing the name and address of the office supply store. The street was flanked by a series of storefronts and small shopping centers but the number he wanted didn't seem to exist. Finally,, he stopped in a dry cleaner and asked the woman at the counter where it might be. She was about forty years old, short and sturdy, with a wide face and long hair tied into tight black braids. She seemed so much a part of the Southwest that he could imagine her as an Anasazi cliff dweller at Bandelier or Chaco

Canyon. Yet here she was breathing in cleaning fluids and wearing a Loretta Lynne t-shirt. With a friendly smile, she told him the store he wanted was actually behind one of the strip malls so couldn't be seen from the street.

Michael found it in a row of shops including a video store, a café, a grimy supermarket, and a combined beauty parlor and tanning salon (an odd business in the Southwest, he thought). He threaded the Mercedes through the parking lot where people were, seemingly without looking, backing their vehicles abruptly into traffic lanes. Brassy music threaded with static sounded from loudspeakers on the lamp posts. After the drivers became pedestrians, they walked slowly and carefully, bow-legged in their cowboy boots. Michael finally found an angled parking space at the side of the store.

Inside, the transaction was fairly straightforward. The file cabinets were expensive, although the factor of how remote San Juan was from the rest of the world had to be considered. The clerks didn't bat an eye at his use of Erica's credit card. Apparently minions had been sent in there before. Michael looked around and picked up a few other items for the office, including a twenty dollar pen for himself. He reasoned that he was going to be writing for her a lot so should have something he liked. The clerks took the cabinets outside and easily fit them into the broad back seat of the Mercedes. He put the bag of supplies into the trunk and walked around to the street side of the strip mall, thinking he'd find a place to have lunch.

He ambled by the supermarket, peering inside, wondering if he should pick up the junk food that was in short supply at Erica's house. He vaguely noticed someone standing in front of him, obscured in the full glare of the sun. As he started to go around, he realized that the person, a young woman, was looking directly at him. He glanced at her, hoping automatically for an encounter but saw with a shiver of combined dread and desire that the woman was Sheila. She smiled but he could see that she was also wary of their meeting.

"You!" he said.

"Michael. How are you?"

"Fine. I'm just fine. What are you doing here?"

"I borrowed Terry's car and spent the morning in Santa Fe with my aunt and uncle. They were passing through on their way to San Diego. I picked up some supplies for Ellen's birthday party this weekend. You know Ellen, the girl from Iowa?" He didn't answer because his neurons were delivering a series of contradictory and immobilizing signals to his awareness. She rushed to fill in the silence.

"What about you? I hear you're working for Erica Hanlon."

"Yeah. I was getting some supplies myself."

"I'd really like to talk to you. Could we sit down somewhere?"

The people walking by were flattened to silhouettes by the strong light. Clouds of exhaust drifted slowly past. Sparrows pecked through a spilled bag of popcorn next to the trash can. Michael considered what to do, as well as he could given that her face seemed to be drawing him forward to kiss her. On the other hand, the amount of pain he'd recently experienced in connection with her made him want to flee. He broke his gaze and looked around.

A young woman bulging out of her halter top and cut-off jeans walked to the dime store entrance. She was barely an adult herself yet a cluster of kids hung on her, asking mommy for toys. The mountains were lost in the tangle of electric wires. A small cantina down at the end of the line of shops caught his attention. The entrance was marked by a neon cactus wearing a sombrero, holding a cigarette and a martini glass in separate spiky hands, winking and grinning lasciviously. Michael shrugged, pointed at it, and began to walk in that direction, half-expecting her not to follow.

16

LUNCH

Sheila did come along, slightly behind him, her arms folded across her breasts, her head down, as if anticipating chastisement. A crow plummeted from the top of the gray curved light standard to scatter the sparrows and claim some popcorn. A sour mixture of feelings boiled beneath Michael's surface numbness. Despite his anger at losing her, he harbored an insane hope that somehow, if they spent some time together, she would apologize and beg him to take her back. His immediate thought was that he would spurn her, force her to feel some measure of the loss he'd been feeling so intensely. He recognized how ridiculous this was, not only because she wouldn't want him back, but because he would reconcile with her immediately and without reservation, if she were willing. In fact, he wondered if he could somehow convince her to go to a motel with him.

In the midst of this rapid succession of feelings, he turned his head and made eye contact. He didn't like what he interpreted from her glance. She looked as if she knew she'd done him harm and wished desperately for him to be okay about it but wasn't really going to do anything to change the original blow. Pity was in her eyes and that almost made him change his mind about sitting down with her. But they were just at the door, now they were going in, the smell of spices and cooking enfolded them. He'd been wrong about many things, including his naive assumption that she loved him, so he could be wrong in his present interpretation although, on some level, he knew he wasn't wrong. A dumper almost never changed her mind about the dumping. Out of guilt, she might attempt to make contact with and support the dumpee, but she was highly unlikely to allow a return to full erotic engagement.

All these thoughts occupied the few seconds they took to walk into the cantina where a woman with breasts like battlements covered by a mustard uniform greeted them and showed them to a booth in the back, away from the street. He tried to implement the aesthetic strategy he'd been working on at Erica's and just see what was in front of him. The motif was chrome, spotted with rust. The tables were less than half occupied; the dinner rush hadn't yet started. Most of the men wore cowboy hats and drank beer. The few women had on lipstick about the same shade of scarlet as their Bloody Marys. On a juke box against the wall, bubbles floated quickly and silently up silver columns. A woman sang something plaintive in Spanish about love.

When they sat down, Sheila grabbed the menu and studied it. Michael rested his forearms on the table and looked at her, daring her to return his gaze. The waitress, a woman in her forties with a pock-marked face and a brittle smile approached the table, pencil poised.

"Howdy, folks. Any drinks to start with?"

Sheila ordered a glass of wine and Michael ordered a beer. Sheila continued to study the menu after the waitress left.

"This looks pretty good," she said.

"You think so?"

"Too bad I had lunch in Santa Fe."

"Have another one. On me."

She shook her head, put the menu down, and finally looked directly at him.

"So, does the job with Erica Hanlon pay well?"

"More than the ranch."

"That's not saying much. What exactly do you do for her?"

"Handyman stuff. Errands. Office work."

"I see."

She looked skeptical so he added something he thought might hurt her in some obscure way.

"Plus I'm painting again. Every day."

"Oh, that's good."

"Yes, it is."

The waitress walked by carrying plates piled high with enchiladas, beans, and rice. He felt an urge to get up and leave, just walk away, because he knew this was going nowhere but he couldn't. It wasn't politeness that kept him seated. Only six weeks had passed since they last made love. The sense memories of her body in his hands, of her skin against his skin, suppressed for weeks, had been triggered by her presence. He again wanted to ask her to go to a motel with him but a look of wary pity was in her eyes and he didn't know how to make it go away.

He stared at her face but had trouble bringing it into focus. Was she kind of plain or very beautiful? Was she smiling or crying, young or old? He had trouble peering through the fog of his mental turmoil to see whoever it was actually sitting in front of him. The waitress brought their beer and wine. Sheila took a sip and looked him in the eyes. He struggled to look back.

"I'm sorry about that night," she said.

Michael felt a flush of anger and looked up at the ceiling fan turning at slow speed. To his left, a fat fly wallowed in the spilt honey beside a dispenser on the counter. He looked down to where a single kernel of corn, a vivid yellow, lay on the floor.

"I should have realized you were getting more serious than I was but I never promised you anything."

Michael laughed.

"Well, excuse me for assuming that because we were together every night you might have some small amount of loyalty to me, or at least tell me before you slept with someone else."

"I'm sorry. That's where I messed up. I was afraid to tell you because I knew what your reaction would be."

The waitress came over again and paused for a second, surveying the tension, before asking, "Ready to order, folks?"

In a strangled voice, Michael said, "Not right now for me. Do you want anything?"

Sheila shook her head back and forth.

"No problem," the waitress said a bit too brightly. "Just give me a wave if you change your mind."

As she turned, Michael had a sudden urge for something comforting.

"Do you have sopapillas?"

She spun back.

"Yes, we do. Want me to get you a basket?"

"That would be great."

She left quickly. Sheila had her head down again, her hair falling around her face. Michael felt an urge to attack.

"So where were we? Oh, yeah, you're sorry you were with someone else all night long without bothering to tell me."

"It just happened. It wasn't as if you and I were married, or engaged, or anything like that."

"So the only reason to be monogamous, from your point of view, is to be in, or committed to, the holy state of matrimony?"

"Don't do this."

"That's rich. What am I doing? You couldn't possibly feel the way I did after listening to you with that asshole all night long."

"You listened all night?"

"Right outside the window. I heard every little moan and gasp. How many times was it, two or three? I wasn't quite sure he came the last time."

This wasn't true but he'd imagined the scene enough times he felt like he'd been there.

"That's really sick, to listen like that."

He leaned over and whispered urgently.

"Oh, yeah, that's right, I'm sick although I wasn't the one fucking a complete stranger all night. How old is he, anyway? Thirty? Forty? He could be fifty with his leathery face and gray hair in that stupid ponytail. I sat there for hours trying to decide whether I should beat the shit out of both of you."

Her eyes widened.

"Look, all I wanted to do was tell you I'm sorry."

"Well, I'm sorry, too. Sorry I made such a poor choice of who to stick my dick into."

This last remark, obviously heartfelt, emerged in a voice that was a bit too loud, because heads all over the restaurant swiveled toward them. Tears ran down Sheila's cheeks. He sat back, in a furnace of shame and rage. The motel was definitely out of the question now.

Wasn't it?

17

RAGE

He drove northward, feeling both urgent and chaotic. He'd stalked off quickly after they exited the restaurant, not turning back to see where she was headed. Now he kept imagining he would encounter her driving on Rte. 96. This was impossible, he knew, because he'd driven like a fiend through San Juan, abruptly changing lanes and passing on the right to get out of there as fast as he could. On the highway, he pushed the Mercedes up to eighty and ninety, passing dangerously on blind curves, not caring what might happen. His fantasy was he'd force her car off the road, following her into the ditch so they could die together in a burst of flame. He was disgusted with himself, at the intensity of emotions threatening to overwhelm him. Could he be any more melodramatic?

Finally, on a curve, an old pick up truck, dark blue and rusty, with a man and a young boy in the front seat came hurtling at him. Michael moved desperately close to the car he was passing but still occupied the entire middle of the road. The boy's mouth formed a perfect dark oval of fear as his father twisted on the wheel to move his truck far enough toward the shoulder to clear Michael's car. Michael flew between the two vehicles with only inches of space on either side and then watched in the rear view mirror as the truck, despite several wild swerves, managed to get back on the road. Michael slowed down to seventy, the normal speed for the area, and didn't pass on the curves for the rest of the trip to Chamisa.

As he approached the village, he found that the Mercedes, as if beyond his will, was slowing and drifting to the right, coming to a halt in front of Angie's bar, the establishment known to be highly unsympathetic to middle-class college students. Through the open door of the bar, he could see orange pulses of neon from the jukebox forming hieroglyphics at the back of the room. Dark forms passed back and forth in front of its light. Inside the leather womb of the vehicle, he listened to the ticks and rustlings from the engine and the interior. When he opened the door and stepped outside, the warm air braced him upright.

The sun was moving down behind the mesas and ridges above the village. The shoulder of the highway near the bar was crowded with the pickup trucks of the men, and some women, who stopped by after work. He was only able to park the Mercedes directly in front by pulling in beside the old gas pumps. Road widening had left them close to passing traffic so the Mercedes was stuck halfway out on the highway. Someone not paying attention and coming around the curve could easily smash into it. He thought briefly of Erica, that the car was hers and she'd be wondering where he was but realized he didn't care about anything. His boots crunched on the gravel as he walked around the car, hitching up his pants. Beside the bar, a short slope, covered with wildflowers, led down to the river. His better nature tried to lure him to rest peacefully in the grass but the percussion of his heart would not allow that. He stepped through the doorway, into the maelstrom.

As soon as he entered, he breathed up into his sinuses the earthy tang of beer, the smoke of cigarettes and small cigars, the sweat from bodies that had been working hard all day, barely masked by the piercing emanations of cologne and industrial strength deodorant. Glints of light burst from the darkness in jagged shards that hurt his eyes. As his vision adjusted to the dark, other illumination slowly emerged, including reflections from bottles and glasses, the bare filaments of low hung lamps with little wattage, flashes from matches and cigarette lighters. The effect was of a flock of heterogeneous fireflies with various shapes, colors, and temperatures of light. A rich low sound filled the space as the bass from the juke box caused the thin walls to vibrate and the glistening surfaces of the drinks on the bar to shimmer.

Moving into this intricate darkness, he saw the cowboy hats along the bar tilting up so the eyes beneath could examine him and register that, although he might be familiar from the Ranch, he was not a local. Facing him down at the end of the counter was Raoul Perchado, with his handle-bar mustache and dark glasses. Raoul was completely still except for the twisting smoke from the Lucky Strike hanging from the corner of his mouth. Raoul worked with the maintenance crew at the ranch on a seasonal basis. Michael knew from experience that Raoul invariably exhibited profound disdain for the male college staff but displayed avid attention to the women, especially when they were in bathing suits at the pool. He was known throughout the region as a notorious alcoholic, a borrower of money he never paid back, and a bar fighter, just the person Michael wanted to run into in his present mood.

The juke box displayed its glistening fluid magic directly in front of him. To his right was a jumbled collection of tables at which were seated a few couples and some lone men slumped over in various stages of inebriation. On the wall behind them was a gallery of signs advertising beer and fortified wines. The restrooms were behind a pair of swinging doors beyond the tables. A short foyer separating the Mens from the Ladies rooms was lit by a red light bulb around which flies spun like manic satellites.

The establishment was presided over by a man he knew as Jorge, a legend in the area, a huge presence behind the bar with his wedge-like black beard and tattoos of clothed and naked Olive Oyls on his biceps. Jorge was glaring at him so hard he seemed to have flames in his pupils. Michael gave a brief wave in the direction of both Jorge and Raoul and spoke:

"Gentlemen, how are you on this fine evening?"

Jorge's stare narrowed down to laser-like intensity. Raoul's stillness spread out like ripples from a stone thrown into a black pond. One of the men at the bar snickered. A whispered "cavron" followed Michael as he walked deeper into the establishment. The instrumental tune on the jukebox ended and a plaintive ballad began. Michael reached the end of the bar, inches away from Raoul, and looked back out the open door. Reddish light poured through the entry way, and he imagined the patrons awash in blood.

The gold paint of the Mercedes was tinted with a shade of deep burgundy. The two gas pumps next to the sedan looked like props from an Edward Hopper painting. Beyond them, the tinted blurs of speeding cars occasionally flashed by. The reds of the earth in the opposite slope intensified by the moment. The blue of the sky above the ridge line was dimming into shadow.

"What do you want here?" Raoul didn't move his lips in saying this. The smoke from his cigarette curled over into Michael's eyes.

"Just came in for a beer. What's it to you?" The line of eyes staring at him were strung together like beads of black pearl. Jorge snorted and turned his attention to the cleaning of his fingernails with a buck knife. Michael anticipated what would happen in just a few minutes in a chaos of blood and pain. His every muscle was tensed for the coming conflict when a voice spoke in his right ear.

"Hey, man, why don't you go home? This isn't good."

Michael turned to see Diego Confrides, another member of the maintenance crew at the Ranch. Diego had always been on friendly terms with the summer staff and he was a genuinely good guy. Diego grasped his elbow and tried to move him toward the door. Ignoring him, Michael stayed stubbornly planted.

"Hey, what is this?" Michael asked loudly. "You won't serve me because I'm Anglo?"

"No," Jorge shouted, "We won't serve you because you're stupid!"

"Go back home, cavron," Ramon chimed in. "Your old lady is waiting for you. And I do mean your OLD LADY!"

The line of hats at the bar broke into raucous laughter.

"Your very old lady, man!" Someone else chimed in.

"Tell us, hombre. Does she ever get wet?"

"Whatcha got in the car, cavron? A case of Vaseline?"

The hilarity became general. Michael felt his internal processes accelerate, heard the roar from the blood rushing through his skull. His last fight had been in grade school but now seemed like the perfect moment for another. He swiftly pulled his fist back to land a punch on the side of Raoul's head, something he'd always wanted to do, but found instead that his fist was immediately enclosed in a hand the size of a catcher's mitt.

Jorge had come around the bar to intervene, moving so quickly that the patrons' hats spun in his wake. Jorge grabbed Michael by the waist and propelled him to the door, his hand still raised up but trapped in Jorge's giant paw, his other arm pinned to his side. Jorge swung him once from the hip and Michael arced toward the Mercedes.

As soon as he was free, he twisted himself in mid-air so he'd hit the car door with his ribs instead of with his head. The chassis reverberated with a deep thump, jangling his bones as he slid to the dirt. Looking back to the doorway, Michael saw Jorge filling the frame, his arms folded. From inside, laughter mingled with trumpet blasts, the music streaming around Jorge's bulk.

"Don't come back," Jorge said. "Not until you learn some manners."

18

RETURN

Michael walked into the house and noticed Erica sitting in her chair in the middle of the courtyard. She'd obviously heard the car arrive but she gave no greeting, just sat looking in the direction of Obsidian. He wanted to go to his room and hide but knew he had to talk to her. His hand lingered on the rough wood of the post.

"Sorry I'm late," he said, his foot placed tentatively on the flagstone of the patio.

A long silence came back at him. The colors of sunset had slowly filtered down through layers of cloud, suffusing the sky with a deep vermilion. Finally, as the first star revealed itself overhead, she spoke.

"Are you drunk?"

"Not at all. I couldn't get served, as a matter of fact."

"You look as if you've been in a fight."

"Not really a fight, no."

Shadows deepened under the porch around the courtyard. Venus glowed like a torch above Obsidian. Michael's back and hip were sore from the impact of hitting the car but he felt it would be some kind of concession if he were to sit down or go to his room, so he kept standing, his arms crossed, looking out at the sky that was giving a preview of the spectacular visual drama about to be presented on its stage.

"Jed Mills said my car was blocking the highway outside of Angie's."

Her face was as impassive as the profile on a coin.

"The car's fine, if that's what you want to know."

She smoothed the skirt on her thighs and stood up.

"I don't understand you," she said.

"Funny, I was just thinking the same thing about you."

"There's work in the morning."

"That's right."

She walked to the corner of the courtyard and back toward her room, her right hand held out tentatively in front of her.

He stood in the courtyard and tremors of emotion convulsed him from the craziness of the day, spasms of shame, guilt, fear, anger, and grief, an unholy cocktail. He didn't know what to do with it all but felt exhausted so went to bed.

19

ACHE

They didn't speak more about that day although the next time they drove out together, she stared pointedly at the wide dent in the door of the Mercedes before she got in. In the mornings, he continued his studies of the complex and mysterious terrain. He felt he could spend his entire life just painting what he saw in every direction from the house, exploring slight variations of angle or illumination. He wasn't trying to make "pictures" anymore. He just laid paint on paper, examined what happened, and repeated the process.

Erica came out at some point every day to be present while he worked. She noticed he was painting his watercolors on the cheap paper he pulled from tablets.

"Don't worry about materials," she said. "Charge what you need in San Juan. They're expensive, and limited, but at least if they don't have something, they can order it from Albuquerque."

When she made a comment about his paintings, which was seldom, it was always about some technical detail and not about overall quality, a reticence he appreciated. She pointed out colors and shapes that either worked or didn't. If they didn't work, she always suggested practical methods for improvement and she was invariably right, despite her poor vision. He came to feel protective of her eyes, thinking grandiosely that maybe his task was to see for her. He knew, although not from anything she said, that she'd prefer to be making her own art rather than advising him. She gazed obliquely at his messy paintings with a stern grief he didn't dare question.

At lunch they had brief exchanges about what chores and business needed to be done for the rest of the day. Michael finished the roof, fixed some electrical outlets, and patched more adobe (a task as endless as painting the George Washington Bridge). When the sun was at its most intense, he sat at the desk in the cool of the office and typed out letters on Erica's ancient Underwood. He took the drafts of his replies to Erica in the evening and read them to her. Usually she nodded her head without comment. Her business methods were simple: she never accepted invitations to appear or speak; she declined all interviews; she negotiated only with museum administrators, never with galleries, about purchasing her work.

When the office tasks were done, he'd take a beer and read a book out in the shade of the courtyard or in the cool of the living room, depending on the weather, until dinner. Lupe was an excellent cook of the local cuisine: enchiladas, chicken mole, chile rellenos, all seasoned just on the hot side. During dinner, a tradition began that he and Erica would share a bottle of wine. Erica would become more talkative and he played the role of eager student. She told him about her upbringing in rural Maine, her days studying and teaching in New York, her life with Harold in Greenwich Village and in France, and their eventual estrangement. She'd made her living for many years as an independent artist, favorite of feminists, scorned by the male sculptors of her time but really outflanking them. She held forth with her many opinions about art, culture, and politics.

Her views were so precise and yet so sweeping they made Michael realize how vague his own ideas were. She dismissed Paul Klee as a mere cartoonist, Rodin as a crude imitator of Michelangelo. She thought Truman should have dropped the atom bombs on Mt. Fuji instead of on Hiroshima and Nagasaki. She called film a stewpot of various art forms, none of them done very well. Often he disagreed with her but couldn't say why, and he stayed awake in bed at night trying to come up with counter-arguments. He realized he hadn't thought very hard about anything before.

After dinner, he'd do the dishes and they'd go for a walk. Erica had a favorite route heading toward the red hills behind her house and rising along a ridge line almost to the foot of the sandstone cliffs. At the top of the ridge, two large smooth rocks lay waiting patiently for erosion to grind them into sand. In the meantime, their surfaces were perfectly shaped for sitting.

Erica always chose the one closest to Castle Rock where the Valle Luminoso stretched out before them in the ruddy light of the setting sun. They'd listen to the occasional engine passing along the highway or high above in the air. Sometimes they'd hear snatches of hymns from the chapel at the ranch or maybe a Led Zeppelin guitar riff from the cranked-up stereo at the college staff house. But these sounds were crude in comparison to the intricate music of nature.

The hoot of an owl in the crevices of the cliff, the rapid flutter from the wings of bats emerging in the dusk to search for insects, the plunk and roll of a pebble falling and beginning its journey down to the river far below them, all these sounds created a complex orchestration that Michael found enthralling. During these sessions, neither of them spoke much because they were caught up in the sheer movement of sound and light. Sometimes Michael felt an almost physical ache barely restraining a rush of desire for Sheila, an ache keeping him separate from the moment. For the most part, however, he simply watched and waited, not thinking, just listening, feeling the breath move in and out of his body as some presence inside him spoke to the massive presence all around them. He didn't know what Erica was thinking and didn't dare to ask.

20

STIRRED

She, on the other hand, sat on the rock with the young man at her side, looking toward the dark mountains far away, not seeing them at all but somehow smelling the iron oxide in their cliffs. The evening gathered around her, the chill rising in the deep shadows below the mesa. The bones of her pelvis felt sharp against the sandstone. Her body, after serving her so steadfastly through seven decades, was now slowing down, cracking at the creases, aching in the joints. For some years, she had no longer recognized herself when she looked in the mirror so now it was a relief she couldn't see clearly.

Although she wasn't sure she could really compare over decades, her sense of self seemed remarkably the same. The fact her body had aged around this central awareness was a constant surprise. She continued to feel passion, for the life running through her every day, for the art she could no longer practice, and now for this young man next to her. She didn't know why she felt so strongly about him. He was soft and unformed, callow and needy, arrogant yet ignorant, reminding her of the long-haired youth, both male and female, who showed up at her house, inspired by her sculptures, imagining she had some wisdom drawn from nature and her idiosyncratic yet stubbornly maintained aesthetic to help guide them in their wanderings. She bestowed upon them, for the most part, only the curtest of dismissals, having no desire to be a mentor to anyone, much less a guru.

Michael was different. When he was beside her, she wanted to reach out and touch his hair, pull him close to her, feel the casual strength of his arms and legs against her. Ridiculous thoughts to have, adding in her mind the phrase she hated: for a woman her age. Although she'd never been pretty in the traditional sense, she retained a knowledge in her bones of having been strangely beautiful, someone whose presence made people turn to look again.

The sculptures Harold fashioned with her as his model, so casually sexual despite the rigidity of the material, made her body famous. Caught in carefully selected moments, the sculptures, wherever they were, in museum or private collection, remained vibrant and erotic while her own body was irretrievably battered by time. She knew little remained in her flesh to attract a young man. What she had to offer was her wealth (not inconsiderable), her experience, developed over years of practicing her art (the mightiest of her gifts, she thought), and the mystery of her inner self, a mystery she had never been able to share, even when she was still in love with Harold.

What did she want from this boy? Altruistically, she wanted him to find himself and have access to creative power, something she'd possessed from childhood. Michael's talent had been merely pictorial until now but he was slowly learning to see. In his recent dabblings, a connection was being formed in a dynamic arc, from the world around him, through his eye and mind, to his right hand. The mesas and sky were being etched into his vision.

With Michael, she was playing a tutorial role new to her. Even when she'd taught art in her twenties, she was doing it for the money. In her obsessive ambition, she'd given little thought to the careers of the mostly young and female artists in her classes. The work of others, especially her contemporaries, and especially sculptors, never interested her much. Over the years, she'd perfected the art of ignoring what did not please her, totally excluding bad art, fractious people, and unwanted events from her awareness. Despite the trends of the art world and the resistance of the arrogant men who were always in power, she went her own way. Indeed, in the end the world followed her, admiring and envying the fierce individuality she brought to her work. The only problem now as she grew older, as her vision failed, was that the other side of this relentless process of defining herself was isolation.

She wanted someone to be with her but she was wary. Her most recent companion/secretary had insinuated herself into Erica's finances and siphoned off a large amount of cash. Erica didn't want to involve the law with its attendant publicity so didn't call the police and was forced to put up with the woman's histrionic rage when Erica fired her. In the end, she was forced to call Jed Mills to escort the harridan off the property.

Now, after a long period of fumbling on her own, albeit with Lupe's domestic assistance that she knew she took for granted, she had this young male muddle close to her. She didn't feel any fear of his taking advantage of her. She found him to be sufficiently intelligent but couldn't imagine him to be devious enough, or confident enough, to manage a swindle. However, she was painfully aware of how much her emotions were stirred up by his proximity.

21

CHALLENGE

One evening, as they sat on their separate rocks, taking their break halfway through a walk, she spoke. She could smell the soap from his shower and a hint of sweat from their hike up the ridge. She turned to him and said the first inanity that came to mind.

"So how are you?"

He looked over at her, startled. She'd never before asked him anything about how he was doing.

"Fine, just fine."

"What do you want to do tomorrow?"

"Pretty much what we did today, I expect. Did you have anything in mind?"

"Yes, I thought we might climb Obsidian."

"The mountain?"

"Yes, of course the mountain."

"Are you sure you're up to it?"

"I can do it one more time. At least."

"Do you think... Should we ask... someone from the ranch to go with us?"

"Why should we do that?"

"In case something goes wrong."

"I am now seventy-two years old. If anything goes wrong, as you so euphemistically put it, that will be a good place to die."

"I was thinking…"

He stopped himself.

As always, his hesitation, generated by his vast internal uncertainties, irritated her. Above her head, she could sense the soaring presence of a large bird, a hawk or an eagle. He wouldn't even notice, despite his perfectly adequate eyesight, city boy that he was.

"Out with it!"

He jumped. Such a sensitive thing.

"I don't know. I was worried about a broken hip, maybe. Aren't you afraid of that?"

Wonderful. That's how he saw her, of course, as ancient, a grandmother doddering around, likely to fall and break something. She had the urge, could taste it on her tongue, to blast him, as she had so many others for lesser presumptions, but she held back.

"I'm in better shape than you are."

He smiled.

"Of course you are," he said, with barely concealed sarcasm.

"I'll race you back to the house. If I win, we'll go tomorrow and climb the mountain. If you win, we'll stay home and eat mush. What do you say?"

"I don't want to race. I'm not into competition."

He had clearly said this before when challenged. No wonder he lost that stupid girl over at the ranch. Jed Mills had told her what drove Michael over the cliff to land like a clod of dirt at her doorstep. Erica stood up and pushed him hard off the rock. He fell awkwardly in the dust.

"Fifty years earns me a head start," she said and trotted nimbly down the trail.

22

DRIVE

A shattering sound brought him up fast from the depths of a complex and murky dream. He flung himself out of bed and banged around the room in the dark trying to find his boots, determined to defend his new home against coyote, bandit, or raging arroyo. From outside came the rasp of Erica's voice through the door.

"What is wrong with you?"

As soon as he heard her, he realized what was happening: she was merely banging on his door to wake him early so they could climb the mountain before the day became too hot.

"Nothing. I'm fine."

Fine. He kept using that word. What would be better? Okay? Good? He fumbled for the switch and turned on the light to awaken the dusty room. Erica's footsteps receded down the porch.

He'd only slept a few hours, having stayed up late drinking beer and reading *Steppenwolf*. Hung-over and haunted by the prose that seemed as convoluted as his mood, he caught a glimpse of his puffy red eyes in the mirror. This was going to be painful, he could tell.

He put on a clean T-shirt and jeans and pulled on his hiking boots. He stuffed his usual gear into the small knapsack: snake-bite kit, Swiss Army knife, first-aid kit, canteen, jacket, and Yankees cap. His sketch pad and pencils went on top as he headed out the door.

Erica was in the kitchen where the windows were so dark they appeared to be painted black. She wore her cowboy hat with the draw string under her chin, a black work dress belted at the waist, and sturdy boots on her long feet. Into her canvas pack she was loading various food items. She gestured with a sandwich wrapped in wax paper.

"Let's get going."

He held up his flashlight.

"Do you think we'll be back late?"

"Probably by sunset if we don't spent more than a few hours at the top, but you'd best bring it anyway."

While he filled the canteens with water from the sink, Erica gathered up the rest of her gear. As they headed out to the truck in the chilly air, the stars were still clustered thickly above despite the faint glow of morning behind the mesa. Michael saw two meteors, one after the other, sizzle across the sprawl of the Milky Way. He turned to comment to Erica but realized before he spoke that she couldn't have seen them so he refrained. After they climbed inside the truck, Michael made sure his sunglasses were in the visor. Although the need seemed theoretical at the moment, he knew the sky would be blazing by mid-morning.

When Michael turned the key in the ignition, the big V-8 sent detonations bouncing off the mesa walls. Michael thought they could probably be heard all the way to the staff house, if anyone were up to listen. He looked at his watch. Only four thirty. A surge of fatigue pulled down on his eyelids. Erica was staring straight ahead in her attitude, now familiar to him, of fixed determination.

He backed the truck in a wide curve in front of the house, looking over his shoulder at the piñon bushes and cholla flaring red in the brake lights. A randomly chosen section of desert illuminated by the headlights stood poised elegantly in the moment like a diorama at the Museum of Natural History. He didn't even bother to look down the road for cars. If by some chance Jed and Susan Mills were up and moving this early, their truck would be cutting a wide swath of glare with its rack of lights. Michael cranked the wheel, bumped the undercarriage hard on the culvert, and shot onto the road, the gravel spinning out behind.

As they moved along, Michael reached for the radio and flipped on an Albuquerque station that played country music through the night. He turned up the volume to be audible over the engine noise but Erica immediately reached over and flicked the dial down below the threshold of hearing. She ignored his glare. They rumbled along the road, sweeping up the ground in the fan of their lights, freezing a rabbit for an instant in a pose with dangling paw before it exploded into a mad scramble to save itself. They bounced over the cattle guard and into the ranch.

He thought of Sheila in the her bunk at the staff house just across the field (if, in fact, that's where she was) and how she used to whisper in her sleep, soft syllables emerging with each breath while her eyes shifted under their lids. To obliterate this memory, he stared fiercely ahead into the wedge of light revealing the gravel road rolling toward them.

They turned down the hill toward the highway where the stars, their luster even penetrating the dirty windshield, defined the mountains to the west. He paused for a moment at the end of the ranch road as the dust they'd provoked swirled around them. A moth fluttered in the harsh glare, fascinated by the sudden dawn from the truck's headlights.

"Go left," said Erica.

"I know, I know."

He paused for another moment to express his independence and carefully moved the truck onto the highway, feeling the sudden ease of the blacktop beneath their tires. After rolling his window all the way down, he rested his forearm on the cool metal of the door. The night air was filled with the tang of sage, juniper, and piñon, along with the scent of coyotes and jackrabbits, owls and mice.

As the truck began to cruise, his fatigue lifted and he enjoyed the freedom of his obscurity in the world. No one beyond the ranch thought much about him or expected anything of him so he could do whatever he wanted. He could hitchhike to Anchorage, or sign on with a tramp steamer to Indonesia. He could even whistle *The Yellow Rose of Texas*, as he began to do, with enthusiasm. Erica glanced over at this unskilled musical foray and he expected to see her frown but she was actually smiling a bit. She reached to the radio and turned it on. Country music filled the cab with sound. He laughed at this commentary on his musical ability. She pushed air briefly out her nostrils, which he knew was what passed with her for hilarity.

The waxing light gave just enough definition to the mesas on the road to indicate their complexity. Usually in the night they were looming dark presence, giving one's passage a claustrophobic edge. Now the sandstone was receding back into itself, taking on dimension and shading in preparation for the intense light of day.

The truck twisted down the tight curves high above the meandering river, gravity shifting the heavy chassis a bit harder with each turn. The angle eased as they gradually rolled to the intersection where the road to the dam extended off to the west. Michael looked over at Erica and asked her, with fake innocence, "Turn right?"

This time she laughed deep in her throat. A few gently curved miles brought them to the earthen dam built by the Army Corps of Engineers in its usual style of vast overkill, needlessly backing up the river and inundating the valley for what they termed recreational purposes. Although it was now run by the state of New Mexico, the area retained a definite military atmosphere with its harsh halogen lamps and nearby Quonset huts, reminding Michael of some sci-fi film from the fifties in which the military hastily constructed a bulwark against an advancing horde of giant insects.

As they drove over the dam, a soft mist lay on the lake's quiet. A bird flew low across the water, its dipping wings just grazing the surface, each touch sending ripples flowing out in widening circles. Looking past Erica, whose tightly pulled hair was straining at her scalp, Michael shared for a moment in the intensity of her attention to the squeak of the bird's shoulders and the rhythmic splashing on the lake.

23

APPROACH

They began to ascend onto a tilted plain leading beyond the basin into a jumble of low mountains. A single car could be seen approaching from miles away, pushing its light in a moving cone that grew ever larger until, after long minutes, it suddenly passed by, momentarily overwhelming them with the intensity of its glare. The headlights of a few more cars defined an intermittent curve along the highway. Michael wondered at the early traffic and Erica explained this was the vanguard of the long commute to Los Alamos, the only place in the region where jobs were still plentiful, albeit in janitorial or landscaping positions. Up until the Second World War, local families were able to survive by raising cattle, tending gardens, hunting, cutting wood, and selling crafts. Now most of the locals worked full-time somewhere else: for the Ranch of the Spirits, the Forest Service, or the nuclear labs. Caring for their spreads had become a part-time occupation.

They drove through the small town of Hermosa where Michael looked optimistically to see if the grocery store had opened yet for coffee but it was still shuttered tight. Behind them, in the rear view mirror, Michael could see the humpbacked mesas of the ranch popping into view, the gypsum caps dingy against a dark blue-gray sky on which heavy clouds were scattered. Maybe it wouldn't be as hot as he'd anticipated.

"The turnoff's in another ten miles," Erica said.

Michael reached forward and set the odometer. The road passed through an intermediate zone between desert and peak, scrubby terrain slowly revealing its tans and browns in the expanding light. The immediate area didn't have the drama of the landscape around the ranch except for the looming presence of Obsidian itself to their left, revealing an unfamiliar and narrow edge, with battlements and fluted columns invisible from Erica's house.

At the ten mile marker, they turned onto a forest service road angling off to the south and began to gain altitude rapidly. In a grove of cedar trees, the road became such a washboard he was forced repeatedly to brake hard to avoid slamming his teeth together. Although the light now glowed strongly above them, the spaces between the trees were still dim from the night. In the midst of the slender trunks, a fire ring of gray stones had been laid out next to a poled frame, a campsite that could have been anywhere from a few hours to a few thousand years old.

They kept rising into ever thinner air, moving over bare open shoulders of hills where they looked up to views of the surrounding ridges and the startling bare rock of Obsidian's summit cap. Michael began to feel a tremendous sense of exaltation. The intensifying brightness at the zenith was dissolving the night clouds into a pure blue so intense it seemed to bow down to scrape the roof of their truck. Today, they were going to climb this obscure local peak that was to him and, he knew, to the woman beside him, the most beautiful mountain in the world, whose form and detail he'd been examining closely every day and attempting with only marginal success to put down onto paper and canvas. In her sculptures, the woman beside him had made a thousand representations of its unusual shape. As the next curve brought the entire back of the mountain into view, he realized how little of its texture he was able to see from their house, how the shape he so casually filled in with mottled gray wash held an infinity of detail.

24

ASCENT

Erica pointed past him to a rocky track that was clearly not maintained. The truck climbed at such a steep and twisted angle that for a moment he thought it would tip over but he pulled hard to the left and crawled over the crown, scraping the chassis, to more level ground. Here the dirt road was so deeply rutted he had to veer from one side to the other to avoid being pulled into a trench too deep for their clearance. Erica had to brace herself between door and seat as they were thrown around inside the cab. She leaned forward intently, as if she could through sheer force of will smooth out the gullies and top the hills. The truck strained to climb over small boulders and tree limbs in the road. The fresh smell of pine rose up into their sinuses, with intoxicating effect. Between the trees, shards of brilliant blue stood out like emblems against the darkness of trunks and branches.

Michael felt exhilarated. He broke into song, belting out, "Oh, what a beautiful morning," in a deep off-key voice. He looked over at Erica and was surprised when she joined in with a high sour soprano. They swung tight around the edge of a slope where an even vaguer side track climbed steeply toward the sky.

"Up there," Erica said.

"Will the truck make it?"

"It has before."

He shrugged and turned the steering wheel, dropping the engine into first gear. Dirt spun out behind their rear tires as they ascended at such a steep angle all they could see through the front windows was sky. Brush on either side of the road was bent back with their passage, forcing them to pull in their elbows and roll their windows part way up to keep from being lashed. Finally, they crawled over a hump that loudly scraped the oil pan and drive shaft. They came to a clattering stop in a small clearing surrounded by Ponderosa pine. Between the trunks they could see open ground rising some distance away.

Michael turned off the engine and silence immediately enveloped them. The clearing was saturated with shadowless light. As another wave of tiredness swept through him, Michael leaned his head back against the cab window. Erica, meanwhile, was bustling with energy, gathering her day pack from between her feet, tightening the laces on her boots, gathering stray items from the seat and putting them into the glove compartment. Michael wondered if by some magic their ages had been reversed. She even took the rear view mirror, angled it toward herself, and examined her face. She began to apply suntan lotion to her nose, cheeks, and forehead. Michael had a sudden flash of empathy for this girlish routine. She noticed his attention and thrust the tube toward him.

"Here. The sun will be immense today."

"Thanks."

Putting a glob of white cream on his fingers, he began to rub it on his face. When he turned his head to apply it to his neck, his tiredness gave a strobing effect to his vision, the trees and brush and rocks vibrating as his eyes passed over them. When he handed the tube back to Erica, she peered at him.

"You have a big clump on your nose."

She was quicker than he was as the tip of her finger smoothed out the lotion from the side of his nose to his cheek. His face burned at this intimate gesture and he fought the urge to flick her hand away, feeling like a kid whose mom was tending him too closely. Grabbing his sunglasses, he twisted away from her, opened the door, and stepped out. Stretching up from his driving crouch, he grabbed at the sky with his hands. He hoped they actually made it to the summit. What if Erica was not only old and almost blind but crazy as well, completely unable to do this climb? He didn't relish the idea of having to carry her back down, or leave her to go and get help.

As if to illustrate his concern, Erica moved beside the truck in the hunched-over posture she used when preoccupied. She was rummaging through her pack and mumbling to herself. She reached in the bed of the truck and came up with a coil of rope, stuffing it in the pack. She handed the canteens to Michael. A hawk circled overhead and then, with an idle flick of its wing, sailed off to the west. She looked over at him.

"Try to keep up."

She started off at a brisk pace. Michael hefted his pack and hastily made sure the doors of the truck were locked. He ran to catch up to her, feeling heavy in his hiking boots, as she pressed forward, gliding through the trees toward the slope of freshly spun sunlight.

25

CLIMB

They easily made their way through the pines, Erica proving to be quite nimble over the uneven ground. She felt her way with the toes of her boots through clumps of thick yellowish grasses edged by wild roses and small blue flowers. He was breathing hard in the thin air but Erica didn't seem to be winded at all.

Various kinds of scat were on the ground. Some of it was deer but the other droppings were of strange colors and dimensions. Lynx? Cougar? Bear? From above they heard a skree: through the patterned branches a hawk casually tilted its wings and ascended in a spiral. They walked in a floating hemisphere of sheer beauty containing no sign of human habitation. They moved along easily, companionably, ascending with each step, drifting toward each other and then away, bumping occasionally. The sun still hadn't topped the summit, and probably wouldn't for several hours, but they sensed a presence behind them and turned to see a distant slope to the west bathed in luscious yellow light.

"This reminds me of the Midi," Erica said, slowing her pace a bit.

"When were you first there?"

"Before the war." She looked at him. "The Second World War."

He laughed. "I wasn't going to ask."

"I wove wheat into my pieces to capture the light but never felt I succeeded. I filled our country house with the various efforts."

"Were they in the Guggenheim show?"

"That's right. Now they're all in Chicago."

"Huh. You know, I saw them with my junior high class on a field trip."

"Are you sure it wasn't your kindergarten?"

He ignored this and continued:

"I didn't know enough about art at the time to appreciate them, and my teacher certainly didn't help, but I remember how the colors almost made the pieces vibrate."

"That's what I was working on. Color."

They kept trudging while they talked and finally found themselves at the edge of the tree line. Across most of the slope the trees went right up to the escarpment but their path went through a clearing leading directly to the summit cliffs. Michael finally had his first close view of the reverse side of the mountain.

Directly above was a colonnade seemingly filled with statuary, like the facade of a Roman amphitheater of vast proportions, most of which had been eroded by time. Juniper and piñon bushes clung to any horizontal space on the ridge cap except where the drop was too steep for anything to hang on. Michael felt an envy of nature's creative power spilling forth such beauty so effortlessly while he struggled to create even a remote approximation. Perhaps the secret was to let himself go, just as nature did, to paint whatever he wanted without getting in his own way. That might be the best method for keeping despair at bay.

Erica gazed intently at the ridge line but didn't appear to find anything in her murky vision to delay them. She marched quickly up the steeper slope of this final section, somehow aiming directly at the only line of ascent where they wouldn't need to do any technical rock climbing. Michael followed her, admiring the stamina of this woman in black whose form seemed to absorb the light, creating an immense gravitational pull he found impossible to resist.

His lungs ached from the steep angle and the altitude. He thought he'd been in pretty good shape, at least before he landed at Erica's house. At the ranch, after working in the sun nine hours a day, six days a week, he'd gone hiking in the evenings and on his days off. He'd become lean and strong, stronger than he'd ever been in his life. The routine with Erica wasn't exactly unhealthy but definitely wasn't as strenuous. His focus now was only on painting, and that required visual and mental concentration rather than physical activity. Some hiking was involved in their evening walks and when he carried his supplies out to the desert but he knew he was getting soft.

As he watched her make her way through the field of debris that had fallen from the top, he thought about how she possessed a paradoxical combination of stillness and energy, generating an incredible force. Whenever he came upon her sitting alone in the courtyard, he was surprised the adobe walls didn't start bending in, pulled by the force of her presence. She was the least ignorable person he'd ever met and he knew this was true because he often tried to ignore her. It wasn't just the impact of her fame. Fame was a mere byproduct of the creative energy of her self. He felt abashed and jealous about being in her presence. He himself was a wad of inchoate emotions while she seemed to be a pure channel for whatever was inside.

26

DESIRE

The pure channel at that moment was having thoughts anything but pure. She could feel in the generalized ache at the small of her back and in the tension in her chest that the effort of climbing would exact punishment on her later. However, she was gratified to realize she still had energy for this enterprise. Muscle and bone continued to respond to the labor she forced upon them so this might not have to be her last climb of the mountain. Her attention was occupied, however, by this young man behind her. She had the urge to strip off his sweaty clothes (she could smell him on the following breeze) and move her hands upon him.

Of course, this was insane. She hadn't made love for some years and was surprised she still wanted to now. What was she going to do with all this energy? Should she find some elderly man who somehow still had enough spunk to get it up? Was she never again to be held by someone young and virile? She wondered how much this boy would have to be paid to sleep with her, but scolded herself severely. That was a corrupt thought and she couldn't allow it. In her work she relentlessly purified corruption with intensity and precision. The cow skull in one of her most famous pieces held meat in its eye sockets when she found it but she remembered well boiling it in a bucket on the stove until the rotting gristle gave way to white bone. When it was clean, she placed a ceramic flower in the eye and mounted it on an altar of sandstone, an image endlessly reproduced in posters on dorm room walls around the globe. But she had little interest in what appealed to the young in her sculptures, although she enjoyed the money generated. She'd felt a sense of triumph in making the original piece, as if she could redeem the corruption of the world one work of art at a time.

Now as she climbed, she felt heat between her legs, a final gift from the mountain that had inspired her so much both in life and in work. Obsidian was giving her a late rush of eros. She didn't dare turn around to look at Michael. She could hear him panting in the thin air and couldn't help but think he would sound the same in bed, pushing himself into her body. She looked up to distract herself from the urgency of this thought and barely saw, through the thick fog of her sight, the Gaudi-like extravagance of the summit ridge.

The pain of not being able to make art was in her breath, in her heart, in her mind. She hurt all day, every day, that she could not simply begin again each morning, as she had throughout most of her life. She could, of course, dabble around as she had for the past several years but the electric charge between her eyes and her hands and the materials was missing. Her present state of working was not good, not sufficient for who she was. She could still put words together, of course, but mostly in the service of her art, to instruct the ignorant about what she had most definitely not been doing.

Of course, no one spoke plainly anymore, although she did, causing great consternation. She told people what she thought and what her reasons were for acting but no one believed her. They thought it was too unlikely for anyone simply to be who she was, and just do what she said she'd do but that's how she'd always been, from childhood to the present.

She'd been strong enough that she could both be herself and still love great men and women, Harold and the others along the way but even so she was far from self-sufficient. Her devotion to her art caused her to long for a corresponding spirit, another artist, to temper her and give her balance, someone equally strong who was fully engaged in his, or her, own process. Harold's huge sculptures, for example, were vastly different from her own work yet she loved and respected both his energy and its products, at least until age, infidelity, and alcohol cut him down. Susannah, a poet who lived with her in the fifties, fashioned short yet multi-faceted poems that reminded Erica of crystals. Susannah was with Erica for ten years until she ran off with a younger female poet, a danger, Erica learned the hard way, about having companions from other generations.

However, the greatest influence of all upon her was not a person but this mountain she was now climbing. When she first saw Obsidian, she knew it was her very own mountain, placed in the world for her to work with and worship. She knew the peak was thought to be the home of the Tewa gods and sacred to several local tribes but it spoke to her in a voice beyond religion and beyond culture. She knew the mountain had been calling her for months, and now was speaking to her as she moved upon its surface. She could hear its voice in the vast stillness it generated. She wanted to be buried deep inside it, or at least have her ashes spread upon the summit if those fatheads from the Forest Service prevented an actual burial.

She was full of desire right now, desire to create, to make love, to become one with this mountain. She wanted it all but knew she was on the wheel of suffering and could not have it. Instead, she was climbing a steep slope in a wrinkled aching body dressed in black. This was not how she imagined the end would be. She somehow thought she'd be beautiful forever, not in the fashion magazine sense (a beauty she never possessed) but in the sense of being able to light up another human with desire. Even through the dimness, she saw how Michael looked at her, with the pity and reserve appropriate for someone old and feeble. Her beauty now was like that of the cow skull, stripped to its essence, the empty eye sockets a mocking analogy. She always knew when Michael didn't point things out because of her eyesight. She'd soon have to tell him to cut it the hell out.

From her forty years in the desert, she was well aware of what was happening around her, even if she couldn't see it clearly. The movements of the weather and of celestial objects were etched into her mind and didn't need the confirmation of physical sight. This land was inside her, as close as her breath. She'd thought for awhile, when young and entranced by the spells of literary artists, that if her skill with materials ever failed, she could simply put what her mind held into words. But words now seemed increasingly disconnected from their intended objects. They obdurately remained in a realm of abstraction separate from pure sensory input. The word "tree," even with a thousand modifiers, could not convey the sheer experience of standing in front of an aspen on a misty October morning up in the high valleys above the mesas. The word "mountain" was merely a bland and empty frame for the immensity she was climbing. How much easier it had been to bypass words and allow her hands to give form in three dimensions to the impact of the natural world upon her mind.

Unfortunately, the world outside was turning into fog even as the world inside was ever more vivid. For instance, she remembered well the peak towering above them. Her mind held it in meticulous detail although she could not actually see anything in particular. She could feel how the stone leaned down upon them, how the clouds were passing across the edge of the summit, how the molecules of golden air flowed around their bodies. The way up was as obvious to her as if she could actually see it. The abiding presence within reality was now contained inside the dimensions of her skull, where it had always been, she thought. The distraction of sight had given way to an illuminated blindness, a state she'd dreaded for years but now, in certain sacred but unpredictable moments, surprised her with the spontaneous appearance within her mind of the universe in all its detail. When she realized how powerful this summoning process was, she almost felt repaid for the loss of her art. For years, she'd reorganized the elements of the world into specific works but now the process was purely internal. What she needed was a device to project her mental visions out into reality. With such a mechanism, the world would be able to see that the physical objects she made and placed in museums were far surpassed by the wonders she currently entertained within.

But these invitations to ecstasy were rare. In this moment, she was grateful for having something physical to do: climb a mountain, a straightforward task. This was a mountain she'd summited at least a dozen times, that she'd looked at on countless occasions, a place as familiar as her own hands. Her body, so prone to mysterious ailments these days, felt ready for anything. Maybe she wasn't growing older, maybe some miracle had brought her body back to its fifty-year-old, maybe even her forty-year-old, self. She knew this illusion would be shattered by one good look at those brown-spotted hands swinging at her sides but, peering up through the bright misty light of her vision, she suddenly felt ageless. This body could still easily carry the awareness riding behind her eyes. In the sense of liberation generated by this climb, she realized the obvious: that she'd been depressed for years, stumbling about the house, stuck in her routine, not talking much to anyone, but now she felt a blessed release.

27

YELLOW

She turned to Michael and saw him as a dark wraith in a field of vibrant yellow.

"You see why I wanted to climb today?" she asked him.

"Absolutely," he said, with school-boy enthusiasm. "This is beautiful. Beyond words."

"That's right."

They climbed the last steep section of loose scree before the colonnade and sat down for a rest, using the bottom of the cliff to support their backs. Michael took a long drink from his canteen, his Adam's apple bobbing as he gulped. Erica noticed its motion as she took a short drink and basked in the well-being coursing through her. Perched on the rock, feeling the light swirling around her, she remembered the walks she and Harold used to take in France, long springtime rambles through acres of flowers with the tan blunt bluffs hanging over them. She remembered the feeling of being absorbed in love, of having someone beside her who was totally acceptable and who totally accepted her.

This was in the days before the affairs and the letters and the lies, culminating in her unannounced visit to his studio in Paris where she found the woman she called "the young one," all moved in and modeling for him between fucks. She thought of that as the only day she ever came close to losing her mind. She could easily have killed him; killing the girl would have been incidental. Erica destroyed as much as she could in his studio, smashing some of his most precious pieces with a sledge hammer until he hit her across the back with a piece of rebar and knocked her out. She could still feel where the blow had landed on her spine, always the first part of her to ache when the barometer dropped or when she exercised hard as she was doing today.

She was compelled to destroy his art because he'd destroyed her central illusion: that their relationship shared in the same creative force driving their work. She knew it was difficult, in most cases, for artists to be together but she thought she and Harold had escaped the curse by working in different areas, by respecting each other, by being absorbed in their passion that had not seemed to wane despite the length of their time together. She couldn't believe he'd been lying about any part of it but he must have been. He chose to have his affair with a woman who was red-haired, full-breasted, placid, uncreative, and agreeable, none of which could even remotely be said of Erica.

The wench eventually left him, perhaps discouraged by Erica's sudden and unpredictable appearances in the studio, shrieking like a harpy. Of course, he came crawling back to Erica, begging her to forgive him, but she never did and it was never the same. She ended up being caretaker during his transformation into a senile old man who was pissing and shitting in his pants, a form of revenge on both their parts, perhaps, but not a very satisfying one.

Now why was she thinking of this when she felt so good? To make herself feel bad again? Maybe, but she wasn't feeling bad. Perhaps she was putting her worst state of mind up against the present feeling to see if they could be reconciled. She was always able to summon up the indignities of her past with great clarity but in this moment the rage and depression associated with these memories seemed to have fallen away. Something deeper than the turmoil of emotions was carrying her to the summit. What was it?

28

SUMMIT

As Erica contemplated the mountain in her mind, Michael looked up at the cliff face, surveying for a route. The only possibility was a narrow, almost vertical chimney. He was glad their packs weren't heavy.

Erica stood and said, "Let's go."

She began to climb the chimney with deliberate speed, carefully placing hands and feet before shifting her weight in smooth lunges. Michael had a sudden fear she'd fall and break her bones. He stood below her for a moment to cushion such a fall but she soon rose out of his sight so he had to follow. He attempted to trace her path but kept finding he'd make wrong choices in the placement of his hands or feet and then would have to retreat a bit and start over. Erica seemed to have dissolved into the stark blue spilling over the summit's edge.

Michael found himself several times in places where he had to pull himself up using just his arms and could barely scramble to the next ledge. Fortunately, this rock was harder than the sandstone at the ranch where the handholds tended to crumble when he hung his weight on them. Two questions came to mind: how was Erica managing to do this and how could they possibly get themselves down? His legs trembled from exertion and fear but he was spurred on by the fact that a woman in her seventies was ahead of him. He was dimly aware of the amazing view at his back but his fear of the drop made him unable to turn and enjoy it. Finally, he climbed over a smooth boulder and the sky seemed to fling itself with abandon out to the horizon in every direction. He was on the summit.

Erica sat on the opposite side of the ridge, her figure dark against the bright emptiness. With his heart pounding and sweat rolling down his shirt, he stumbled over to join her. A single white cloud hung just above them under the dome of sky encompassing the world.

They sat together on the rocks and looked out to the expanse of the valley below. Although Erica saw only an undifferentiated haze of illumination, she felt on her skin the complex web of air currents rising from the vast area in front of them. The sun had just lifted itself above the defining edge of terrain and now its light struck their faces full on. Michael could see immediately why the Tewas held this to be the home of their gods: because the vision impressed him as divine, encompassing an infinity of land and a multitude of lives in a single sweep of the visual field. He began to speak out loud, simply naming what he saw, partly for Erica's benefit, partly to engage what was before him.

"There's the river, going into the lake behind the dam."

"Goddamn Army Corps of Engineers," was her reply.

From where they sat, the cliffs at the ranch were amazingly small, sitting at the worn and nibbled edge of a gigantic mesa complex, tinged in green, rising gradually to low mountains. Below them was a jumble of country with flat tables and headlands and slopes, slanted and jagged in every angle, trees covering much of it except for some clearings that seemed odd to Michael.

"I wonder what those circles are below us, the bare spots?"

"The old pueblos are down there," replied Erica.

"Wow. No kidding? Could we walk right into them, if we found the way?"

"Of course we could. I'll show you sometime. I've hiked all those trails and seen the secret places."

"That would be great. It's odd. I can see where the river flows but Chamisa itself is blocked off by the mesa tops."

"That's right. The village is wedged up against the wall below us. Its height made it more defensible against raiders than anywhere on the open plains."

"Over to the east, there's a broad valley with blue mountains rising above it."

"You can't see Taos but it's tucked in against those mountains, called Sangre de Cristo, the blood of Christ. And the rest of the Jemez mountains block out Santa Fe."

"This is the most amazing view I've ever seen."

"I never grew tired of it."

Her use of the past tense struck him. He thought hard about what to say. He didn't want to make her feel bad but she'd brought it up, at least indirectly, so maybe she wanted to talk about it. He didn't think it could hurt to reply.

"I'm sorry."

Her silence lasted so long he regretted having spoken. Finally, she said, "For most of my years, I lived through my eyes, and through my response to what I saw, so losing my vision is like being drained of blood. Nevertheless, something is left."

She paused. A column of cool air rose over the edge of the precipice and momentarily soothed their faces from the sun's heat.

"What's that?"

"When I made art, at times I'd feel that something or someone was looking out through my eyes. Even though I can't see much now, that presence remains, below my thoughts, at the center of it all, somehow containing it all, and that's enough for me."

An elongated cloud, shaped vaguely like a fish, so thin it was almost transparent, flew slowly past. Its shadow undulated across the landscape, moving up and down ravines and arroyos, topping sheer cliffs with miraculous buoyancy. As Michael watched it, he realized how incredibly fortunate he was. In the last few months, he'd lost much of the pointless ambition he'd carried since adolescence about being an artist. What he cared about now (mostly, anyway) was this seeing, this pure act of perception, and how it could be rendered.

His eyes moved across the shapes, colors, textures, dimensionality, reflections, shadows, and lines of what lay before him. He knew this was where he belonged, not just on top of Obsidian, although the peak did feel like home to him, but in this moment, seeing in a way he'd always imagined an artist would see.

However, his previous imaginings had always been from the outside, struggling to look in, while now he was inside looking out.

He reached in his pack, removed his pad, and began to sketch, swiftly letting his hand follow what he saw: a mosaic of lovely patterns. In the lower realm, he always struggled with the horizon and its relentless demarcation of reality. Here on top of Obsidian, he was far above that division, comprehending from the perspective of the sky the unfolding patterns of the world below while his eye and hand worked as one to transfigure reality into marks on paper. He glanced over at Erica who was clutching her folded arms close to her chest, even though the sun was blazing hot. As he sketched, he spoke:

"I just want to tell you…"

Swiftly, she interrupted him.

"Keep going. Stay with it."

So he did.

29

AFTERNOON

They lingered on the summit through the hottest part of the day. From her backpack, Erica pulled a square of white linen that she unfolded to the size of a bedspread. She used the rope she'd brought to artfully arrange a shelter between two piñon bushes so they could sit in its shade and look out on the world being created below. Michael's splurge of drawing energy lasted for hours, until he filled the sketchpad. He even went back and used the reverse sides for miscellaneous details he wanted to remember. With his drawing arm and his eyes aching, he put the pad aside to find Erica arranging their lunch. They sat and ate the sandwiches she'd packed that morning, along with cheese, tinned oysters, apples, and Belgian chocolate, washed down with sweet lemonade she'd made from scratch the night before and poured from a metal canister.

After they ate, they leaned back in the shade, so close that Michael could smell the English soap she used every morning. Erica told him more of the history of the region that lay below their feet, the many wars and traumas and injustices of the valley, along with stories of the idiosyncratic men and women who lived and died in this vast basin. Michael couldn't keep it all straight in his head, the dozy feeling of a hot noon overcoming him but he did take in that this had been the greatly disputed intersection of many cultures, where Native Americans battled each other for centuries about who would hunt and live on its plains and among its cliffs, where the Spanish struggled to maintain outposts for their culture and religion, where mountain men emerged from the high country covered in beaver pelts, as eager to rut and get drunk as they were to trade, where water was as precious as gold and just as fought over, where vast changes had come about in the course of the last generation far exceeding the impact of the many centuries of bloodshed.

The afternoon clouds gathered in the west above the mesas and slowly built into a solid mass, even as the sky above and around Obsidian was clear. Despite the charred branches of the trees around them on the summit, Michael wasn't worried. He couldn't imagine the day would end in death by lightning but even if it did, this would be the best way to go, at the height of awareness, on top of the mountain.

30

STORM

Incrementally, over the hours they spent on top, clouds moved in from the west, sending a cooler wind in advance of their looming front. Mists rose in dark spirals around them. The sun was eventually blocked off by battlements of cumulus taking on Wagnerian proportions. Strangely, the far-off cliffs around the Ranch were still visible and shining brighter than ever, in stark contrast to the deep blue-gray of the clouds gathering thickly around them. Soon they found themselves sitting on a small hill in the center of a plain of seething vapor, their feet dangling in the mist. From below came an abysmal rumbling and the clouds became even more active, taking on deep ultramarines and ebonies as they roiled and stormed in spinning ribbons.

Erica stood and gathered up the white tablecloth before the wind could sail it away. Thunder shook the mountain as if ancient volcanic activity had been revived. Erica suddenly pointed and Michael looked down to see a bolt of lightning far below them, and then another, coiled within a small space from their perspective because the lightning was flashing down. At first, a few seconds gap remained between the booms and the flashes. Then the explosions and bursts of light happened simultaneously as the circumference around them grew white with incandescence. The crackle of electricity filled the air and Michael felt the hairs on his arms, chest, and head start to rise. He grabbed for Erica and they ended up holding each other's hands in a double clasp. A high-pitched tone rose to the threshold of pain as the rocks they sat on shuddered with a series of earth-splitting detonations.

A hissing sound made them turn to see a rolling globe of ball lightning, about three feet high, slowly moving down the trail that extended along the ridge top. The globe, looking like a dandelion head of sparks, followed the undulations of the path and then dropped out of sight off the end of the peak. They looked at each other for a moment, their eyes taking in the awareness living in the other's gaze, and they laughed. The tremendous commotion all around them drowned out the sound but that made them laugh even harder. Rain began but it wasn't raining down, it was raining up, sharply, so they were struck by stinging droplets in unexpected places: under their chins and up into their nostrils.

Their bodies were buffeted by gusts attempting to shove them off the peak. To keep from being blown away, they had to hold onto each other tightly, his arms around her shoulders, her chin against his sternum. The sun came out in front of them, shining through the rising rain, creating an upside down rainbow shimmering just beyond the edge of the cliff and vibrating into arced fragments of color. They lifted each other up and danced in place to the rhythm of the pandemonium.

31

RANCH

The wet rocks made their descent slow and treacherous. They didn't reach the truck until stars were appearing in a deep blue turning almost black. They barely talked on the return trip but they both felt, for the moment, content.

As the summer went on, they fell into an easy rhythm without questioning their connection. Early each morning, Michael went out to paint for several hours before retreating to the casa when the heat became too intense. In the afternoons, he played secretary to Erica's correspondence and business. In the evenings, he would read to her, usually Dickens or Austen and, when his voice faltered, she would talk about whatever came into her head, mostly stories from her life and opinions about the decline of the world.

As the end of August approached, he kept thinking of Sheila, who would soon leave the Ranch and head back East to school. He knew it would be better for him if he just let that happen but in the night, while staring at the ceiling, the impulse to go over to the Ranch and see her kept rising up.

He was certain that each person on the college and permanent staffs had heard all about his breakup with Sheila and his new job with Erica. Previously, he hadn't wanted to face all the gossip but now he didn't care. He hadn't done anything to be ashamed of. So Sheila had betrayed him with someone else? So he'd taken off and gone to work for Erica? So what? Because Erica was famous in the world, and notorious to the locals, people were bound to talk but he couldn't think of any consequences that could really hurt him. Maybe he should reach out to his friend Chuck and try to mend some fences. Staying at Erica's house, although good for his artistic ambitions, was way too isolated. He began having fond memories of his brief time on college staff and the camaraderie around the bunkhouse. So one night, he told Erica he was going for a drive and didn't wait for her to answer before he left.

As he drove away from Erica's house in the pickup, his vision was confined to what had become usual, the gravel road directly in front of him with its fringe of desert on either side. Suddenly, as he turned the corner away from the highway, the ranch was all spread out for him again: the curve of mesas, the irregular shape of sky, the sense of entering an amphitheater at once commanding yet intimate. He had the paradoxical sense of coming home to a place utterly strange yet completely familiar. Growing up on the East Coast had in no way prepared him for this terrain yet he already knew the topography of the ranch better than he knew the dense sprawl of New York City.

He didn't eat much for breakfast so now he was actually looking forward to the sometimes questionable contents of the dining hall's steam tables. The truck bounced up and down in a general ascent until he could see the intense green of the alfalfa field outlined by darker trees in silhouette against the ruddy mesa walls. As usual, he was amazed by the lushness of the field given that most of the water came from the two foot wide stream trickling down from the box canyon at the head of the Ranch. A single ancient tractor sat in the middle of the field, presiding over a line of wheeled sprinkler pipes. He couldn't make out any people and yet he knew they were all there, hundreds of them, hungry after a long day of going to seminars or loafing or, for a minority of them, actually working. Near the trailers before the corner of the field, a pink towel hung stiffly from the branches of a piñon tree.

He bumped over the cattle guard and went the long way around the field which was the approved approach to the dining hall. The road turned by a pair of trailers and the adobe home of Tex and Luisa, the couple who ran the maintenance and housekeeping departments. He followed a blind curve until he could see the beige wall of the staff house and the packed earth court where fierce volley ball games were waged in the evenings after dinner.

Two of the college staffers, Eric and Becky, who'd become an instant couple at the start of the summer, were batting a volley ball lazily back and forth across the torn net. Sparky, the horny chihuahua who belonged, in the loosest sense, to Tex and Luisa, sat and watched the game from a safe vantage point behind the net pole nearest to the road. Beyond the players, House Mesa caught the full impact of the afternoon sun, sandstone ablaze with those same brilliant orange highlights he noticed on the cliffs by Erica's house.

Michael remembered that he and Chuck had planned to climb the mesa face some night after supper. They had scoped out an approach up a talus slope that ended unusually high along the cliff, reaching close to a broken area below the summit where one could at least conceive of a route to the top. This was one of the many hikes he and Chuck had talked about doing, hikes far more difficult than the usual ones listed in the ranch guidebook. They had also thought of going way back into the canyon behind the old homestead to the south, or of ranging in the empty high country beyond Obsidian, or of hiking across the bridge by the Monastery to explore that side of the river. Unfortunately, Michael's sudden departure precluded such expeditions, for Michael, anyway.

He drove the truck by the front of the staff house where groups of two or three college staffers sat on folding chairs on the porch or lounged on blankets in the yard. Some of them were drinking from cans of Coors, the summer beverage of choice, despite the right-wing politics of the brewery owners. Others were reading or whittling or just perfecting the art of hanging out and talking. He looked for Sheila (he couldn't help it) but didn't see her. Instead, he saw Barry and Clarise Tondreau walk out of the end suite reserved for the college staff leaders. He didn't want to answer their questions about what he'd been doing. They had the surface friendliness of clergy involved with youth, a demeanor he'd encountered several times since he'd arrived at the ranch. Not knowing what was underneath those forced smiles made him more than a little wary.

He pushed down on the gas pedal of the truck, hoping irrationally to flee from observation but the sudden acceleration caused the back wheels to spin in the gravel. This display caused several heads to turn but he didn't want to linger to examine their reactions. Instead, he quickly passed by the male side of the staff house and drove around toward the back of the dining hall.

He was now experiencing the all too familiar anxiety trio: his pulse quickened, sweat ran down his chest, and his breathing was rapid and shallow. The mesa in front of him was actually shimmering from the internal agitation of his eyeballs. He feared this visit would inevitably lead to a series of embarrassing encounters he wasn't sure he could face. He thought momentarily of just turning around and heading back to Erica's house. However, he was hungry and the potential in the dining hall for some social interactions more complex than Erica's frequent and sullen silences held enough attraction to keep him going.

He passed by several college staffers, including the girl from Wisconsin whose name he never could remember, the one who looked like Olive Oyl and kept fainting from dehydration during her first weeks at the ranch. Nevertheless, she continued to insist on jogging every day in the afternoon heat, often ending up unconscious on the road, covered with dust. Picking her up and carrying her to the nurse's station had become just another chore for the male staff members. Michael had the sense she enjoyed the attention.

A few dozen feet past her was the edge of the arroyo passing behind both the staff house and the dining hall, defining the eastern and southern limits of the lived-in portion of the ranch. Green trees rose along its sides, drawing their life and color from the rare flash floods that roared down when storms dumped rain high up on the table land. The seething brown flow would race through the deep-cut channel, bearing the bodies of animals, including cows, horses, and coyotes, amid an interesting variety of debris, including tree limbs, fence rails, entire tents, clusters of brush, baby dolls, and even hardback books. No one could explain how these human artifacts floated down from a high country virtually barren of habitation. Sometimes floods would be generated by storms up north even when the skies above the ranch itself had been clear blue all day.

Now Michael could see thick gray smoke rising from the kiln at the bottom of the arroyo which meant that Will, the resident potter, was firing the pots from this week's workshops, probably the last of the summer. Michael pulled the truck in behind the kitchen and sat for a moment. He could see clouds of steam from the old Hobart dishwasher emerging from the windows of the dish room.

In his first weeks at the ranch, he'd been assigned to work in that humid environment, sharing heat but not dryness with the surrounding desert. That was how he'd first come to know Sheila, who'd been working pulling the clean racks of dishes out of the steel machine. He remembered his initial stunning sight of her in a damp t-shirt, wearing no bra, an erotic image pulling him inexorably into a huge mess.

To clear his mind, Michael forced himself to remember something else, such as the night a college staffer named Johnny, fueled by more than a few beers, had volunteered to be sent on a dish rack through the Hobart. After the hot water was turned down, Johnny made the journey and emerged much cleaner, unscathed except for a minor contusion from hitting his head on the gate when he came out.

Michael also remembered how Chuck would pull out the racks of dishes and yell, "Reject!" in mock rage at each plate, cup, and piece of silverware with the least bit of food on it. To retaliate, Michael would send him progressively more encrusted items. The mock feud would escalate until they'd use the flexible water sprayers to drench each other to the skin.

32

DINING

Through the screen door in the back, Michael could see the silhouettes of people moving back and forth in the main dining room. He was just on the verge of entry but couldn't quite push himself over. He heard the crunch of boots on gravel and before he could turn to see who was there, he felt a hand on his forearm as it rested on the truck door. Tex Terrell was squeezing the muscle so hard that a stab of pain leaped up to his shoulder.

"Hey there, stranger," he said. "How's it hanging?"

Bowdie, Tex's sullen assistant, sidled around so their two huge faces were hanging in his window. Their breaths smelled sour from cigarettes, boiled coffee, and recent slugs of whiskey. Michael pulled back a bit before replying.

"Hey, Tex, Bowdie, I'm doing pretty good. They have any supper left?"

"That's just where we're headed. Why don't you join us, unless you and Erica have other plans?"

Michael looked at their grinning faces. Now it's begun, he thought.

"I'm just the hired help."

"That's not what we hear," said Tex. "But why don't you come on in? Lots of people been wanting to talk to you."

Michael had an urge to slam the truck into reverse and drive away but he didn't want these two baboons to think he was intimidated by them, even though he was. He basically liked Tex and his blunt cowboy humor but he could be very cruel when he was in a teasing mood. Bowdie was a not very bright cowboy who'd wandered in several years before from a neighboring ranch to watch the girls in their bathing suits at the pool. For reasons unfathomable to Michael, Tex had kept him on.

Michael pulled the keys from the ignition and hoisted himself out of the truck. Tex and Bowdie stood flanking the door of the dining hall to usher him in. Reluctantly, as if going to see the principal, Michael walked forward and through the door. Inside, he immediately heard the sharp percussions of the dish room, sounds that had been only a distant background noise from the outside. The steamy air enveloped him as he walked down the hall to where the food line began.

Tex and Bowdie followed him, chuckling to each other. Michael figured they were laughing at him but he didn't care. All he wanted was to get his food and sit down. He made an impulsive turn and walked the wrong way into the serving room, going against the traffic which, fortunately, was sparse. As he knew, most of the ranch patrons showed up exactly on time, if not early, for meals. Those who came through late usually didn't have to wait at all but took the risk that several of the more popular menu items might be gone.

Michael picked up a tray from the pile and moved to the end of the line where just a few people waited in front of him. Tex and Bowdie also grabbed trays and stood close behind him. Michael felt obliged to make some form of conversation although the other two men seemed to be content just gazing at the back of his head. He turned around and addressed Tex:

"So, are they keeping you busy?"

"As always. We're finishing that new construction up on the mesa. Had to hire some extra help when you left. Good man from Chamisa named Hermanos."

"Well, I'm glad you found somebody."

Bowdie cleared his throat in order to talk:

"So did you know Erica Hanlon before you went out there?"

"No, never even saw her before."

The serving line cleared and Michael stepped forward to avoid this line of questioning. Behind the counter was Theresa, a pleasant plump woman from the village who greeted Michael with a big smile.

"Well, hello, stranger! We thought you were so happy eating caviar and steak every night you didn't need to come and see us."

"I've missed your chile rellenos. Is that what we're having tonight?"

She made a face.

"No, unfortunately. We have chicken and rice." She shrugged her shoulders to indicate it was not her choice. Michael peered into the steel vat in front of her. The white rice had taken on the gray of the chicken grease but it was steaming and looked good to him.

"Pile it high for me."

She gave him a large helping with some broccoli and he walked quickly to the end of the line, grabbing a small bowl of formerly canned peaches on the way. Without waiting for Tex and Bowdie, he stepped into the dining hall.

The evening light sent a mellow radiance through the wall of windows. The sizable space was lined with painted cinder block, giving it the bare look of a school cafeteria, a look enhanced by a series of weavings on Christian themes that Michael had always made a point of not looking at too closely for fear their churchy earnestness would spiral him down into depression. The room was only about a third full but still carried a buzz left behind by the many conversations of the last few hours.

Usually the ranch crews and college staff ate at the tables to the left so Michael headed that way, trying to appear casual, scanning the room for anyone he knew, hoping Sheila might still be there, yet dreading the encounter. This is insane, he thought. Why am I here? He saw a cluster of college staffers by the back exit but they were a very Christian group from the Midwest and he didn't anticipate a great welcome from them. Several of the tables were empty and he thought he might just go and sit at one.

Then he saw her.

33

GOLDEN

At the corner table beside the huge fireplace, Sheila was leaning back in her chair, her face turned so the curve of her cheek glowed in the sunset light. Since their last miserable encounter in San Juan, she'd cut her hair short so it fell just under her chin. She was smiling at a young man Michael didn't recognize but her expression didn't arouse any jealousy because he realized what that particular smile meant. She was being agreeable but didn't really buy whatever it was that the guy was saying. Michael himself had received that look quite often. Her friend Stacy sat sprawled beside her, blocking his view of most of Sheila's body except for her arms which were bare and golden, even from several tables away. He turned to the right, away from her, toward the bank of windows glowing with dense light and heard someone call out to him.

"Hey, Michael. How are you?"

He looked over to see Will and Val Sprawlins sitting together, their shoulders not quite touching. They were the second most important couple in the hierarchy of the Ranch, just behind Jed and Susan Mills. Will and Val were drinking coffee with some of the older staff people: Harriet, the librarian, and Ted, the volunteer gardener. Ted was famous that summer for finding a deer, a common predator in his precious flower beds, and fixing it in the beam of his flashlight. He walked right up close and whacked it on the nose: "Take that, you dang deer!" he shouted, words that became a catchphrase for the college staff.

Michael nodded hello to everyone and sat down. Will and Val both smiled at him from across the table. He'd always liked them. They seemed an unusual couple (although what did he know?) because Will was a stoic but friendly cowboy while Val was more emotional and mercurial. Michael appreciated that they each had tried to make him feel welcome.

"So who knew the prodigal would return on a Wednesday night at supper time?" Val said this with such a warm expression that Michael couldn't take offense at being called a prodigal.

"How have you been?" he asked.

"Same old, same old," Val replied. "We're getting ready for the high country trail ride in a few weeks. You wouldn't care to come and join us, would you?"

"Um, well. I'd have to see." Beside him, Ted was staring blankly out the window while Harriet gazed adoringly at Ted's craggy yet chinless profile. He'd never before noticed that she was in love with Ted. Funny to think the whole process causing him so much pain did not decrease with time's advance. He hoped to God he wouldn't be suffering from unrequited love when he reached her age. He looked over at Will.

"How's the water supply holding up?" Will could rattle on about this topic for hours and Michael felt the need for some filler.

From the corner of his eye, he watched as Sheila sat with her chin on her fist, listening to her table mates. He both hoped and dreaded she would notice him and come over. That would mean dealing with her in front of everyone at the table and he was embarrassed enough as it was.

Will began describing the intricacies of the irrigation ponds and the small changes he'd made in the pipes. As Michael half-listened, he amused himself by watching a glaze of boredom develop over Val's eyes. He'd never understood how they actually got along, given how different they were. The fact they had two kids together didn't make it any easier to figure out. Their children, Dusty and Sue Ellen, ages twelve and ten respectively, were miniatures of Will, both complete ranch hands, skilled at riding horses and already able to drive stick shift. Not only were they able to drive; they did drive. Will allowed them to take his truck anywhere on the ranch or over to the river but not out on the highway. He said it wasn't worth the risk, admittedly remote in this area, of being stopped by the State Patrol. He warned them an arrest might delay their driver's licenses, a prospect generating the desired reaction of filling them with horror.

They went to school in Chamisa and, despite being Anglos, were accepted by the highly particular local families. The school bus coming down from the north drove all the way up into the ranch for them, even though it wasn't supposed to, mostly because Will, with his constant availability for calm and insightful advice and material assistance, was the most respected man in the basin. His boss, Jed

Mills, was a very close second.

Unlike her husband and kids, who embodied the concept of laid-back, Val was wired up tight, sometimes throwing a fit over events insignificant to all others but extremely real for her. After getting to know her, Michael found she had an acute understanding of people and their behaviors, even though she was usually blind to the meaning of her own emotional storms. Michael was attracted to her but she scared him plus Will had been his mentor out working on the ranch lands, a combination sufficient to deter him from even thinking of acting on his errant thoughts.

As he was musing on these things, Michael noted that Tex and Bowdie were walking toward the table, obviously intent on sitting down. He wondered what had taken them so long (maybe another drink?) but he could tell from their faces they intended mischief. As Bowdie passed near, he bumped Michael's chair in a way that was obviously not accidental, causing a spill of milk across Michael's hand to the table. Tex gave him a leering grin. Will was talking of how little rain they'd had and how the irrigation pond was getting very low.

"Yeah, ain't it terrible when things get all dried up?" Tex interjected, taking a big bite of his chicken with rice. Rice grains clung to the corners of his mouth.

"That's right," Bowdie added. "Sometimes you have to use oil to work yourself in."

"Sometimes a little spit helps, too. Ain't that right, Michael?"

Will looked genuinely puzzled. "Why would you put oil or spit in the pond?"

"Never mind, Will," Val said. "Boys are just being crude. Tex, Bowdie, this isn't the junior high lunch room and ladies are present so, if you can't be nice, go right on over to another table and eat by yourselves."

Bowdie put his head down and shoveled in some food. "Yes, Ma'am."

Tex grinned. "Well now, Val. You may be the one with the dirty mind. I was just talking about the drought."

Val sighed, wadded up her paper napkin, and threw it on the plate. "I grew up in a family with four brothers so I know more than a little about the workings of the male mind. I can see you and Bowdie aim to tease Michael about working for Erica Hanlon. But I don't believe there's anything to tease him about. He might as well work for the one person around here who means anything to the outside world. Just because he isn't out there digging holes and laying cement with you saddle tramps doesn't mean he isn't doing legitimate work. Isn't that true, Michael?"

Michael felt acutely embarrassed. Sometimes assistance could be more difficult to deal with than mockery.

"Yes, ma'am," he replied, echoing Bowdie. "I'm working there and that's a fact."

"I know that's right. You're working at her house and doing handyman chores and helping with her paperwork and learning something about painting. See, we don't have any secrets around here for about a fifty mile radius. I don't see a thing to be ashamed of there."

"No, ma'am. I'm not ashamed."

Tex and Bowdie were paying close attention to the meals in front of them. Harriet, however, had detached her interest from Ted and was staring at Michael with astonishment.

"Did you say you're working for Erica Hanlon?" Harriet, even though she was two chairs away from him, leaned over and grabbed Michael by the arm.

"Now, Harriet, don't go swooning. Harriet is a big fan of Erica's, Michael. She has every available art book about her in the Ranch library. Spent a large part of the last ten years' budget on them, too. She met Miss Hanlon once at a party at Jed Mills' house and was snubbed cold for her trouble. Isn't that right, Harriet?"

"Oh, I didn't mind," said Harriet, her eyes shining. "She didn't know me from dirt. A great artist like that can't be involved in minor social interactions."

Michael said, "Actually, she has a talent for being rude. She's rude to a broad range of people."

Val nodded. "That's a fact. I've seen her look right through people like they're not there. And don't even talk to the residents of Chamisa about her. With that big house on the hill, she's the only Anglo resident of the town so there's bound to be some resentment there even aside from her high and mighty attitude."

Unable to contain herself, Harriet broke in: "But her art work is so lovely! My trailer is filled with the best posters and prints I can find. I first saw her sculptures back in New York when she had her show after the war and I couldn't believe that a woman made such powerful works. The art world back then was dominated by men so a woman with such an intense connection to nature who was able to express it so forcefully simply amazed me. Young man, what is your name?"

Michael had been shoveling in the chicken and found himself with a mouthful at this point. He gestured to her for patience and swallowed hard. "I'm Michael Spielman."

"Michael, I know this is presuming a lot but do you think that one day I could come and visit you out at the house? It would mean so much to me."

"Um, I don't know. Erica, I mean Miss Hanlon, leads a pretty quiet life and she doesn't much care for strangers. I'd hate to have you come out there just for her to bite your head off."

"My goodness, Harriet," Val interjected. "Leave the poor boy alone. He probably has his hands full out there as it is."

Bowdie grinned. "Does she ever try to bite your head off, Michael?"

Tex chimed in: "I'll bet she keeps your hands full."

Val stood up and piled her dishes. "That does it. You men are free to be just as filthy as you want once Harriet and I are gone. You coming, Harriet?"

"Oh, no. I don't mind. I mean, I'd rather stay."

Val leaned over confidingly to Harriet. "I don't think you'll learn too much with Tex and Bowdie around. Better to invite the young man over to the library on some pretext or another." Harriet nodded her head at what she took to be sage advice.

Michael bristled at this. "Val, I'm sitting right here. Don't talk about me like I'm not present."

Val straightened her spine and took a deep breath.

"Well, maybe that's the problem, Michael. We'd just started to get to know you when you disappeared. We thought you either ran away or died somewhere. Later we hear you're working for Erica Hanlon and now you just show up on a Wednesday night at the end of summer for supper. Maybe we don't know if you're really present or not."

Tex snickered down at his end of the table. Bowdie nudged him and covered his own mouth to laugh. Michael looked up at Val who was beautiful in the moment. Even though he felt embarrassed and ashamed, he also felt aroused by her intensity. He experienced a pang of guilt for screwing up somehow and breaking the social code of the ranch.

"Sorry, Val."

"You don't have to be sorry. That's not what I'm saying. All I'm asking is that you don't disappear. We like you and don't want to lose touch again."

"Okay. I hear you."

"That's what people say when they want to be agreeable but don't really want to agree. Anyway, I'll see you back at the house, Will."

"Yes, Val."

Val took her tray and marched off across the dining hall with determined strides. Michael found that Tex, Bowdie, and Harriet were all staring at him intently. Ted, oblivious, was looking out the window and humming tunelessly. Will concentrated on finishing his coffee. Michael didn't want to put up with any more teasing or (in the case of Harriet) more prying questions about Erica. Will came to his rescue.

"I'm heading out. You want to join me?"

"That would be great. Hold on."

Michael swallowed a last mouthful of chicken and rice and stood up to follow Will who was already ambling across the dining room with his tray. Michael didn't even bother to say goodbye to the four people left at the table. He looked off in their general direction and then nodded his head. Harriet called after him, "Remember to stop in at the library!"

The dining room was sparsely populated with just a few die-hard conversationalists left sitting at the tables. Michael looked over to where Sheila had been sitting and saw she was gone. He'd been so anxious about the table conversation he hadn't even noticed her leaving or whether she'd seen him.

He glanced out the window toward the staff house and saw Chuck moving through the yard. At some point, he had to go over and talk to him. He couldn't show up at the dining hall and not talk to Chuck. Maybe their friendship could be repaired. The sun was falling faster now and the shadows of elongated figures rippled across the walls as the last diners walked toward the dish room.

In the foyer, Michael quickly put his dishes in the tubs on the counter without bending over to see who was working the line. He very much wanted to be outside under the sky for awhile without encountering any more problematic people. Although, weren't they all problematic? As he half-ran out of the building to catch up with Will, he felt a sudden draft of cool evening air drifting in from the darkening arroyo.

34

STAFF

As the evening deepened, bats flew from their crevices in the mesas and fluttered through the now chilly air, looking for insects. The reds and oranges of sunset had given way to a deep blue with patches of violet. The staff house music became louder and Dave Mason's voice drifted out across the field and echoed from the cliffs. Michael knew the seminar participants preparing for bed were listening, with varying reactions, to the college staffers at play.

Will watched the action for a moment and pointed at his red jeep.

"Want to move the sprinklers with me?"

Michael had performed this nightly chore when he worked at the ranch and had felt honored to be allowed to do it because moving the line of sprinklers up the field was not a simple task. But now he didn't feel like providing the ranch with any free labor.

"No, I think I'll go over and say hi to people."

"That's fine. Enjoy."

Will swung himself into the jeep and gave Michael a tip of his cowboy hat. Michael waved in return as Will took off with a burst of engine noise.

Michael reached the road and stepped onto the gravel. The almost solid shadows gave the mesas and cottonwood trees and low adobe houses a mystery absent in the day's blast of sunlight. Michael found himself being lured on by the music from the staff house reminding him of the night Dave Mason's *Only You Know And I Know* played while he and Sheila made love on a blanket at the edge of the arroyo.

The volleyball game was now over. The players had ambled back to the staff lounge or were sitting out in the Group W area. The sky was poised at that deepest shade of blue just on the edge of becoming black. Michael felt his stomach tighten as he approached. Through a gap in the full crown of the tree in the staff house yard, he saw a glowing star appear, more likely a planet, given how bright it was. The lights were low in the lounge and, as he passed, red flickers from the fireplace played across the high windows set in the cinderblock wall. He stepped off the road and onto the scraggly grass futilely aspiring to the status of lawn. On the women's side, a screen door banged but no one was visible.

He heard voices and, as he rounded the corner past the lounge, saw a group of about fifteen people sprawled across the yard. Chuck was sitting on the bench, his feet up on a green plastic milk carton, balancing his open pocket knife by the tip of its blade on his finger. When he caught sight of Michael, he flipped the knife up in the air, caught it by the handle, closed it shut with one hand, and stuck it in his pocket. A girl sitting behind him, maybe it was Wendy from California, said something that broke his gaze away from Michael.

Past the far end of the bench, several people were reclining on blankets, holding cans of Coors or joints cupped in their hands. On the last blanket to the left, lying on her back, looking up at the sky, was Sheila. She wore a white t-shirt with an even whiter bleach stain on its side, a pair of khaki shorts, and black sandals on her feet. Michael was painfully reminded of a time when he would remove those sandals in order to kiss her instep. She was talking to one of the college staffers who worked for the housekeeping department, a gangly kid from Ohio named Bryan. Michael looked intently at her as he approached but she didn't seem to see him. Michael walked up to Chuck.

"Hi." Michael felt a dozen pairs of eyeballs move toward him.

Chuck turned from Wendy and gave Michael a cautious smile.

"Heard you were around tonight."

"Yeah. Thought it was time to stop by."

"I have a six pack of Coors in the fridge. Help yourself."

"Thanks, I think I will."

Michael was glad for this chance to postpone the initial conversation and gain time to deal with his turbulent emotions. He walked toward the combined kitchen and laundry room at the side of the lounge. He heard, or thought he heard, an urgent flush of whispering behind him. Fuck them, he decided, and felt better. So what if they talked about him? Who better to talk about? He went into the room where the washer always seemed to be going. In fact, as he entered, several loads of laundry were lined up waiting.

Michael opened the refrigerator. Chuck's six pack was adorned with its usual sign: "You touch, you die." Michael unfastened a can from the plastic rings and waited for a moment. No death ray. No lightning bolt. He popped the top and took a long swallow.

Beer in hand, he walked outside where the sky had been alchemized into an ebony from which more stars were emerging every second. Wally, one of the contingent of summer staff from Minnesota, was playing *Sweet Baby James* on his guitar. Michael sat down on the earth next to Chuck who was talking with Wendy about Mendel and his fruit fly experiments. Apparently they'd each tried to replicate them for their high school science projects, with poor results. They were both pre-med so connected with each other at least on that level of biology. Michael tried not to look down to the other end of the group.

He could hear Sheila's flat Midwestern accent but couldn't make out what she was saying through the intervening conversations. Across the alfalfa field, the lights were on in the library where evening seminars were held. The silhouettes of the people inside passed against the windows. The Ranch's offerings were a mixture, in his opinion, of boring Church topics and genuinely interesting seminars on spiritual, artistic, and social themes. He wondered idly what they were talking about tonight. Above the library, the crowns of the cottonwood trees were illuminated from within by exterior lights, making the foliage stand out against the massive shadows of the mesas. He took a sip from his beer. Chuck turned to him, leaning forward so they could talk.

"So, how are you?" he asked.

"Not bad at all," Michael replied.

"Do you like working for Hanlon?"

"It's a job. Plus I have a lot of time to paint."

"What? Her house?"

"No, I mean paintings. Remember those drawings I used to do? Well, that's what I studied back in college."

"Funny, we never talked about art."

"I was taking a break. But now I'm into it again. And she critiques my work."

"Yeah?" Michael said this skeptically. "You know, people talk about what goes on out there."

"I'll bet they do. All I can do is tell you what I'm doing and what I just said? That's it."

"Okay, okay." Chuck was reacting as if Michael had been vehement although Michael thought he'd been rather matter-of-fact.

"So what about you and Wendy? You seem to be pretty friendly."

Chuck looked over his shoulder to see if she was listening.

"No," he said quietly. "We've talked about it but she has a boyfriend back home so we're just hanging out."

"Oh, okay. Cool. But maybe that could change."

"Nah, it's too late. We're all going home soon. Wouldn't want to start something now."

"Guess you'll be heading back to school."

"Aren't you?"

"No, I'm done with school for awhile. Actually I'm learning more here than I ever did in art school. This is the best education I've ever had."

"What do you mean?"

Michael thought for a moment about really telling him what he was doing, about his daily routine, the visual discoveries he was making but he didn't want to come across as pretentious. He settled for severe understatement.

"She teaches me stuff."

"I'll bet." This sounded sarcastic to Michael.

"Listen, I'm trying to tell you how it is. If you don't believe me, that's just too fucking bad."

He'd raised his voice so of course everyone else stopped talking to check out what was going on. He looked down the line of interested faces. He noticed that Sheila was now sitting up straight and staring at him. Her expression was not encouraging.

Chuck took a deep breath.

"Hey, man. No reason to get all huffy. You're the one who went away without telling anyone. Then you show up and expect to take up where you left off. Listen to yourself, man."

Michael looked down at the packed earth between his feet. The prints from countless sneakers and boots were overlaid in an intricate pattern.

"You're right. I should have called or something. I was trying to get myself together. That's my only excuse so it will have to do."

Chuck nodded and couldn't help but glance over at Sheila.

"I can understand that."

Michael's face burned under the multiple gazes. He didn't know what they were thinking but imagined they were judging him.

He stood up.

"I'm gonna hang out in the lounge for awhile. Miss all that music."

He walked back to the staff house, his spine stiff against the silence behind him. He turned the corner into the lounge. Inside, the only light came from the fireplace that sent shadows shifting across the concrete walls. Pads and cushions were on the floor in front of the fire, spread out like rays so that each person could face the burning logs. The usual lounge gang had gathered, comprised for the most part of the couples who'd formed that summer.

Michael and Sheila had been devoted members of the fire-staring society until their break-up. He greeted a few of the people but didn't feel close enough to any of them to start up a conversation. He sat on the bench that lined the inside walls of the room, placing himself directly opposite from the fire. He stretched his legs out in between two sets of intertwined couples and stared into the flames. He wondered what Erica was doing. He thought of calling her from the phone in the ping-pong room but didn't know what he would say. Someone had put on the *Tapestry* album and he let the music roll through him.

His fantasy of Carole King was that she sounded like the perfect woman. He couldn't reconcile the picture on the album cover with the voice; they seemed very different. The singer was someone inside him, the woman he wanted, the woman he'd wanted Sheila to be: passionate, surprising, loyal, tender. Sheila had been all of that for him in his imagination but he'd obviously been way overextended in his feelings. Why was he always so intense, so attached? He envied the guys he'd known who claimed to seduce women without caring whether the women became involved, much less worrying about their own feelings.

So what was he doing sitting here in the dark surrounded by romantic couples? He should just leave. He couldn't see hanging around anymore tonight hoping to talk to someone. How could he possibly connect with any of the women here, given what a pathetic picture of himself he'd painted for them? He'd freaked out because Sheila was fucking around and then he'd disappeared, for Christ's sake, only to turn up months later like a ghost looking for a warm body to inhabit.

Should he hang out in Chamisa and try to talk to the local Hispanic girls? That was likely to end up with him wrapped in barbed wire and hanging from a tree, especially after the scene he'd caused at the bar. It was hopeless. Better to settle right now for the perfection of art and not of life. His mission had to be to keep painting and, unfortunately, that meant getting along with Erica. If such was the case, he'd better stand up and start moving. Maybe he'd leave from the opposite door and walk behind the staff house to the kitchen so he wouldn't have to encounter any of the gang outside.

He felt the warmth of the fire on his legs and hesitated about leaving. However, the lovers snuggling below were starting to piss him off. Didn't they know they were just a whim away from suffering? He stared into the flames, watching the fluid interchange of colors at the core. After letting himself be hypnotized for awhile, he shifted his weight in preparation to go. He realized he wanted to talk to Sheila one more time although he wasn't at all clear about why that was a good idea.

35

SHE

He stepped quickly out of the room, thinking he'd ask her to walk with him so the darkness would hide him from himself. Several of the more religious girls, determinedly uninterested in the activities inside the lounge or around the group W bench, were sitting on the logs that lined the walkway, engaged in some form of spiritual discourse. They looked up as he emerged and he felt their eyes on his heathen form as he passed by.

He walked around the building and out toward the group by the roadway. House Mesa loomed over him. Stars kept filling the spaces between the stars, and then more stars emerged between them. The music had changed to Nina Simone, another album he associated with their brief courtship.

A pick-up truck idled on the gravel. Sheila was leaning against its door, her head in the window. All he could see of the driver was a mass of long hair. He could hear a baritone voice.

Michael took a deep breath and looked directly up. The stars hadn't formed themselves into any constellations he recognized. All was darkness around him. He heard a cowbell ringing in the distance. What the hell was that about?

From the shadows, he watched as Sheila opened the door, climbed in, and laughed along with the driver. She slammed the door shut and the truck quickly did a three point reverse before speeding down the road past him. The dust propelling out behind it went into his face and made him sneeze.

He crossed the road and walked diagonally across the top corner of the alfalfa field to avoid the staff house. He felt an enormous grief. She'd seen him, obviously, but hadn't wanted to meet with him and had gone off with someone else. His previous relationships had all ended badly so he wasn't exactly surprised this one had detonated as well. He was disgusted with himself that he kept allowing himself to feel shitty about her.

Looking back, he could see the shapes of the kids sitting in front of the staff house, backlit by the dim lights on the porch. He knew from experience that he was too far away for them to make him out. Someone was playing the guitar, a Joan Baez tune: *Silver Dagger*. Ahead of him, the dining hall was dark. The nightly raid on the kitchen was usually conducted later, close to midnight, by the dining hall staffers with access to the refrigerator keys. In the corner of his vision, a shooting star propelled itself past its static cousins. All he wanted now was to get in the truck and head back home. Funny he was thinking of Erica's house as home. He expected she'd be pissed off at him.

He walked toward the swimming pool, planning to go through the passageway separating it from the dining hall. He could smell the acrid edge of the chlorine, incongruous in the desert. A gentle splashing sound echoed from the pool. He looked over the fence and saw two people swimming in the ink-dark water, side by side, their wakes shimmering with reflected starlight. They reached the shallow end and climbed out, a young man and a young woman, slim, nude, casually beautiful. They held up their arms to each other and embraced.

Michael felt the fire of regret. He wanted to be in the place they were in and this living tableau only made the ache of his loss more acute. He walked quickly to the truck, pulled opened the door, and slammed it as he sat down. He started the engine and revved it, wanting to intrude on their magic. He moved out quickly, sending gravel skittering back across the concrete apron where the lovers stood and wondered who that was driving away in the dark.

36

RARE

Although Erica had waited for hours for his return (whether to shoot him or scold him or hug him, she wasn't sure), by the time he did return, she was telling herself she'd lost interest in the entire dynamic. One of the advantages of advanced age (she told herself) was that she'd had many experiences of loss and had learned she invariably did survive such times.

After he'd left, she'd recovered from her anger at being abandoned by walking briskly around the courtyard many times. After tiring herself, she went back into the house and put on her favorite music, the plaintive sounds of Bach's cello suites. She wandered through the rooms, picking up items that provoked memories, attempting to remove herself from the limited context of the present day and its multiplying irritations. If she so desired, she could call up people on the phone who would gladly drive out from Santa Fe to give her adulation.

Or, thinking more long-term, she could accept one of the many invitations arriving daily for her to speak at universities or appear at exhibitions or do any of the things people asked her to do because they responded to her work. However, praise counted for almost nothing in her thinking. In fact, crowds of admirers, with their various ambitions and curiosities and jealousies, tended to give her a thunderous headache.

She'd always prided herself on not caring about the affections of the general public. En masse, they were just a mob to her, of people approaching uninvited and saying the most inane things, of journalists eager for a story and being absurdly ingratiating or impossibly rude in the process of trying to convince her to talk, of obsessives attempting to climb into the garden in the south of France, only to be repelled by the fierce bulldog named Mango she and Harold had kept there.

Here in New Mexico, in the past several years, she had occasionally walked out of her house in the morning to find some dirty long-haired child who'd hitchhiked from God knows where to talk to the great artist. She'd always called Jed Mills to make them go away but she felt worried about this trend. The invasion of her life by the young and the lost offended what she realized were her aristocratic prejudices.

Although she was herself the child of farmers, and not very successful farmers at that, she had the sense of having been elected by the gods to the inner circle of those who lived and worked primarily in service of their art. She kept thinking that if these young people were serious about their vocations, they certainly wouldn't be bothering her, or anyone else, with their naïve questions. They'd be off painting or writing or dancing or whatever it was they wanted to do.

Most of these children were simply tongue-tied in her presence and weren't able to articulate exactly what had brought them from Somerville, Massachusetts or Burley, Idaho or Gainesville, Florida to meet an artist. A few were much more loquacious and talked fervently in the brief time she allowed from her first encounter with them in the yard to when she retreated to the house and slammed the door. Often they'd babble on about how much her sculptures meant to them, especially the flowers, the huge damn flowers she almost regretted sculpting now for all the misinterpretations people put upon them.

Didn't people realize her goal was not so much erotic as spiritual, that she was following Blake's axiom of finding the world in a grain of sand, infinity in a flower? She had nothing against vaginas, possessed one herself and, in fact, had in the course of her many affairs with lovers of all sexes come into rather close contact with them. What bothered her was that with all their speculation about sex, people weren't seeing the details of the flowers, the universe contained within each one.

The lost souls who showed up at her house were confused in many ways. They seemed to think her life was freer than that of the rest of the world, that she had somehow joined in their quest to overthrow existing institutions and mores. Although she was sympathetic, she felt these goals to be quixotic, inasmuch as the world of commerce and ruthless growth seemed to her implacable. All one could do was go one's own way.

The great virtue she saw of American society was that no one cared much about art. She didn't have to pass her work by a board of review, or defend it to government commissioners. All she had to do was find a way to make enough money to survive while she did what she wanted to do.

The threat of poverty had been an issue in her early days as an art student in New York but ever since her life with Harold, financial support had not been a problem. She had enough in her accounts and investments that she would never again have to worry about finances, even though the modesty of her early upbringing made her worry in a vague fashion anyway. She was one of those rare artists who had been able to make a living in this culture but she knew she would have kept on making art no matter what her financial circumstances.

A shadow crossed her mind sometimes, as she wondered how she would have been able to follow her vision of desert spaces and nature in the open if she'd had to labor long hours for sustenance, but she always assumed the vision within her would have found its way, no matter what the obstacles. If she thought about it at all, she simply assumed this was the same for everyone, that if they had talent, they would find a means for expressing their gifts.

Despite Michael's definite affinity with the shaggy-haired interlopers, she'd allowed him into her life because she saw a spark in him that might be kindled into a flame, no matter how wavering, of creativity. She wouldn't say his work was improving but at least he was drifting in the right direction. His eye was becoming clearer;

his patience was expanding. However, he continued to be willful and spoiled and fearful, as maddening as the damn flower children, with whom he shared many traits. He didn't have the gumption to strike out on his own and yet he was full of obstinacy about her and about his role in her household. She was sometimes tempted just to call up Jed and have Michael's ass thrown out of her house. But she knew she wouldn't do that yet.

Ever since his arrival and especially after their embrace in the storm at the top of Obsidian, she'd felt herself to be inflamed with desire. She'd felt exactly this way whenever love loomed in her life and she had never backed down. She'd always followed her erotic impulses all the way through even when decades of intensely ambiguous feelings ensued, as they had with Harold.

37

COLT

She heard the truck coming down the road. In the course of all the times she'd spent waiting for Michael, she'd memorized the deep thrumming of her own vehicle's engine. He was still far away, just dipping down into the arroyo and coming up the other side with a more insistent sound. Where should she wait? As angry as she was, she nevertheless felt like retreating to her bedroom and postponing the confrontation until morning. She wished her vision was better so she could look deep into his eyes to detect whatever follies he'd been involved in. As it was, she'd just have to rely on sheer force of personality in dealing with him, not an inconsiderable support.

She walked into the living room and sat in the armchair facing the hallway where he would come in. Let him think she'd been waiting for him all day. She felt her blood pumping hard in her narrow chest. All the frustration she'd felt over the past decade about her diminishing powers and her fading vision now seemed to have a direct channel for expression. She felt as if she were confronting her youthful artistic self and demanding of this self why she was being abandoned when her need was greatest.

The truck was at the front of her house, the wheels crunching the gravel in the road. As the truck turned into her driveway, the sound was almost overwhelming, filling the room with the agitation of the V-8 engine, setting the adobe walls to vibrating, releasing particles of dry mud to float in the air. (Although she couldn't actually see these particles, she did think she could smell the dusty earth). After parking, Michael gave the engine a final surge of acceleration while in neutral, an annoying habit she'd asked him to stop but he seemed to enjoy, asserting his connection with all that force as a way of announcing himself.

She sat in the posture she knew he found annoying, upright with her hands in her lap, staring off-center to the hallway so she wasn't looking directly at him. Although this might seem like a meditative pose, she felt anything but calm inside. She heard the truck door slam, unnecessarily loudly, she thought. His boots scuffed through the dirt in the driveway. He paused on the front steps as he looked for his keys. He had this infuriating habit of putting the keys in one of his pockets as he stepped out of the truck and not being able to find them immediately when he needed to unlock the door.

Nevertheless, after a moment, the key entered the lock with a sliding metallic sound. The tumblers clicked as it turned. Hinges screeched. He'd never oiled those hinges as she'd asked him to but she actually liked the sound because she always knew, even when she was sound asleep, when he was going out or coming in. The door swung open, bringing with it the cool air of the desert wafting the always familiar, always surprising scents of sage and piñon and desert flowers. Michael stepped into the hallway and in her peripheral vision she could just barely see his shape as a dark foreground against the light cast by the lamp in her office. He stood there and she could sense his apprehension and annoyance. He jingled her keys in his hand for some seconds and then took a step toward her.

"Hi, Erica," he said in a tone meant to sound casual but was somewhat forced.

"Michael Spielman," she said, using his full name to indicate her estimation of the seriousness of the situation.

They appraised each other warily.

"How was your evening?" She thought she'd attempt a conversation on a neutral level.

"Interesting."

"How so?"

He took a deep breath and another step forward, as if about to launch into some discussion. But he must have thought better of it because he turned away and walked back to the hallway toward his room.

"Think I'd better get some sleep."

She clutched her hands in rage as he left the room. She couldn't remember ever being this furious, even with Harold at his worst. Well, maybe then. She walked to her bedroom, feeling like her skull was in a vice, constricted to its maximum point, rage pouring from her eyes, nose, and ears. She reached up to the shelf in the closet and pulled down the box containing the Colt. She flipped open the chamber and made sure it was loaded. Six brass circles stared up at her. She flipped it closed, a familiar motion from years of using it for target practice and to scare off coyotes when she was camping up in the high country. She flipped off the safety and strode quickly out to the wing where Michael had his room. She stood outside the door, pointing the pistol at the doorknob as if it was about to jump at her.

She realized she didn't know what to say. What did she want him to do at gunpoint? Leave? Stay? Take his clothes off? She didn't want to burst in without knowing her goal.

She must have made some kind of sound because, from inside the room, Michael's voice rang out.

"Erica? What are you doing out there?"

She lowered the Colt and shook her head.

"I don't know."

A pause before he replied: "Go to bed."

Anger urged her inside but she relented, turned, and walked back down to her room.

38

CLASH

Early one morning in October, Michael woke from a dream of childhood: his mother was sitting hunched over at the breakfast table in the apartment he grew up in. Her face was in her hands. The gray curtains of the kitchen window billowed in and scratched across her shoulder. Tears leaked from between her fingers and pooled on the table. The angle of the light made him think her day was ending, as it had in the late afternoon when she died of cancer in the Sloan-Kettering Hospital.

Waking found him staring up from his bed, feeling the emptiness of isolation and abandonment, somehow intensified by the bare splintered beams of the ceiling. However, when he turned his head, light was precisely framing the rectangle of the door with a border of radiant gold.

He sat up and felt better as he once again remembered where he was: in New Mexico, on a ranch, with Erica. No mother or lover was in his life now but he had enough to get by. He dressed quickly and opened the door to let the light fill his room. Feeling a bit hung over, he walked down the porch to the bath. He'd had three German beers the night before where usually he just had one or two. They weren't celebrating anything, just sitting in the living room while he read Hemingway's *In Our Time* out loud and she sat in her chair, her head tilted to listen. When his throat grew tired, they played classical records on the stereo.

He was now frequently bored in the evenings; he and Erica had run out of conversation about her opinions. His experience didn't add much so they were mostly quiet, beyond a few remarks about the day's events. He usually sat sipping beer and reading until his eyelids began to fall. He'd stumble to bed, hoping to avoid any dreams about Sheila or his mom but they would both insinuate themselves into the nightly flow of images.

After his morning ablutions, he walked into the dining room where Erica, as usual, sat straight up in her chair, carefully lifting the food to her mouth. He took his place beside her where his bagel and jam were already waiting, along with a banana and an orange. A pot of coffee steamed next to the plate. He shook the napkin out and put it on his lap, noting the napkin was much cleaner than the jeans he'd been wearing all week. He looked over at Erica who was staring in his direction although, as usual, he wasn't sure she was actually seeing very much of him.

"Good morning," he said.

"You slept in today," was her reply.

He looked at his watch. The time was eight twenty three.

"A little, maybe."

"I eat breakfast at eight."

"Okay. That sounds like a fine time to eat."

He carefully spread butter and strawberry jam on his bagel. He knew where this conversation was going but he didn't want to make it easy for her.

She gave him her haughty look, of the imperious queen displeased. He took a bite of his banana and had a sudden impulse to open his mouth and show her the mash to see whether she'd react but he suppressed it.

"I would appreciate it," she said, "if you would make an effort to sit down with me at eight a.m. precisely."

Michael swallowed the banana and wiped his face with the napkin, being careful to swab his mustache which was hanging down over his upper lip.

"Look, Erica," he said, "We've been through this. Lunch and dinner aren't a problem but I don't like having to wake up at an exact time. If it bothers you to wait, then go ahead and eat."

"I am the head of this household and my wishes should have some importance."

"Breakfast just doesn't mean that much to me. I like to have a cup of coffee, a little toast, a piece of fruit, and that's enough. Besides, we hardly ever talk to each other in the morning. It's not exactly a social occasion. Yet you sit here and stare and get all upset if I'm a few minutes late. What's the point?"

"The point is that I am your employer. If you wish to keep this job, you should take pains to ensure I am satisfied with your work."

Michael took a deep breath to hold back a surge of anger. A few months ago, he would have bowed his head and apologized but he was ever more willing to say what he thought.

"Let me put it this way, Erica. Meals are not my work. I'm not going to make any effort to be on time for breakfast. You don't have to make it or wait for me. If that's a problem for you, you can fire me right now."

He stared defiantly at her. She looked toward him but slightly to his left. Her eyes were open wider than usual. Her chin trembled. He turned to his orange and removed the peel with fierce movements. He really didn't care what she did.

Erica stood up, holding onto the chair for support. She was suddenly looking much older, or maybe she was looking as old as she actually was.

"Excuse me," was all she said and left the room, hurrying to the doorway and holding on to the jamb for support.

Michael assumed this was all for his benefit but that was fine with him. If she wanted to play the victim, he wouldn't deprive her of the pleasure. He finished breakfast leisurely, taking his time with the coffee and looking out the window at Obsidian. He felt self-justified and angry. Maybe she was his employer but he was doing a good job, carefully maintaining the home and cars, cleaning up her correspondence and her accounts and doing her damn errands. What did she expect from him? She acted more like his mom than his boss. Well, that was going to change. He gathered up the dishes on a tray and carried them out to the kitchen.

In the past few days, he'd been painting across the highway on what the Ranch called Deer Flats, working on the details of rock and earth and bones. Just the day before, he'd come across a great swollen corpse of a cow, its brown and white hide broken with gashes oozing pink liquid. He'd been repelled yet fascinated. His goal was to work through his discomfort and just see the decaying object for what it was: a composition of volumes, shapes, and colors. Right now, this particular advice seemed good for how to deal with Erica herself. He wanted to move past the emotions she provoked in him and see her for the lonely old woman she was.

He noisily gathered his painting gear and packed a lunch, giving her an opportunity to join him if she wanted. No sounds came from the direction of her room as he made himself a pair of salami sandwiches with cheese and tomato. He packed up his paints and canvases and carried them out to the truck. The curtains of her room seemed to be trembling but he didn't look too closely. He didn't want her to think he cared whether she was watching. When he went back into the kitchen and filled his water bottles, the silence in the house had taken on an odd quality, a tension as if someone had just stopped screaming. The planked floor creaked with his heavy steps. He walked outside, threw his supplies into the bed of the truck, and climbed in. He started the engine, letting it run for a minute longer than usual.

The thought occurred to him, "Why the fuck am I trying to get her to come after me?" He threw the truck into first, purposely grinding the gears. Without warning, Erica stepped directly in front of him so he had to slam on the brakes in order to avoid hitting her. She must have come out the side door to intercept him. Lightly touching the truck with her fingertips, she made her way around its side, opened the door, and climbed in. He looked at her but she just stared straight ahead. He said, "Fuck!" under his breath and pulled out to the road.

39

IMPULSE

Erica sat with the back of her head pressed hard against the rear cab window as Michael turned the truck onto the highway and headed north. She folded her hands in her lap and allowed herself to feel the full impact of her rage. Anger burned through her, creating a throbbing vein in her forehead, a tightness in her chest, an acidic churning in her stomach. Despite her reputation for having an eruptive temper, she had only once in her life ever been physically violent, in that incident in Paris with Harold, but she now very much felt like indulging in the madness again.

As her blindness became more profound, as her dependence on this little bastard next to her increased, as she was forced to live through him and his first baby steps in painting, she felt the same storm of emotional ties she had felt with Harold, without the alleviating factors of respect for his artistic power or the ability to resolve tensions by making love.

She knew quite well the absurdity of her situation: infatuated with a twenty-two year old at her age. She remembered back when she first went to art school in New York and had fallen in love with a young drawing instructor named Benjamin. She didn't remember much of what he looked like, other than that he was tall and energetic, but she remembered clearly how she felt when he would stand close to her and move his hands in the air in front of her drawings to emphasize points and admire what he saw. She was still a virgin at that time and the present feeling was somehow analogous to what she had gone through sixty years before: both then and now love-making appeared to be impossible even though she desperately wanted it to happen.

She was angry that her body was so ancient she couldn't easily act on her impulse to make love with Michael. Maybe she could have forced it to happen when she was still in her fifties or even sixties but despite the fact that her desire had changed very little, she was withered, God damn it. There was no better word for it. What had once been a slim and attractive body was now a husk. Never mind that her nude form was displayed in museums across the world in the form of Harold's heroic sculptures. No one could make love to a statue, although she'd been familiar with the phenomenon of young men coming on to her based on the impact those sculptures had upon their libidos.

Surges of wild emotion ran through her. She didn't dare look over at him as he drove the truck with his jaw set and knuckles tight because she knew anything she said would provoke him. She'd felt compelled to join him even though she was well aware he didn't want her. She'd become addicted to his process: preparing the canvases, loading supplies into the truck, driving on rough roads or no roads at all to special places in the desert she recommended. She pretended she was the great one, the one in charge, but he was the one with the creative burn, venturing out every day to engage in the dynamic struggle between paint and nature.

She wanted her dependence on him to end. She wanted to put a stop to her desire for the infusion of his life into hers. Of course the attraction was erotic but it was more as well. She knew her life was coming to an end, the ebbing of her sight just a harbinger of the final blindness and she had sometimes thought in the last few years of defying death by bringing it on herself. She'd always preferred to do things her own way and if that meant killing herself, she didn't mind the prospect. She'd definitely had a full life, and she couldn't regret any of it, even the pain of breaking up with Harold yet having to nurse him until his death. However, now she wasn't sure what the point of it all had been.

She'd never thought much about a personal God, or about his supposed offspring, despite a childhood surrounded by Christian zealots, but she did believe in something or someone expressing itself in everything (she supposed), although she was only familiar with its workings through nature and art. She'd never been stupid enough to attempt to pontificate about this during interviews. Her only reply to questions about religion or spirituality was to say she knew something she could not talk about. She'd sit there, sphinx-like, as the reporter or art critic tried to make something out of her cryptic remark.

She had taken her cue on this from Vladimir Nabokov whom she'd met briefly at a luncheon given by his publisher in New York in the fifties. He chatted to her, in his idiosyncratic English with a

Russian accent, about his learned enthusiasm for lepidoptery. On her place mat, he drew several illustrations of the "Blues," the small butterflies that were his special interest. (She still had the mat in a trunk somewhere).

Later, when no one else at the table was paying attention, he leaned close and whispered forcefully that she was one of the magicians and therefore, of course, knew where the magic came from. When she looked confused, he said she had to be aware that all of this world was a rabbit being pulled continuously out of a hat, although the magician kept himself hidden behind the curtain of appearances. The presence of this prestidigitator could be inferred through nature but also through the magic rendered by creative people in poetry, novels, science, paintings, and sculptures. He said he'd recently seen a small show of her work at a gallery in mid-town and he knew that she knew. Nabokov put his finger to his lips to urge silence and winked at her.

She didn't know what to say at the time but she often thought of this extraordinary and, from what she could find out about Nabokov, uncharacteristic encounter. His wife, Vera, had not been present (touch of the flu) and she often wondered if he'd merely been flirting with her although it had felt like something more. She had been an apprentice magician, she supposed, but now her wand was broken and she was left to wonder about the primary magician, the one who performed the continuous feat, on a moment to moment basis, of pulling the furry trembling world out of the top hat of nothingness. What did he or she have in mind for her? Was there some point to the arc of her life? She sometimes felt Michael had descended from the mesa, like a bruised and dusty angel, to be the meaning of her third and final act, but that was not at all apparent today.

She was well aware that Michael was restless in the evenings. While he drank his beer, she usually sat in the old armchair she'd had shipped from the South of France, allowing it to carry her off to the past. The chair had been Harold's throne through many long nights as he sipped his cognac and held forth in his loud blunt way to the equally drunken artist and journalist friends who'd materialized at the iron gate of the house for supper, alcohol, and maybe a place to sleep.

The chair still retained the odors of his cigars, of his spilled liquor, and of his piss and shit from the times late in his life when he'd fallen asleep there and soiled himself, leaving her to clean him up in the morning. Although the smells had enraged her at the time as the evidence that she was bound to a raging, dying alcoholic, she now found the faint but still pungent aromas to be comforting in their familiarity.

Although he'd been dead for more than twenty years and she seldom missed him, he had been a part of her life, both together and separately, for the thirty years before that. His absence was now like that of a long-missing limb: every so often, the phantom appendage would ache. While she was still able to do art, she'd been able to lose herself in an eternal moment of dynamic action, and had thereby avoided the pain. Now she had no distraction from any of it. She took a deep breath and tried to clear her mind despite the alarming speed at which Michael was driving the truck. One breath and another; that's all there was, until the last one.

40

PONDEROSA

Michael drove up Rte. 96 in a defiant mood. He didn't want to go to any of Erica's favorite sites for painting she'd so solicitously pointed out for him over their time together. He remembered hearing from Tex Terrell about the beauty of the high forest around Ortega Mountain so he thought he'd drive up there and see what it was like. He wasn't about to ask Erica what she thought of this plan. He was doing about eighty as he started the long climb to the plateau above the Ranch. The truck roared with protest against the grade but he kept it floored, not caring if he burned out the engine. He wanted Erica to say something so he could explode at her. Except for clutching her dress at the knees with her hands, she gave no indication that anything was amiss.

The truck crested the first steep rise then continued upwards onto the huge shelf that followed the Continental Divide to the Loveland Pass, ten thousand feet high in the Rockies above Denver. The land leveled off from the broken region of sheer rock faces around the Ranch and began to spread out into grazing land. They reached the turn-off for the National Forest road that led up into the Ortega region.

After they left the highway, the truck immediately began to bounce along the graveled, rutted road. They drove for miles, steadily gaining altitude, moving through languorous curves in a narrow valley bordered by occasional green glades set among the Ponderosa pine. At about eight thousand feet, Michael began to see the white trunks and gold leaves of aspen trees.

He didn't have any particular goal in mind. He was happy just to let his eyes move across the landscape as he drove, waiting for an intuition about where he wanted to paint. The truck bounced, turned, rose, fell, and twisted as his mind went into neutral, sparking out occasional angry thoughts aimed at Erica who sat as far away from him on the seat as she could get. Each jounce from a rut in the road set the dust in the cab to floating in slow motion, the motes glittering in the light. Here he was in a box of metal and glass, gliding through a landscape of stark beauty: raw rock face, yellow grass, pine needles, piercing blue sky.

The sheer oddity of being alive right now overwhelmed him. What was it that kept this moment, his particular section of reality, intact as he lived it? Why didn't everything just fall apart and separate out into isolated atoms and chaotic energy? He didn't know. The weirdness of it all set him shivering. He woke to this moment and found himself in the mountains of Northern New Mexico, two thousand miles away from where he was born, in the constructed surfaces of New York City. Now he was wandering on a dirt road, looking for just the right place to put some paint on canvas. A world-famous artist, almost blind, sat rigidly, within arm's length, pissed off at him. Everything was very strange.

Could it possibly be that this reality in which he found himself was all there was? No spirit realm? No divine intelligence guiding the entire operation? He'd flirted with despair many times throughout his adolescence, especially after his mother's agonizing death but he couldn't completely reconcile himself to it. Maybe this was all there was but he frequently wondered whether the world of appearances could possibly contain, or be, something profound, something infinite? And what practical difference would that make?

41

BEAVER

The road leveled out and Michael looked to his left into what seemed to be an unusually open area for the terrain. Through the trees, he saw a pond spread out in front of a broken stone formation. On the close shore were stands of intertwined pine trees. He stopped the truck and looked more closely. At the far end of the pond, in the midst of a cluster of reeds, was something he recognized but had never actually seen: a stack of twigs, branches, and logs, all held together by a complex architecture of mud. Erica took a deep sniff of the air and pronounced decisively, "Beaver."

Michael pulled the truck to the side of the road and shut it off. Still ignoring Erica, he stepped out and looked around, walking a few steps away from the vehicle. He found himself enchanted by the space, an intricate lush corner of the vast plateau. This was as good a place as any to paint for the day. Erica was briskly getting out of the truck so he figured she must be in agreement.

The passage of an hour found him completely absorbed in his work. He'd set up his easel about ten yards from the pond at an angle where he could see both the facade of the surrounding cliffs and the surface of the water. On the other side of the pond, out of his direct line of vision, Erica had spread out the blanket from the truck. She sat cross-legged upon it, her hands on her knees, her eyes closed, apparently deep in meditation. He felt comfortable ignoring her in order to concentrate on the problem at hand. He'd been painting for so long in the area around Erica's house that he felt competent to handle the part of the composition including the mesa rock. What challenged him was something he'd found very easy to do back east: the water.

As he'd told Erica, he'd spent his summers painting portraits of boats and houses for their owners out on Long Island. He'd found a simple formula of blue with white highlights for the waves and an off-white, close to ivory, for the froth of surf. Now he had to contend with a deceptively still pond surface reflecting the colors of earth and sky, with a dark undertone likely generated by the organic matter beneath the water.

He was trying to look carefully at what was there and found it damn hard to render in a way that satisfied him. The only body of water he'd tackled recently was the distant view of the Chamisa lake from the flatlands across the highway. Now he found himself struggling to show the pond in a way that made it actually look like water and not just like a muddy composite of the colors in and around it.

He first made a series of drawings in his sketch pad to gain a sense of the relationships among the shapes. On a canvas, he began to lay down the paint in fast thin strokes. He kept working it over, playing with the composition and color until it was a brown muddy mess. In disgust, he discarded that attempt by throwing it into the bed of the truck and started another. This time, he decided to follow the strategy he'd been using with his paintings back at the ranch: keep it simple. He used long lines and large areas of wash, not attempting to do a precise landscape but just responding to what he was seeing in the most basic way. He definitely missed the subtle textures of the water in the course of doing this one, but at least it wasn't over-elaborated. He stopped while it was still unfinished and then started another.

He eventually noticed that the sun was burning the skin in the part of his hair so he moved the easel over into the shade of the pines. He didn't want the paint to dry so fast that he'd lose the ability to manipulate its edges and depth. With great satisfaction, he noticed how absorbed he was in the process: stray thoughts and feelings weren't distracting him as they usually did. Instead he was simply taking in what was before him, putting paint on canvas, looking at the results, and thinking about how to proceed, wanting to find a way that was clear and direct.

As the sun slowly passed overhead, he grew sleepy in the direct glare of light that made it harder to see. A great tiredness moved through him, slowing his arm as he tried to lift the now heavy brush, laden with paint, to the canvas. He realized a siesta was unavoidable. He looked over to where Erica had been and saw she was no longer sitting on the blanket. He looked around the area and saw her standing in a copse of pines beyond the pond, her head tilted as if listening to some music in the trees not apparent to him.

He packed the paints in their case and covered them. He went over and removed the blanket from where Erica had spread it out. In an area among the trees with fallen pine needles and soft shade, he used both hands to flick the blanket into the air and let it float slowly onto the ground. He lay down, using his sweatshirt for a pillow, and wriggled in the ground to create a contoured bed. He looked up through latticed branches pierced by shards of pure blue sky. Winged insects buzzed by to investigate but then left, uninterested. An ant crawled across his hand.

He thought vaguely of Erica. He hoped she'd stay away from him and wouldn't come over to claim the blanket. The thought of Sheila rose up with an air of inevitability. He kicked himself for having been such a jerk to her. Why couldn't they be friends, after all? The answer was simple: because he felt betrayed. But hadn't he contributed to the betrayal by smothering her with his attention? Well, maybe, but he didn't want to let his mind go down that deep rut again. What was here, around him, where he was?

A soft wind moved across his body, probing between the buttons of his shirt, stirring his chest hairs, and cooling him off just a little. What was the temperature anyway? Probably somewhere in the nineties. He didn't know if this was unusual for the autumn here or not. He remembered digging a ditch by the corral when it was almost a hundred degrees. Everyone on the crew was pouring out sweat at a rate that soon made the bottom muddy. Chuck had observed sarcastically that they shouldn't mind because it was, after all, a dry heat.

Back in Manhattan, through the summer, Michael and his mom would sit by the blower of their single air conditioner as it strove in vain to cool their apartment that was just under the molten tar roof of their fifth floor walk-up. They'd watch the news morning and night to find out what the temperature would be although he could never see that the forecast made much appreciable difference to their comfort or behavior.

Here in New Mexico, cut off from the media, he only knew what was happening in the weather by stepping outside and taking a look. At first, he'd felt disconnected, as if the real weather was on the maps with cartoon drawings. Eventually, he began to see the obvious: the weather consisted of whatever was happening outside the room he was in.

Sleep was a heavy satellite circling above his head, emitting a transmission of peace settling down upon him. He was stretched out on the ground, feeling as if he were floating, his body weightless yet calm, the heat radiating from his skin matching the warmth of the afternoon all around him. The thinking machine ticked on even as he slipped toward unconsciousness.

After awhile he realized he wasn't thinking much anymore (aside from that lazy thought itself) and had gone to the dark warm place from which he'd originally arisen, a place he recognized immediately although he had no memories of it. Now he was close to losing his conscious self entirely so he tried to pay attention as he fell into sleep. He wanted to find the precise moment when he passed from awareness to slumber. Was it here, or here? No. Maybe?

His usual anger and grief and fear had receded so far as to be a barely discernible murmur at the circumference of his awareness. Now nothing was wrong, nothing could hurt him, nothing could move him from the strange yet wonderful feeling of being alive right now, hanging on the side of a planet spinning in a void even as he plummeted internally, far below the surface of his identity, down to some bare plain of being.

He entered a realm of flux. The mild air moving across his body became a wind lifting him up and carrying him through a weird museum of soft murky displays, with objects and people and even feelings from his life that he almost recognized but couldn't quite place. In the end, after sifting through a myriad of possibilities, after wandering through a plain complicated by tangled piles of thought, he no longer remembered to look for the dividing line, absorbed as he was in the murky movements of dreamland. But what was the dark shape moving across his dimming awareness, a hairy matted mass of shambles and grumbles?

So he dreamt, in plumes of trailing smoke drifting over heavily wooded slopes. On those shaded angles were gophers who popped up from their holes with dangling paws and peered at him, chattering warnings to each other. He followed one of them down into its den and found stored in the crevices a blue bandanna, a toy top without a string, a vague desire. Large feet stomped across miles of black and white checked linoleum. Jagged blades thrust out at him from serrated walls. He barely retained a consciousness of himself as a being separate from the imagery rising up to engage and involve him.

He heard a noise from a darkened room, a crying sound. He knew it was Sheila but stood hesitating outside, torn about whether or not to enter, fearful he would find her being vigorously mounted by some muscular demon. The landscape slid down an even darker tunnel and he was back in high school. His friend Tommy was busily stuffing Will Purdy into a locker. Even though Will, the frequent target of their bullying, was small, he was oily and parts of him kept oozing out of the locker. Michael joined Tommy and they tried to close the door on him but kept finding that Will's various appendages blocked the final latching.

Finally, Tommy cursed and pulled a huge bowie knife out of his back pocket. He sawed at a piece of Will that was sticking out. Blood spurted and Michael protested but soon realized Tommy was actually gutting a tuna. They were at the end of a dark pier, their fishing poles leaning against a railing, the black water muttering below. Tommy worked frantically on a table, elbow deep in the huge fish. The deeper he dug, the more long ropy strands of gut, glistening with yellow fat deposits, unspooled from the corpse to the planking at their feet.

Michael felt he was going to throw up: a boiling sourness rose from his stomach as if something alive was trying to climb to his throat. He pushed down on his sternum to restrain it and felt the agitation of an enraged badger under his hands. He moaned and woke for a moment, seeing the evening sky, now obscured by hovering clouds. He had the vague impression Erica was nearby but he didn't want to look for her. He fell back asleep, this time without dreams, floating into a solid gray space where he mercifully lost his awareness.

He woke to what he thought was the sound of a shotgun going off. He scrambled up from where he lay and looked around, crouching to form a lesser target. The sound was repeated, originating from somewhere near the pond, the noise echoing from the walls of the cliff. He looked over as a beaver swimming on the surface of the water lifted its tail and slapped it hard a third time, clearly enjoying the loud percussion. Erica stood at the edge of the pond, as slender and straight as an aspen, listening intently as the beaver swam back to its mounded home and dove down to enter.

Michael had assumed the dam was abandoned but the owner was now making his rounds and announcing his presence at sunset. As Michael watched the ripples circle out from where the beaver had plunged, he heard another sound up on the ridge, a long bugle's note descending mournfully into deep bass tones. That had to be an elk. He'd heard about their call before but had never encountered it. The sharp slaps of the beaver's tail and the elongated bugling of the elk were somehow complementary to the dark clouds moving over the mesa top. He waited for the elk to make another noise but heard only a faint whispering from the collective sound of the trees in motion.

He realized he was hungry and thought about the sandwich in his backpack. His sleeping bag was in the bed of the truck and if not for his irritating companion, it would be so easy just to unroll it among the trees and spend the night. If the clouds held off, the stars would probably be incredible at this altitude, at least a thousand feet higher than the ranch, with no artificial light nearby, the perfect showcase for meteor showers. He noticed Erica had turned to face him with an odd expression on her face. His interpretation was that she wanted him to interact with her. He was sorry now he hadn't just locked the doors and driven away when she'd appeared so precipitously in front of him back at the ranch.

42

RIFLES

Just as he was thinking he might take Erica home and return on his own for the night, he became aware of a sound different from that of either the elk or the beaver or the trees, a low thrum growing louder by the moment. A truck was making its way up the road they'd driven in on. He'd been hearing it for awhile but only now did it register. Erica's quizzical expression must have been due to her picking up the sound long before he did. He walked over to where Erica stood by the pond. He hoped whoever was out on the road would simply drive by, on their way to something else.

As he walked up to her, Erica took his hand. He couldn't read her expression but felt embarrassed to have to deal with strangers while his hand was being held. He also didn't find it comfortable to be in physical contact with someone he was so angry with. He tried to pull away but she held on tenaciously and stared intently in the direction of the sound. He stepped in front of her and turned to the side so their joined hands couldn't be seen from the road. The beaver put his head out of the water just next to his mound of sticks and looked around. He stared at Michael for a moment, his whiskers slightly twitching, a critical expression on his face, and dipped under the water. The sound of the truck grew louder.

From the screen of trees at the end of the road emerged a large green Ford pickup truck with a camper shell. As it approached, Michael could see three men across the front seat, each wearing a cowboy hat. Behind them were two rifles in the gun rack on the back window. Michael didn't want to appear afraid but he was. He also felt exhausted, despite his nap. He suddenly jerked his hand away from Erica who emitted an uncharacteristic squeak.

When the men caught sight of Erica's truck, they slowed immediately and their three heads turned in unison to inspect it as they passed. Michael could see that the body of their truck bore the usual scrapes and dents of life on the range. Michael thought for a moment they might just keep on going but the driver stopped the truck completely when he saw Erica and Michael standing by the pond. The three men engaged in a brief discussion after which the driver put the truck into reverse and backed up to where Erica's truck was parked. They turned behind it, going off the road, and started forward, directly toward Erica and Michael. The large vehicle slowly bumped its way across the uneven terrain around the pond.

As he watched them approach, Michael had an immediate impulse to run away. Yet where would he go and to what purpose? The men had rifles so they could pick him off fairly easily if they were intent on mayhem. Besides, even if he did elude them, he didn't want to walk all the way back to the ranch although it occurred to him that he could walk a much shorter route back by going straight over the top of the plateau where no roads existed, eventually reaching the path he'd taken to the top of Mesa Montejo on the morning when he'd first met Erica. All these thoughts rushed upon him, riding the wave of his fear. He reluctantly supposed he couldn't just leave Erica to deal with them alone so he'd have to stay.

As the truck neared, Michael noticed that its grille and indeed the entire front of the vehicle were splattered with the corpses of bugs, their exoskeletons imbedded in the goo of their inner workings. The windshield had two arced segments cleared of insects by the spray of the windshield washer although even there certain stubborn remains clung to the surface.

Behind the glass were the three men, all in their late twenties or early thirties. Two of them had long handlebar mustaches, giving them an appropriately desperate demeanor. They peered past the reflections on the windshield with the blank expressions Michael had seen in the tough kids who hung around on the street corners of the Lower East Side and scared him even when they didn't notice him. It was as if they weren't seeing human beings in front of them but rather mere obstacles in the way of expressing their impulses.

The truck came very close and for a moment Michael thought it wasn't going to stop. He tensed to leap behind a tree and pull Erica with him but, just as the front bumper rolled to within ten feet, it stopped sharply, sending the three heads inside nodding forward in unison, as if in common assent to what was about to happen.

Michael lifted his right hand to shoulder height and waved it in a brief span. No response. He walked around to the driver's side and casually said, "Hi." Erica stayed back but he could tell she was bristling. He very much hoped she wouldn't try to wither these guys with her attitude. The driver looked him in the eye and smiled a phony grin for a moment.

"You're going to have to leave, mister."

"Sure, but why?"

"Because you and the lady don't belong here."

At this, Erica moved forward so she was jostling Michael's shoulder. Michael spoke out fast to forestall her.

"Actually, we just stopped to look around for a bit. No problem about going. We were heading out anyway."

Erica could no longer contain herself. She stepped in front of Michael and, with the clipped tones she used when provoked, said, "I've been living in the desert for forty years, long before you were even born, young man, so I don't see where you have any right to tell me I don't belong."

The driver whistled low and said, "You know what? I don't give a fuck how long you've been here. Your kind comes from the outside to buy up our land cheap and use us for servants. That's not belonging, old lady. That's exploitation. And no one gives a shit if you pretend to be an artist. Your sculptures suck!"

His companions dipped their heads in vigorous agreement. Erica grabbed the door of the truck and leaned in to blast him. Michael grasped her at the waist and picked her up, intending to run back to the truck with her under his arm. Unfortunately, she held on tight to the door handle and for a very long instant he couldn't budge her. She was shouting both at him and at the driver:

"Let go of me right now! I'll tell you something, young man. You're the arrogant one. This area has been a crossroads for many cultures for centuries and the very idea that one group…"

Michael gave a vigorous yank and she finally let go of the door. He dragged her, still squawking about the rudeness of both Michael and the driver, back toward the road. The driver threw the truck into reverse (in a glance, Michael could see him in the cab, hunched-over, his arm pumping the gearshift lever) but, in his haste, he let the clutch out without applying the gas and stalled it. The two passengers were, with comically broad gestures, berating the driver for his clumsiness.

As Erica and Michael crossed the dirt road, one of her boots caught in a deep rut and came off. She began to shout, "My shoe! My shoe!" This made Michael feel like laughing, even in this midst of the turmoil, because she sounded like she was emitting comically exaggerated sneezes. He reached the truck and had to release his hold on her a bit to open the passenger side door. She used this opportunity to break free and run around the truck to retrieve her boot.

"Jesus Christ, Erica! Let's get out of here. Now!"

Erica picked up her boot and hopped back around on one foot, shouting at him as she hopped.

"How dare you drag me off like a sack of potatoes? That young villain deserves a piece of my mind!"

She sat on the seat with the door open and fumbled at pulling her boot on.

"They're going to fucking shoot us if you don't get in right now!"

"Don't use foul language with me. I'm not one of your hippie girlfriends to listen to that."

She waved the boot in his face. In exasperation, Michael pushed at the boot and she fell back onto the seat, her legs waving in the air (surprisingly slender and youthful, Michael noted, despite himself). She landed hard and kicked out with her left foot, the one that was still shod, and struck Michael in the knee. A spasm of pain bent him over to grasp the wounded joint. He grabbed her foot and had an impulse to twist it hard but instead pushed her leg into the truck (glimpse of blue underwear) and slammed the door shut.

He limped around to the driver's side. By this time, the other truck was in motion and bouncing backwards fast across the rough ground, the contents of its bed (baseball bat, Coke cans, Big Mac wrappers, various debris) flying up into the air with each jolt. Michael tried to move faster but the pain seemed to hold him in slow motion. He scrabbled at the door handle for a moment with the sudden fear that Erica had locked it, as she was now sitting up on the seat with her arms crossed, wrath upon her visage. The door finally opened and he jumped inside, only to find that his sitting position made the keys difficult to extract from his jeans pocket.

"Goddamn it to hell," he shouted as he angled his leg around and arched his back so he could pull out the key. The malevolent truck had almost reached them by the time he put the key into the ignition and started the engine. He threw it into reverse and they lurched backwards just in time to avoid being hit by the other vehicle suddenly looming up in their windshield. He pulled hard on the steering wheel so the truck whipped around in reverse, crashing into piñon bushes at the side of the road. These actually helped by slowing the truck enough for him to slam the transmission into first gear and start racing back down the mountain.

In the rearview mirror, Michael could see dust rising up in their wake in a towering cloud. The other vehicle broke through it, accelerating up behind his back bumper so quickly he was sure they were trying to run him off the road. He went faster but they sped up inexorably to match him. Their bug-stained grille filled the entirety of his rear-view mirror. All he knew was that he just wanted to reach the highway in one piece. Not that it was that much safer there, given that the nearest police station was about sixty miles away in San Juan but he'd at least have more options on the road, and more possible witnesses.

43

DOWN

The trees accelerated on either side of them. Erica sat glaring, holding her boot in her lap like a casserole, as if they were on their way to a contentious family gathering. He was angry, both at the men and at Erica, angry enough he wanted to slam on his brakes so the sons of bitches would run into him. He wanted to drive inside them at a corner and push them off the road to tumble down into one of the ravines. Michael knew that if he stopped for anything, they would surely rear-end him. From the damage on their truck, he was sure they didn't care. And actually, he didn't care too much about wrecking Erica's truck either. Maybe he should mess with them, force an accident, but he had an image of hanging upside down in the mangled chassis on the side of the road as the three desperadoes came walking toward him, rifles laid casually across their forearms.

So he drove on, spiraling down the Forest Service road through the trees he'd found so beautiful before but were now just gray blurred shapes. His fear and anger were balanced in equal amounts. He wanted to destroy them but he also wanted to escape from them. He was glad to have Erica in the car for some human company at the same time he was furious with her. The sensation of inner tension was almost intolerable. It reminded him of being a kid in Manhattan and the feelings he'd had toward his mother. He wanted to defy her, to assert himself as an independent being but he also didn't want to provoke her rage.

The claustrophobia of the current situation was so intense he felt like screaming but instead he pretended to be casual. He turned on the radio to see if the country music station from San Juan could distract him but the signal was faint, the music rising and falling in waves of static. Erica didn't attempt to turn it off.

With the transmission in third gear, they descended in curve after curve. He barely had to use any gas and hardly ever had to tap the brakes. If it weren't for the determined vehicle looming behind him, he would have enjoyed the ride. He hit each corner at exactly the right speed, as if he'd known this road all his life. The truck rocked back and forth. A dented Styrofoam milk shake cup left over from a fast food stop in San Juan kept rolling around on the floor next to Erica's feet. He remembered the blanket was still on the ground in the copse of trees. The peace of that nap seemed like a dream within the current nightmare.

They reached a curve with a drop-off on the left and he had a fantasy of going straight over the side to lead the truck behind them to share in their doom. He didn't believe in the Christian vision of heaven promoted by the faithful at the Ranch. He didn't know what waited on the other side and he was skeptical of anyone who claimed definite information on the subject. People went about their business on the planet, scuffling for food and sex and security, while in truth they were suspended in a void of cosmic indifference extending far beyond human imagining. The three guys in the pickup behind him seemed as implacable as human fate and he was angry about it, did not want to submit, to the universe or to them.

They finally reached the highway where high forest and cliffs gave way to the scrubby hills, scattered gravel, and assorted litter signaling the approach of civilization. The truck behind was still within inches of their back bumper so Michael didn't slow down at the stop sign for Rte. 84. Without looking to either side, Michael jammed his foot into the gas pedal and plunged onto the road where the northbound traffic was steady with workers from Los Alamos making the long drive back home.

Erica emitted a surprised grunt at his extreme maneuver. An old Lincoln had to swerve onto the shoulder to avoid hitting them. A battered green Dodge van coming from the north stood on its brakes, sounding its horn in a shrill undulating wail. He looked back and saw their nemesis trying to make its way into traffic to follow but without success. He laughed as he sped up. Erica glared straight ahead.

"I suppose you're proud of yourself," she finally said.

"We're losing them, aren't we?"

"At least I was willing to stand up to those hoodlums. You ran away."

He thought about arguing with her but his mood shifted and he had an image of how comical they'd been, with him carrying her and her losing her shoe. He couldn't help but smile.

Erica noticed this and looked puzzled.

"Ran away to fight again another day," he said.

She shook her head.

"I won't hold my breath waiting to see that."

They looked each other in the eye and started to laugh. They couldn't stop and Michael's eyes watered so much he could barely see the road. Erica was holding on to the door handle to steady herself but she pressed it down and the door opened. The sudden rush of road noise made them both jump. Erica couldn't pull the door tight so had to swing it open in order to slam it. This only made them laugh more.

They began the long descent from the plateau to the ranch, the heat gradually rising with the lower altitude. The sun had set on the mountains to the west, sending a coral radiance fading across the mesas, reinforcing the fact that this terrain had been the bottom of the ocean eons ago. He glanced repeatedly in the rear view mirror but couldn't see the evil truck behind them.

An expansive sense of freedom had come over Michael, from being back on paved road and from the release of the tension with Erica. The green van he'd cut off was traveling a respectful distance behind and Michael didn't see any further signs of protest against his insane driving. The driver may have been angered by Michael's reckless move but at least he hadn't pulled out a rifle, so far, anyway.

Michael turned on the radio and twisted the dials until he found the faint signal from the rock station in Farmington. Then he slammed his hand on the steering wheel and sang along to *Purple Haze*. Erica reached over and twisted her fingers as if turning down the sound, but didn't. He reached over and put his hand on hers as she put her head on his shoulder.

44

DOOR

She sat, alive with emotion, feeling in her bones how easily he'd picked her up. She'd been filled with rage in the moment as he deprived her of agency but now she remembered how, on a deeper level, she'd felt contained and protected, stirred by being in his arms. She did want him; she couldn't deny it despite the chasm of difference between them. She removed her head from Michael's shoulder and sat upright, her body moving with the shiftings of the truck, looking like Whistler's mother, she supposed, too old to interest Michael, she feared. Not a bad artist, though, that Whistler. His series of Nocturnes had something.

They returned to the house in darkness. Michael pulled into the driveway and shut off the engine. They sat together for a minute, listening to the ticks and sighs of the machine shutting off. They both wanted to say something but didn't know what. Finally, with deliberate movements, she pulled on her boot, stepped out of the truck, and walked into the house, knowing just when to lift her foot for the front step, reaching with the assurance of long practice for the door handle. He followed behind, feeling in the moment that the house he was entering, the woman in front of him, and the body he lived in, were all utterly strange.

She stepped inside and listened but heard only his footsteps and the faint hum from the kitchen clock. Gliding down the hallway, she ran her left forefinger along the wall for guidance. She turned the corner into the courtyard and made her way as if pulled by a rope toward his room.

Now she became aware of the night sounds in the courtyard. A fluttering told her of a bat searching for insects around the exterior lights. A tile clacked at the edge of the roof. A breeze sent something scrabbling across the paving stones of the patio. She turned around to face Michael, who had slowed down as he approached.

"What's going on?" he asked.

"I want to talk to you."

She turned the door knob to his room and the door swung open. They looked each other in the eye, Michael gazing directly, Erica peering through the edge of her vision where he was clearer. They both knew what this meant and they both decided to allow it to happen.

45

DARK

In the room, in the dark, she took him in the way the desert takes in water. She almost forgot who and where she was in the pure sensuality of the moment. Having been blocked from clear visual perception for so long, she felt this rush of specific physical, oral, and tactile sensation to be tremendously compensatory. A lifetime of erotic memories came over her, of her early lovers, of Harold in his potent days, of the younger men she took when Harold was too besotted to function anymore. She had a rush of memories of engaging in the act of love in a variety of ways and places, on top, underneath, and from behind, by the docks in the Old Port of Marseille with workmen passing nearby, on the crest of a mountain in the Sandia range, on a bench in the night shadows of Central Park, in a thousand places and times and ways she'd thought she'd lost forever. Michael's body became the fulcrum of the world for her as she played with him and teased him, humorously, assertively, defiantly.

She governed the situation, balancing the giving of pleasure with the ensuring of her own. She felt herself quicken where she hadn't felt alive for years and reached down to urge herself along. In the tumult, she could feel herself getting closer, riding the edge of a spiral of pleasure coiling up from deep inside her.

He began to mutter, "Oh, God," and that suited her. She summoned up the power of creation, the erotic force she'd poured into sculpture back when her eyes, hands, materials, and subjects united in a flow of being. Now she could feel he was on the edge and she exulted in her power. She'd lost almost everything that had meant anything to her: the friends she'd known, her life's companion, her work in art. Even her mystical connection with the world of nature was strained almost to breaking. But now, somehow, in recompense, all she'd lost was being summoned up for her by this boy's warm living presence submitting to her sweet force. She didn't care what happened next, whether he loved her or ignored her or departed. All she cared about was being allowed to do this for one last time in her life, to be permitted to take him in and draw him out.

She no longer felt old and desiccated. Her young self had returned and was playing with her lover on this bed in a room in her house. She could feel how close he was so she deliberately slowed down to prolong the moment, because she knew all of this would change when he finished. He most probably would reject her, would regard her aged body with disgust. She wanted this moment of unity to last forever but of course it wouldn't and of course she had to let him go. She could feel the movement rising inside him.

All her frustration, her sadness, her loss, were being consumed in this fire, in the aggressive and receptive movements of her upon him, of him upon her. She felt the propulsive thrust rising up from deep inside him. He thrashed on the bed and she hurried herself along so she went over with him, their cries echoing out to the listening desert. Through most of her life she'd held herself back, kept a reserve from the desperate seeking of others in order to remain independent, so she wouldn't be destroyed by their needs. Now she wanted to give herself up totally to his youth, his strength, his potential for art, if only in this moment.

He was lost in an explosion of body and mind draining all the tension and rage of the past few months into an agonizingly long moment of the purest pleasure. He felt her take him in and pull the energy out of him. To what he knew would be his eventual shame, he loved it. Maybe he enjoyed it even more because of the shame. The feeling was excruciatingly beautiful, built up from months of abstinence and rejection and worry and trouble in mind so dense he hadn't even been able to please himself. Now that the opportunity for release had come, he gave himself over to it completely.

All his concerns, about her age, his youth, her power, his weakness, disappeared utterly and he was lost in the sensation, aching from the sheer intensity. But as the pleasure faded, he felt afraid, afraid of how this would affect their life together in the light, afraid she might control him and use him in ways he didn't want. With the fear came a recoil about the age of her body. His instinct was to reach down and pull her up to him but he didn't want to feel, at the tips of his fingers, the wrinkles on her skin.

46

AFTER

She wanted to move up and embrace him, to lie in his arms, but she felt the edge of resistance in him and didn't want to provoke it further. She lay between his legs, feeling the heat radiating from his skin, smelling the fragrance of what she'd drawn from him. What she should do, she thought, was just stand up and walk out of the room, give him time to deal with what happened, to decide how he felt. He would either leave her immediately or stay as her lover.

She didn't want any half-measures at this point. If he wanted to leave, that was fine. She'd simply give him a large check so at least he wouldn't be starving for awhile and let him go in the morning, or whenever he wanted to go. She wondered why they couldn't just be together but she knew how impossible that was. She wasn't very motherly, nor was she very romantic either, never had been. But it was her age that doomed their connection. She knew of no way to get around that.

He reclined on the bed with his hands under his head, his eyes closed. The air outside was very still. He wondered how loud they'd been and whether anyone had heard them. He didn't know where to go from here. He didn't want to leave yet he didn't want to be known in the world as her lover. He was afraid of her age and his own reaction to it, afraid of what people would think. He wondered if they could move somewhere else. She still owned Harold's house in the south of France. He'd paid the bills for its upkeep. Maybe they could spend a year or more there to let all this die down if (and this was a big if), he wanted to stay on with her. This was all too much so he tried not to think.

Silence all around. Silence in the cells of their bodies. Silence in the neurons of their brains until they heard the sound of an engine on the highway, at first subsonic but noticeable, loud, louder, floating in an arc through the clear space of consciousness before ebbing away, moving north toward Colorado. They lay for awhile longer, each listening to the other's breath slowing down as they fell back from their moment of communion into decidedly separate selves.

He thought for a moment he could hear the drifting chords of the *Tapestry* album floating across the low hills from the staff house.

She thought she could even hear the high-pitched tone emitted by indifferent stars.

He breathed in deeply and slowly let it out.

She slid down and away from him and turned as she slid in order to sit on the floor with her back against the bed.

He used this opportunity to pull the sheet up to his chest and lean back against the headboard.

They ticked off in their minds various things they might say but none of them seemed adequate. She knew how absurd they would be as a couple and also felt she might not be able to bear his inevitable rejection of her, not because her ego was so flimsy but because she didn't believe another relationship would replace him. Someone had always come along before but he was likely the last. But at least this had happened. Finally, she put one hand on the floor, lifted herself, and stood. She smoothed down the dress she had never taken off.

He listened to these sounds but even though he couldn't see her in the dark, he didn't look in her direction.

She said, "Goodnight," and walked out the door, closing it behind her.

47

TABOO

He'd wanted to say something to her but couldn't. By breaking this taboo, he'd crossed over to some new territory of separation from ordinary life. With her gone, he felt free to move once again. He hunched his shoulders and stretched out his legs. He couldn't stand for this to be a relationship yet his own need and, frankly, some element of greed made him consider it. She was wealthy, he knew that for certain. He was bound to have a part of it if he stayed. And he was learning, every day, something of what it meant to follow his art. His mind went back over the sex they'd had and he felt both excited and repulsed. The pure physical sensation had been amazing, he had to acknowledge that. Yet the primal contradiction of sex with someone so much older was almost overwhelming. He shuddered when he thought about the picture they made.

He felt a strong impulse to get up and pack his gear, to leave now and start walking down the road, maybe sleep the night in the staff lounge and hitchhike out in the morning. On the other hand, he was very tired, didn't think he had the energy to leave after all that had happened that day. He didn't have to do anything right now although, if he stayed, he'd have to face Erica in the morning. Given the formal farewell with which she'd left the room, she also seemed to be aware they had crossed way beyond any line.

The day had begun with their argument in the morning, followed by the intense experience of painting near the beaver pond where the mood was shattered when the local thugs drove them out. All the various dramas seemed to have happened decades ago. He felt overwhelmed and didn't think he could absorb anymore. He closed his eyes and tried to sleep but an assortment of images swirled through his mind. The most troubling, especially after what just happened with Erica, was remembering Sheila when he saw her in the dining hall, the hairs on her arms gleaming in the evening light. She was clearly not interested in him yet he still wanted her. He partly felt ashamed about Erica because he really wanted Sheila. He'd never thought of himself as having a thing for older women.

He suddenly felt extremely anxious, as if he should get up and do something major, such as leave, or set Erica straight, or try to find Sheila and beg her to take him back. Yet he was too tired for any of these actions. What he most wanted was to sleep and he could feel its heaviness coming upon him. He wondered if he could just wake up in the morning and go out painting as if nothing had happened. He felt a momentary happiness in thinking of the brushes and the paints and the morning sun glowing on the landscape. That would be best: not to deal with people, especially in the form of Erica, just to be an eye watching the landscape and a hand responding to it.

48

WAY

She didn't bother to take off her clothes. She lay in bed with her hands neatly folded on her stomach, as if laid out for a formal funeral. Her eyes were open although all she could see was an obscure fog above her, a perfectly neutral tone providing a soothing contrast to the wildness she felt inside. Her encounter with Michael had made her come alive but she didn't know if that was entirely a good thing. She'd been in the long-held habit of only vaguely feeling her desire and now she was confronted with its full intensity. She still had the scent of him on her skin, the taste of him in her mouth, and she wanted to go back to the room and take him again in the night. He was young. He could do it several more times, she was sure.

And why shouldn't she have this? She may be old but she was the artist he wanted to be, and she was renowned, and she was rich. Men in similar situations were able to find young girls to sate their desires. Why couldn't a woman do the same? She supposed she could buy such experiences for herself, at the risk of being exploited, but she really wanted Michael to want her on his own. She knew how difficult that would be to bring about. He was handsome enough that women his own age might be interested if he weren't so inhibited and awkward. He was the star of his own movie and, she was sure, didn't want to become a subsidiary character in hers.

Her mind kept moving around two points: how to keep him with her and how to make love with him again. This was supremely undignified, of course, but she didn't care. She'd never gone along with social norms if they intervened with what she wanted although her transgressions had frequently caused pain for others and herself. She was not troubled ethically so much as tactically: how was she to make him want her, in whatever way possible? She ached for the touch of him and tried, unsuccessfully, to think of something else.

Just look at me, she thought. She'd always had dramatic features but now they were so gaunt as to be the opposite of erotic yet she wanted him, God help her. This was insane, she knew. She wanted most of all to be young again and even if she managed to maneuver him into staying with her, he wasn't going to restore the life she'd had before. This realization certainly didn't decrease the surge of desire rising up inside her. She felt not the least bit sleepy but there was no point in wandering the house in the night. There was no sufficient distraction in the world of objects. All she could do was lie still and let the chaos of mind swirl through her.

And what was in her mind? Vague memories now, of searing sunlight against the mesa, of a crowded summer opening at a gallery in New York with sweat dripping down between her breasts, of climbing Mesa Montejo with Jean, a former assistant with whom there had been some erotic sparks although nothing ever happened. In this moment, surges of absurd happiness rose up within her, even though the young man in his room nearby was sure to run.

She wanted to go back in and lie down beside him. He was probably so stunned by what had happened that he would just accept it. She loved once again having human heat in her hands, in her mouth, against her skin. With her blindness and isolation, she had nearly written off such encounters as being impossible and yet here she was, having a last foray into Eros before she departed the world of flesh.

She felt confused but surprisingly unafraid. He could leave tomorrow if he wanted. He could also stay if he so desired, and she hoped he did, but it wouldn't kill her either way. She knew if he stayed he would, of course, betray her the first time a young woman approached him. That was to be expected. She hoped he would stay on anyway, in order to paint, to help her run her affairs, to be with her when she died but, even if he didn't, she knew this was a last gift from life, after almost everything important to her had been taken away. The mesas and the sky and the stars and the art and all that had enchanted her so much through her years seemed contained in the body of this young man. She longed to take him inside her again.

Despite herself, despite her intense loneliness and unshakeable sense of impending death, she was still alive, no matter how far gone she was. She tried turning over all her worries about the situation to fate, the gods, the Tao, the way of nature, whatever ruled the happenings of the world, even if it was the great god Chaos as she sometimes suspected but finally doubted, because nature was not chaotic. In nature's sweet complexity, a presence abided, beyond words, beyond her art, beyond the willful meanderings of her mighty ego. This presence kept her still breathing, still feeling, still aware.

This was it: the way taking her through life and down into the deep well of death. She allowed herself to be aware of her breathing, of her heart beating, of the sense memories from having him. She had no fear in this moment that death was near. She only wanted to live right now, for this moment to expand and blossom out. Everything was complete; nothing more was needed. He would stay and he would go. She would live and she would die. The sheer perfection of it all amazed her, at least right now. Nothing remained for her but to be, as she was.

49

VILLAGE

In the weeks that followed, Erica and Michael made no allusion whatsoever during the day to what was happening between them in the night. Michael continued his handyman activities but they talked of spending time at the Chamisa house, where he'd never been, so he could do repairs there and have a different setting for his art. This was a tacit acknowledgement of the change in their relationship because the Chamisa house was connected, at least in Michael's mind, with Erica in the world, as a personage, as a woman of power and renown. Erica came to him three or four nights a week, always in complete darkness, and he didn't turn her away or keep her at bay. When they were done, she left for her room before the first light of dawn.

One morning, Erica asked him to drive her to her house in Chamisa. He was intensely curious about the place, from all the correspondence and bill-paying he'd done. They drove the half hour from the Ranch and through the tiny village above the highway. Ancient adobe houses were clustered around a dusty square. On a side road, they passed by a small building that Erica said was a morada where the secretive Catholic cult called the Penitentes held their services and secret meetings.

The story, as Erica told it, was that on Good Friday a volunteer from their membership would be crucified for three hours. If he survived, and he almost always did because crucifixion was intended by the Romans to be a slow death, lasting for days, the volunteer would be forgiven for all his sins, not just for those of the past but for any he'd commit in the future. He would thereby become the New Mexican version of Nietzsche's Superman, undaunted by any threat of eternal damnation.

Michael mulled this over and realized he had never believed in hell because this life seemed punishment enough. He anticipated that even if he went through the ordeal of crucifixion, he'd end up being just as inhibited afterward as he was before.

An elderly woman stopped and stared as they drove by, then spat and made devil horns with her fingers, thrusting them at the car. Erica snorted through her nose.

"That's Juanita. She used to work for me some twenty years ago until I caught her stealing from my purse. Ever since, she's told everyone that I'm the devil. Convenient for her to think so. Sometimes, I find road kill such as possums, cats, even coyotes, thrown into my garden. I'd wager she's the one pitching them over the wall, assuming she's already found enough for dinner."

She sighed and said, "These families in the village have known me for generations now. I hired their grandparents to rebuild the adobe walls of my house. Most of the older people at least respect me, even if they don't like me. The younger people are sometimes more overtly hostile but that's tempered by the fact they've seen me around since they were babies. I know some of them hate me but that's all right. People hate anyone who stands out."

They curved around to the upper section of the plateau and came to a high adobe wall with green crowns of trees rising up on the other side. A heavy padlock secured the hasp of the front gate. Erica took a bunch of keys from her pocket, selected the largest, and handed it to him. He left the motor running and stepped out. The air was still chilly from the cool of the autumn night although the deep blue of the sky indicated the day would be warm. He heard the faint sound of a car passing on the highway below and the clicking of an insect from on top of the wall. He inserted the key into the lock that gave way with only a little resistance. Swinging the gate open, he found a sprawling single story house of ancient but well-kept adobe. A gravel parking area was to its right. Unlike Erica's house at the Ranch, this residence gave the impression of wealth, not because it was ostentatious but because only wealth could carve out such a green oasis in this desert village.

He pulled the car in and went back to secure the gate behind him. Erica stood at the far end of the lot looking out at the broad view of the Jemez river below. She thrust her chin at the house.

"I bought this property from the local store owner who was heavily in debt from trying to start new grocery stores in the little villages up north. He was grateful for the money but few others in the village appreciated my moving in here."

They walked up to the massive front door with carved wooden panels of entwined cactus branches around the edges. Michael fumbled with the keys for a moment until Erica reached over and put her finger on one. Michael inserted the heavy iron key and the door swung smoothly open. A draft of cool air emanated from the interior walls still holding on to the chill of the night. He walked slowly through the small rooms, none of which seemed to have a true right angle. The ceilings and floors were all askew after centuries of settling and use. The hand-patted textures on the adobe of the walls gave the interiors an uniquely human resonance.

Deep window casements on the building's north side looked out to the blue sky above the green trees along the river. Erica followed him and began to talk of the building's history:

"These interior rooms were built by Alfonso DeGuerro, the original land grantee back in the 18th century. This room without windows served as a cell for various captives, such as pillaging mountain men, runaway slaves, prisoners of war. You can sleep here, if you're willing to put up with the ghosts."

He looked at her, troubled by the idea that he was another captive. Her face betrayed no indication of whether she was making fun of him.

"I'd prefer a room with a window, if it's all the same to you."

"It makes no difference to me.

She walked away, as haughty as ever, and disappeared into one of the rooms, likely her bedroom although Michael hadn't looked inside it yet. He wandered through the house, getting used to its space. On the shelves and and tables and all along the baseboards were a variety of objects: rocks, sticks, pieces of cactus, bones, parts from ancient equipment he couldn't identify, along with a vast miscellany of other items. He assumed these had all been discovered by Erica during her walks in the desert and brought back to use in her pieces or because they just intrinsically appealed to her.

He went through the kitchen which was fully equipped, more so than he'd ever seen, in fact, and went back outside into the sunlight with its autumn glow. The garden beside the house was filled with hummingbirds and butterflies. He strolled its paths and looked out on the long brown loop of the river below. The house seemed to embody the extended passage of time, containing the centuries of its history along with Erica's decades in the desert.

Michael found a wrought iron bench in the garden and sat. He wished he'd brought his paints because the garden made him want to put colors down on paper or canvas to correspond to what was striking his eyes. This wasn't nearly as lush as the French gardens of the Impressionists but the contrast between the desert terrain and the eroticism of the flowers was intense. Now because of Erica he had access to another house, another place to paint. He leaned back and closed his eyes, listening to the sounds of wind, river, cars, wings.

50

TANDEM

Through the winter months, Erica settled into a routine with Michael and felt her life taking shape around his presence. She was surprised she responded to him so intensely and wanted him so much after she'd been alone for so long but she'd always been someone with an intense erotic life. She knew other women lost interest and capability as they grew older but it turned out she'd been lying dormant rather than drying up altogether. The waters still flowed from the spring, assisted by ancient herbal remedies she acquired from a woman healer she knew at the San Juan Pueblo.

She realized, of course, that Michael was profoundly disturbed by what went on between them in the night and wanted to pretend in the day that nothing was happening. They would probably never be casual with each other about that. So she wouldn't be able to depend on the bonds usually established between lovers: daily intimacies, casual touches, discussions about their relationship. They were friends during the day but without reference to what happened in the night. She brooded on the problem of how to keep him with her.

As Christmas approached, Michael cut a small fir tree from along the arroyo and brought it inside. They used colored yarn to tie bones and bits of sandstone and cactus on the branches, along with lengths of red ribbon. The Ranch of the Spirits was profoundly quiet this time of year, with some of the families traveling to be with relatives and the rest sequestering themselves inside their homes. Jed and Susan Mills invited them to Christmas dinner but Erica snorted that she didn't want to sit and say prayers over a dead turkey.

Christmas Eve found Erica on the couch in the living room of the Ranch house, her face toward the fire. The snap of burning wood was amplified by the silence from the desert, seeming to her as if everything had stopped and was waiting under the moon for some new birth. She shook her head that such a typical religious image should come to mind. The desert knew nothing of human holiday, abiding in its own winter beauty without the elaborations of the mind.

In honor of the season, Michael read Dickens' *A Christmas Carol* out loud. He finished the story, giving an ironic twist to "God bless us, everyone," and set the book down. He'd taken a very old bottle of sherry from a shelf in the kitchen and they were sipping from it. Erica sighed and stretched so the bones cracked across her shoulders.

"I never did buy you anything for Christmas," she said.

"Oh, that's okay. I only picked up a little something in San Juan for you."

"You did? Where is it?"

He laughed. "I was going to give it to you in the morning."

"Humph. In my family, we exchanged gifts on Christmas Eve."

"So you're saying you want it now?"

"We might as well get it over with."

He stood up. "It's not a chore, you know. It's only a minor gift."

"Of course, that's obvious."

He shook his head and walked out. She heard his steps along the porch to his room. She thought she should have bought him something, asked Lupe to pick it up on a trip to San Juan. It didn't have to be anything in particular, just some expensive trinket, a wrist watch, maybe, because she'd noticed he didn't wear one. She would definitely have to think of some way to pay him back for embarrassing her this way.

He walked back in and handed her a small box. She opened it and found an embossed silver clasp for her hair. She turned it over and felt the details of the workmanship, with designs like those on the modern pueblo pottery.

"I bought it in Taos on our last drive. The man had some nice things so I thought you might..." His voice trailed off into apprehension.

Her fingers moved over the surface of the clasp.

"It was done by a fine craftsman. I can tell."

He sat down heavily on the chair. "Oh, good. I never know about presents. It's usually hard for me to find the right thing."

She realized her hair must be almost as pale as the silver in the clasp. She set the open box on her lap, reached behind her, and untied the length of twine she usually used to make a long ponytail. Released, the gray tresses fell to her shoulders. She took up the clasp and reached behind her to fit the hair through it. The gesture made her feel as she had when she was young, in her twenties, arranging her hair while one of her suitors looked on. She wondered if Michael saw any flicker of that long departed girl left in her face. She hoped so but quickly condemned herself for her vanity.

When her hair was arranged, she felt the weight of the clasp, much heavier than the twine. She had a flash of thought that it was the weight of the grave, as if her mortality were pulling down on her skull. She knew the end was coming and she wasn't afraid of it so much as she feared that final agony before the door opened, either to the next world or to nothing. She didn't want to be alone for the passage.

51

PROPOSAL

The firelight caused the shapes in the room to shift and vibrate. She tried to focus on Michael who was leaning forward expectantly, waiting for more reaction from her. The flickering of the light made her think he was a wraith, an insubstantial presence, soon to dissolve out onto the highway and leave her. She'd botched things by not buying him a present. Now what could she do to anchor him, to make him stay? She felt something inside her click and decided to wager everything she had on his number on the turning wheel. The silence outside seemed to encourage her on.

"You've been a big help to me with my correspondence. You seem to have a natural talent for it."

He seemed surprised. Praise was not usual from her.

"It doesn't take a lot of talent to answer a few letters."

She looked up at the ceiling, trying to seem casual as she lay down her bet.

"I've had the same business manager in New York for the past thirty years. I believe I've made him wealthy. Maybe it's time for a change."

Michael didn't say anything to this. Indeed, what could he say? She wanted to be subtle but didn't see any way of maneuvering him into asking her for the job. She'd have to serve it up to him like a bowl of ice cream.

"You seem to be good at office work. Have you ever handled money?"

A long pause. By all the gods, did she have to lead him by the hand every step of the way? Maybe this was a bad idea. Finally, he cleared his throat and sounded a little embarrassed:

"Even though she was a bookkeeper, my mother never could balance her checkbook so I did it for her, from the age of twelve, actually."

She calculated: he was twenty-two now so how old would his mother be if she'd lived? She was dead, wasn't she? That's what he'd told her. His mother could easily have been her daughter. Granddaughter? This was all so crazy but she felt an ache in her chest driving her on.

"I obviously can't check the accounts anymore so I was thinking of asking you to do it."

"Oh, sure, I can do that. No problem."

She could hear the relief in his voice. He must have thought she was going to ask him for something much more difficult. He didn't act as if he'd been calculating how to get his hands on her checkbook so that eased her mind somewhat. But he also didn't seem to grasp the enormity of what she was offering, given her wealth. Now the question was whether he would make a botch of it.

52

SEDAN

In late February of 1973, Michael drove the old Mercedes down to the luxury car dealership in Albuquerque, traded it in for a trifling sum, and used a cashier's check from Erica's bank in Santa Fe to buy a new 1973 sedan, the W114. He drove it back up under spits of sleet, taking the old road through the ghost towns to prolong the experience. He leaned back and admired the wood of the dashboard and the solid details of the interior. The windows seemed huge, affording a wrap-around perspective of the wintry desert speeding by.

He passed Volkswagen vans filled with long-haired hippies and ancient pick-up trucks driven by ranchers wearing straw cowboy hats with the brims slumped down in front and back. He felt vaguely guilty about blasting by them in a metal shroud filled with German technology. This didn't fit with the peace and love culture that ran through his generation and influenced him even though he'd felt spurned by the hippies as well as the straight so had never thought of himself as a flower child. He rationalized that this solid but unusual vehicle was in keeping with Erica's idiosyncratic practicality, even though he was the one who'd suggested the purchase, not her.

When he brought it home, Erica walked around the car, trailing her left hand along the sides to take in the contours. She sat in the front seat and breathed in deeply.

"So this is what my money buys me," she said. "The fragrance of the new, direct from factories on the Rhine."

He sat beside her and couldn't help but feel a twinge when she said, "my money," although she was obviously only speaking the truth. He was simultaneously attracted to and repelled by her wealth, a paradox in keeping with Erica's many contradictions. His new position gave him the power to siphon off funds from her accounts but he didn't feel any impulse toward larceny. He was filled with ambition, of course, but not toward becoming rich.

The next day, he took her for a ride up to Durango, Colorado. The new Mercedes had an eight track cassette player so they could have music on even after they passed out of radio range. On his last trip to Santa Fe, Michael had bought the tapes of the Bach Cello Suites as performed by Pablo Casals so those plaintive sounds served as accompaniment for the terrain. They drove together companionably, watching the high desert unfold up to the Colorado plateau.

"When I first came to New Mexico," Erica said. "This was not a road so much as a track, heavily rutted, and large boulders often blocked the way. We drove an old truck with an iron bar in the back to lift the fenders over rocks. Back then we had isolation and silence, things hard to come by now."

Michael glanced over at her. She had her eyes closed and seemed to be absorbed by her memories.

"Who were you traveling with back then?"

She was quiet for a moment so Michael thought she might be asleep.

"My friend Deirdre. She was another artist, did watercolors, a bit like yours, actually. She was even more reserved than you are."

So she thought he was reserved. How did that account for what passed between them in the nights, experiences he tried to keep away from his thoughts during the day? He found he was becoming accustomed to the ritual, repetition making the reality seem less unusual. As befitting his age, his desires were always intense and, at the very least, he preferred a partner rather than his hand to deliver relief. In the dark, always in the dark, he'd formed a growing connection with Erica who was as slim as a girl but had few of the inhibitions of someone young and inexperienced. Indeed, her energy was always equal to his. He found if he just concentrated on the pure physical input, the thoughts of judgment and shame stayed at bay because what happened felt so good.

The situation was impossible, absurd, tawdry yet the reality had become part of him and he wasn't inclined to put an end to their relationship, especially right now, in an expensive new car, moving at eighty miles an hour on a two lane road, accelerating through the West.

53

PLANS

From his task of opening the mail, Michael already had access to all the bank accounts but now Erica told him to manage them, only asking him to let her know about transactions over a thousand dollars. When he learned of Michael's new role, the financial manager back in New York sent Erica a series of scathing letters predicting doom until Michael finally wrote and told him to stop.

They began a routine of spending Monday through Thursday mornings at the Chamisa house and then going up to the Ranch for the long weekends. They had no particular reason for this, just that they needed a rhythm to their days. They did agree that the village was busier on weekends so they might have fewer unpleasant confrontations with the locals if they were away.

They began to discuss what they wanted to do in the long term and Michael advocated for increasing the presentation of her works to the world, mounting shows in the U.S. and in Europe, wherever the museums would pay the most. He began answering the letters from various curators and started negotiations about the financial arrangements. Erica revived her ability to be very sharp about such matters and instructed Michael on how to keep negotiating for more money. They made plans to travel to the cities where the shows might be held, figuring Michael would thereby gain exposure to the world. He'd never been out of the country so was eager to see the cultures and art of Europe. The slides of his art history classes back in college had stimulated his appetite for the treasures of Paris, Florence, and Rome.

Their relationship shifted so they talked and joked with one another almost as if they were equals, although Erica generally had the last word on decisions. Michael still went out to the desert to paint on most mornings but found he was becoming increasingly distracted. Instead of settling into the pure act of seeing, he found himself obsessing about the various tasks he had to do. Ideas would arise of improvements he could make to the houses and to their daily lives. While he was trying to paint, he would be drafting correspondence in his mind and thinking of their travel plans.

He was also more than a little distracted by the fact he'd gone from being penniless to having access to millions of dollars. He still had no desire to acquire money on his own but he did fantasize about ways to enjoy himself, fantasies previously impossible to realize during his upbringing in New York. Now, more often than not, he would pack up his paints at the end of a morning and his only product would be a lengthy to-do list, combined with a wish list, jotted down on a yellow pad, but he would have made no paintings at all.

They would walk together after breakfast in the mornings and after dinner in the evenings. At the Chamisa house, they'd stroll around the desert garden and end up looking out over the river. At the Ranch, they'd hike through the desert, following one of a number of their favorite paths meandering along the arroyos or up close to the sheer face of the mesa. Now Erica would always hold on to his arm because her eyesight was growing ever dimmer.

After their walks in the evening, Michael would read aloud. Erica had become bored with Dickens so he tried Willa Cather whose sensibility seemed to match Erica's. She especially liked *Death Comes For The Archbishop*. The stark prose evoked much of what she had experienced in New Mexico, and she enjoyed the realistic portrayal of the moral failings of the frontier clergy, in keeping with her own skeptical views.

54

SNOW

Winter, 1974

Snow came early that year, covering the mesas in a white glow that receded only a little in the sunny but cold afternoons. Michael ordered fur-lined cowboy boots for himself from a store in San Juan while Erica used her old ones, brought over from France long ago. They walked together through the dusting of flakes at the Ranch level, admiring the heavier snow visible on the higher elevations. The change in color from desert tans to white gave the landscape a different perspective, making it seem closer and more intimate.

Val called several times, wanting him to help the team from the University that was exploring an Anasazi site she'd found. He considered going in order to interact with a different set of people but Erica was very discouraging, insisting she needed him to help her and couldn't spare him for the days such a project would take. She was less than gracious about any time he spent away from her, always suspecting he was having a liaison with a female, as if sensing that was exactly what he wished for.

Whenever he ran into Val as he drove through the ranch, she would invite him to dinner, or to come play cards, but he always made excuses. He'd exchange small talk with her or Jess if he saw them on the road or in town but he didn't want to be close to them. Jess always just accepted whatever he said and chatted on. Val, on the other hand, would give him a skeptical look and seem just about to say something but would refrain in the end. He felt he'd passed over into a world inhabited only by Erica and himself with no way to explain it to others.

Over the winter, and into the spring, they went into more detail about their trip, thinking of making a swing through Europe in autumn, going to London, Amsterdam, and Paris. Erica wanted to check on her house in Provence and Michael wanted to continue on to Geneva, Vienna, Venice, and Florence, finishing in Rome. The plan was to travel by train compartment and talk to Museum Directors about sending a show through their cities. Michael was very excited to see the sights and soak in the art, even as he was increasingly neglectful of his own. He actually wanted to go sooner, leaving in the late spring and staying for the summer. This was partly so he could avoid the arrival of the new summer staff, with its painful reminders of his time with Sheila.

He began a few letters to her but tore them up after only two or three lines. He couldn't think of what to say or what he wanted from her. Moreover, he didn't have her home address so, in order to mail anything, he'd have to go through the embarrassing process of entering the office at The Ranch of the Spirits and asking one of the nosy staff for it. He supposed he could write to her care of her father who was pastor at the only Congregational Church in her town in

Minnesota but even if the letter did find its intended target, he still didn't know what he wanted it to say. He should apologize, he supposed, but for what? For being first smitten and later angry when spurned? He knew he should just forget her but when he was falling asleep, her face would float above him in the dark. When he was with Erica, he would often pretend Sheila was the one moving over him.

Even so, he felt ever more tied to Erica. She was his only support in the world and he was growing accustomed to her crankiness and moods, as well as the times when she was playful and expansive in her embrace of the world. He learned what would cause her to be more upset and what would work to reduce her agitation. He felt as if she were an elderly relative who commanded respect, even as their nights together created another kind of bond that also grew stronger.

He felt he was dealing with several different people in her single form: someone who shared his bed, someone who carried an aura of recognition to the world, someone who was just about the only person who cared about him, and someone who was a highly temperamental employer. He wondered how his life had come to be so isolated and complex but he couldn't deny that it was.

Their lives fell into close parallel grooves that intersected through the moments. Michael had little interest in becoming a gourmet but their meals did provide a structure. Erica had given up bothering about what time he appeared for breakfast and, probably in consequence, he was almost always in the kitchen by 8 a.m. They usually made coffee, scrambled eggs, toast, and some fruit if they could get it. For lunch, Lupe put out sandwiches and salads on a tray in the fridge so they could eat whenever they returned from their journeys. In the afternoons, Lupe would receive direction from Erica who used to be a devoted cook, favoring local ingredients and recipes, but the degeneration of her vision made the processes difficult for her. Lupe usually made the main course for dinner, maybe a roast or enchiladas or mountain trout, or she'd put out steaks for Michael to cook on the ancient wood stove that sat next to the newer electric stove.

After Lupe went home, Michael would bring the food to the dining room table, along with a bottle of wine to share. They would talk, both during and after the meal. She asked him about his childhood and he told her the not very interesting stories of growing up in Greenwich Village, and going to the public grade school nearby where he survived by pretending very earnestly he wasn't there.

55

TALK

He found his life wasn't very consequential in comparison to hers so he kept the descriptions short, didn't tell her of the many hours he spent with his mother in the hospital where she was dying of cancer. He also didn't talk about his father's death from a heart attack on the subway, of all places, when he was only eight. If he thought about it, he could understand why he was such a loner, why he had such difficulty in sustaining relationships, even why he'd fallen into such a strange arrangement with Erica. He knew he was odd, that was a given, but now his strangeness was matched by his situation. He wanted to continue painting in the mornings but it had become ever harder for him to have the same level of focus he'd had before their relationship had taken its turn.

And now what did he want? He enjoyed his spending power; that was certainly true. He bought (for both of them, he argued to Erica and to himself) a newer and even more expensive stereo system so the classical music in the evening had a crystalline clarity. He bought clothes although he'd never before cared how he looked, had always been satisfied with whatever was hanging off the circular displays in St Mark's Place.

Now he found himself in the fancy Western store in Santa Fe

where his fellow customers included opera singers, wealthy ranchers, the stray movie star making his or her way through the local shops. He knew nothing of what was fashionable but his saving grace was that he didn't care for garish colors so he stayed away from, for instance, the orange shirts with pearl buttons, the jackets with leather fringe and embroidered cuffs. He bought western shirts in subdued colors (with plastic buttons), along with straight leg jeans exorbitantly expensive for no discernible reason he could tell. His outfits were completed by high leather boots with detailed craftsmanship and cowboy hats he had to beat up to make wearable and less obvious.

He had no audience for his clothes, anyway. Erica said she admired some of his sartorial choices but he knew her eyesight did not permit careful examination. He continued to wish he had some female companionship of a younger variety but seasons other than summer at the Ranch were sparse for visitors. Plus he didn't know how Erica would react to his not coming home at night or his bringing someone back to the house. Poorly, he expected, but didn't have the courage to ask. She was more possessive every day, wanting to know every detail of what he was doing and who he was seeing. Ironically, he found himself sympathizing with Sheila when thinking of how he and Erica had never defined their relationship.

In the evenings, when Erica became exhausted with the wine and the talk, he'd take her by the arm, gently pull her off the couch and walk her back to her bedroom. He'd leave her there but often, later in the night, she would join him.

56

PHOTO

In May of 1974, the Santa Fe New Mexican published a photo of Erica and Michael together, taken when they went to an art opening on the Plaza. The caption read: "Erica Hanlon and companion at the Bucklin show, Cimarron Gallery." This was the first public recognition of them as what might be termed a couple and had the effect, over the following months, of increasing the snide remarks they encountered on the Ranch and in the village. They'd gone to the show because the artist, Jeremy Bucklin, was an old friend of Erica's. His work was large, horizontal, very abstract, nothing related to what either Erica or Michael were doing, so therefore safe.

Jeremy and Erica were delighted to see each other because they'd been platonic friends in New York City back in the forties and hadn't seen each other since. He had never been a friend of Harold's so was safe in that way as well. Jeremy ignored Michael and showed Erica around with his hand placed lightly on her upper arm. He was handsome in a leonine manner, with a broad white beard and thinning hair and Michael could tell Erica was happy to be with him again and have him touch her. Michael felt no jealousy about this although he was protective of his special position in her life, not wanting anyone else to infiltrate the private world they'd created for themselves. He scolded himself for thinking this way but that didn't stop him from thinking.

While Erica glowed from Jeremy's attention, Michael walked around the gallery on his own, keeping his eye on an assistant in the corner whose slim figure and air of sophistication attracted him. He had a glass of wine, ate some canapés, and made small talk with the assistant who was careful to mention her husband early in the conversation. He felt mildly deflated but knew, obviously, that the world contained plenty of women who were not attached. He just had to find ways to meet them although the obstacle presented by the elderly lady in black nearby had to be resolved somehow.

A middle-aged woman approached him and introduced herself as a reporter from The Santa Fe New Mexican. She asked him what his connection was to Erica.

"Just a friend," was Michael's response. The reporter took a deep breath and tried again.

"Tell me, what is Ms. Hanlon doing these days?"

Michael looked past her, scanning the room as if he hadn't heard what she said. She was about to repeat her question, only louder, when Michael muttered, "Excuse me," and walked away. He had no desire for notoriety of any kind. He knew people talked about them but he didn't want to hear the gossip, if he could avoid it. The room was too warm for his comfort, the air conditioning struggling against the heat generated by the mass of chatting, drink-holding people who barely looked at the art.

On the drive back from Santa Fe, Erica was showing the effects of several glasses of wine, rambling about Jeremy and her years living in New York, a city Michael didn't recognize from his own experience of growing up there. Hers was a booming post-war metropolis of ambitious artists, wealthy patrons, heavy drinking, passionate affairs. Neither Erica nor Harold had been faithful during that time but they had an unspoken agreement not to talk about who they slept with. Harold's drinking eventually made affairs almost impossible for him in a physical sense. After their years together, Erica felt obligated to stay with him and provide for his care as his health eroded. They moved to France with the ostensible aim of regaining Harold's health but actually so he could die in a place he loved.

As Erica and Michael drove up the highway from San Juan, with clouds stretched out like twisted ribbons across the sky, her stories degenerated into disconnected sentences until she fell asleep, her head at what looked like an uncomfortable angle on the seat back, her mouth open in a way that made her seem older than usual. Michael realized her feisty spirit usually had the effect of animating her face and softening its lines.

They arrived at the house in the village with the background mesas turning dark and the sky deepening blue above. Michael carried her into the living room and placed her on the couch as she snored, heedless of being transported. He removed her shoes and pulled an Indian blanket up over her. He went to the kitchen, removed a beer from the ancient refrigerator, and took it out to the living room where he sat on the leather sofa. He thought of lighting a fire but that seemed like too much effort so he looked out into the darkness through the window which reflected a miniature version of the living room. In that floating room, a small man who looked like Michael sat on an armchair and stared back at him.

He toasted himself with his can of beer and mulled over an idea he'd been playing with for awhile. Erica's eyes were now half-open while the mournful sound of Mozart's Requiem played, not the most auspicious background for the conversation he wanted to have. He hadn't paid attention to what record was on the platter when he turned the stereo on. Maybe it didn't matter.

"Erica?"

She shifted on the couch and opened her right eye a little more to indicate she was listening.

"Have you given any more thought to my idea of making a book about your sculptures and your way of working?"

She shook her head.

"I don't know. You'd have to do most of it. Is that a good thing for you?"

"I'd be in charge of the arrangements and the formatting but it would be based on your ideas, your experience."

"I suppose some people might care about what I think."

"Lots of people would."

"We don't want it to be junk."

"You'll make sure it isn't. We could coordinate the release with the touring exhibit. That will attract lots of attention."

She stirred herself a bit more, propped herself up on an elbow, and looked directly at him.

"I'm happy you're thinking beyond this little corner of the world. You need to keep making art, of course, but if you want to take this on… ."

Her head nodded and she slipped back to rest on the couch. She was asleep again.

He finished his beer and felt excited in a way he hadn't felt in a long time. He needed more experience, in general, and this seemed like a way for him to meet people, go abroad, learn things. Creating the book would significantly delay their travels but he was okay with that as he'd be even more involved than if they were only promoting Erica's sculpture exhibits. The book project lacked a clear path for him to continue painting but that was up to him, not to external circumstances. Maybe his being an artist was only a dream but was it more a dream than any of the rest of this? Somewhere out on the flats, a coyote howled, a sound blending longing and dismay in a way he found completely relatable.

57

BREATH

Over the following months, he performed his usual chores around the two houses, driving back and forth according to what was needed. He also went out in the mornings and did some basic drawings and watercolors, trying to keep his momentum going even though it was difficult. He took pleasure in his encounters with Erica in the night but they continued to trigger his guilt and shame. He was young and wanted to make love but knew of no parallels for what they were doing anywhere in the world.

Their time at night began to have consequences during the day. Gradually shifting from her previous detachment, Erica would, for no reason, at any time, lean over and touch his shoulder or hold his hand, not even trying to hide their intimacy when someone came to the house or passed along the road. When he realized they were were being observed, or could be observed, he'd sweat and his breathing would become shallow. He felt exposed, as if the world could see into the turmoil of his brain.

As for her, she liked to lean in to his chest and hear the beating of his heart and the movement of his breath. She felt connected to the world through him. She marveled at how little she was irritated with him now. His youthful clumsiness and anxiety seemed more endearing than exasperating, a definite change from when she first met him. She wanted him to be happy yet intuited the chaos of emotions inside him about their nights together. She was okay with the prospect of that part of their relationship fading, and she could sense it was fading already, the rush of passion abating to something less urgent. Now she just wanted his presence but she was happy they'd made love as it felt like an essential ritual for keeping dying at bay. She accepted now, more every day, that her days were ending and she wanted him to be with her as she left the world. Was that too much to ask?

58

BOOK

During the winter of 1974 to 1975, Michael spent the afternoons absorbed in creating a catalogue, going back to Erica's student days, of her sculptures and bas-reliefs, listing where they were located, in collections or in storage. As the days grew slightly warmer, he'd open the office window and occasionally a hummingbird would hover there, centered in the frame, wings a blur, calculating whether the room held any nectar.

Together he and Erica considered the items piece by piece. He realized even more what a prolific career she'd had, sometimes making hundreds of works a year. His own pile of drawings and canvases was minimal in comparison but he had to admit there was no way to compare, given her fifty year head start. He contacted a literary agent in New York recommended by a friend of Erica's in Santa Fe, one of the few who had come to accept Michael's pivotal role in the household.

The agent was excited by the idea of the book and approached publishing houses who subsequently offered contracts. Michael sent them to Erica's lawyer in Santa Fe, with whom he'd had little previous contact. The lawyer wrote back that publishing rights were not in his area of expertise so he'd have to send the material to an intellectual property attorney he knew in Los Angeles who specialized in such transactions. The negotiations dragged on for months. In the mornings, Michael found himself impatient to drive into the village for the afternoon mail delivery.

Finally, Hudson and Sons, a major publisher, made the highest bid for the book and sent two representatives out to New Mexico to help Michael and Erica set the project up. The reps, a middle-aged man and woman, appeared to courteously despise each other and stayed in separate casitas at the Ranch only to reveal before they left that they were actually married.

A major hurdle was to obtain the highest quality photographs of the works. Erica and Michael didn't want to rely on the photos that had already been taken, of wildly varying quality, so the reps suggested some photographers they'd worked with in the past. Erica, however, oppositional by nature, came up with the name of Peggy Denham, a well-known photographer she knew both in New York and in France. Peggy had always expressed great appreciation for Erica's work so could conceivably be interested in the project. Michael asked whether someone with an independent photography career would want to do what was essentially commercial work.

Erica's reply was, "She'd do it for me."

The publishing reps were skeptical, especially about how much they would have to pay someone who was an artist in her own right. However, Erica had heard through her telephone grapevine that Peggy was hard up for funds as she was getting older.

Peggy lived in Paris and Michael was able to track down her number. He dialed the phone for Erica who talked to Peggy and said they'd soon be traveling to France, which excited Michael because so far their travel plans had been entirely theoretical. Peggy herself was enthusiastic about the project.

Erica had definite ideas about the city as she did about almost everything. She insisted they book rooms at a small hotel she'd stayed at before, L'Hotel, on the Left Bank, close to the river and lots of cafes. This was fine with Michael who was just happy to be going as he'd always wanted to see the City Of Lights.

He anticipated, randomly, that it would be cleaner than New York, remembering the grime from the city of his childhood. He wanted to see the museums and do the tourist things, go up the Eiffel tower, walk down the Champs-Élysées, visit the Moulin Rouge, even though he'd heard the last was a terrible tourist trap. The tickets this time of year, in the late winter, were not expensive. They would fly from Albuquerque to New York City, spend a night and go from there directly to Paris.

He launched into the preparations for the trip, making arrangements with the travel agent Erica knew in Santa Fe, giving Lupe a schedule for checking on the houses, closing the shutters, turning off the well pumps.

59

PARIS

April, 1975

In every public place from the Ranch to the Plaza Hotel in New York where they stayed overnight to wait for the flight to Paris in the morning, Erica constantly clutched his arm, making Michael think they looked as if he were squiring his grandmother on a birthday excursion. He'd convinced her not to wear her usual all-black uniform so she had on a light blue traveling suit that seemed to keep her from being recognized. She'd insisted and he'd agreed, of course, on flying first class so the trip across the Atlantic took place in relative comfort. They ate filet mignon served on china plates and sipped champagne from fluted glassware.

Erica rested her head on his shoulder and talked in a rambling way of her time in France:

"Harold and I would always spend a night in Paris before taking the train to the Midi. We stayed in the same hotel where we're going tonight. I hope it hasn't changed because the interiors were from a former era, somehow both ornate and subtle. We would go to our favorite place, the Café de Flore, where I'll take you while we're here. After a light meal and a bottle of wine, we'd walk the streets, arm in arm, admiring the way light was reflected from the windows and the cobblestones on the streets which, at least in my memory, were always wet with rain. We'd watch the people passing by, trying to distinguish the tourists from the locals, sharing our speculations about what their lives were like. We'd stop in some small artist's hangout for wine. Harold would usually have too many glasses and loudly shout his opinions about art in broken French, sometimes inciting heated arguments with the locals. I would have to walk him back to the hotel, his weight almost toppling us over but in the morning we'd always rise early, with Harold usually irritable from his hangover. We'd catch a morning train and arrive late in the evening to the Provence station where we'd hire a cab driver, the same every time, except when he had his appendix out, to take us up in the hills to our house."

Michael listened, sleepy himself from the champagne, with hours left until they arrived.

"It's been twenty years and I didn't know if I would ever go back. Now I want you to enjoy Paris for a few days at least, take in the city, wander off on your own sometimes. We'll meet with Peggy and engage her about the book. After that, we'll go down to the Midi house and we'll see if you can work there. I have local people I trust working as caregivers for the place. But, of course you know about them after arranging for their pay. I forget how much you've been doing."

Erica stopped talking and Michael closed his eyes, lulled to sleep by the sound of the engines.

On arriving at Charles DeGaulle, they wound their way through customs, left the concourse, and took a cab to L'Hotel. Michael stared out the window as they drove past the the factories and apartment complexes in the industrial areas ringing the city. With his high school French, he tried to interpret the business signs and traffic directions. He had never before left the country. His parents had travelled in Europe before they married and always talked of taking him but on the salaries of a bookkeeper and poet/teacher, they never saved enough money to make that happen, especially after his father died. Now he found himself entranced by the usual items of civilization: buildings, roads, power lines, all familiar in function but with a different quality, somehow more rundown and more self-possessed, carrying the air of a culture ongoing for much longer than anything in the U.S.

They entered the city and had glimpses of the Sacré-Cœur, the Eiffel Tower, and eventually Notre Dame when they crossed the Seine. The hotel was in a row of six story buildings, looking similar to the apartment houses next to it except for discreet signs on the wall outside indicating that Oscar Wilde and Jorge Luis Borges had both stayed there. Inside, the clerk recognized Erica and treated them with great deference. Michael had booked adjoining rooms with a bathroom in between, which suited both of them fine. The rooms were ornate and comfortable, with a bottle of wine on each of their desks.

They napped and woke in the evening. They walked to a nearby restaurant where Erica had dined decades earlier. They had a meal of fish and roast vegetables, the fish perfectly poached, melting in their mouths, the wine going to Michael's head because of the jet lag. He stumbled as they walked back to the hotel, almost falling with Erica to the ancient cobblestones.

She felt the sharp tug of Michael's arm as he lost his balance, bringing memories of the times she'd tried to keep Harold upright during his drinking bouts. She felt an immediate spasm of disgust at having to deal with this, having vowed never again to burden herself with an alcoholic. The difference was that Michael never did fall down. He apologized profusely and was soon walking steadily again. She recognized that he was not Harold. He might have some drinks in the evening but he wasn't swilling down alcohol all day long like Harold at the end.

The fog of her vision managed to capture some of the qualities of Paris, in the brown of buildings and river, the blue murk of sky, the green blobs from the crowns of trees as they passed by. She breathed in the fragrance from the bouillabaisse of the streets, the distinctive smells of baking bread, urine, flowers, mold, perfume, and underarms. (She knew she was indulging a cliche with that last but still...). She was happy to be back in order to replace her old associations with new, introducing Michael to a culture that was producing art for centuries before the United States generated anything original.

They spent the next two days touring the city, spending more time in the Louvre than either of them found comfortable. Erica lectured Michael about the paintings in front of them although she, of course, was speaking more from memory than observation. They were both amused by the crowds pressing around the Mona Lisa when an even better painting by Da Vinci, a Madonna and Child, was just two rooms away with no viewers, except for them.

Each night they had dinner at one of the cafes Erica had patronized in her previous life. After the bland fare of the Ranch dining hall and the good but predictable Southwestern cuisine prepared by Lupe, Michael was stunned by the excellence of the food, the seafood, casseroles, soups, bread, butter, and cheeses all waking up his tastebuds as if they'd been asleep his entire life.

Michael kept calling Peggy but the phone rang for long periods with no answer until the third day when she picked up on the first ring. She said she was interested in the project but was vague about meeting them. Michael called again the next day. When Peggy answered, he handed the phone to Erica who deployed her tough side and told Peggy she would either meet with them or they would find someone else for the project. Peggy gave Erica her address and said they could come over that afternoon.

60

DEBT

They took a cab with the usual sullen driver to Montmartre and admired the wedding cake glory of the Sacré-Cœur against the gray-clouded sky. Peggy's address was further north in the 18th Arrondissement in an industrial-looking building with metal siding. Michael knocked on the steel door but they heard no answer from within. When he tried the knob, the door swung open. He took half a step in but the interior was dark and silent. He called out to Peggy but received no response. He turned to Erica:

"What do you think?"

"If this is the address, she must be here. Go in and see."

"Maybe if I had a flashlight..."

"Oh, for the love of Athena, what's going to happen? I'll hold the door wide so you can start your way in. I'd do it myself except for..."

Even as her sight grew worse, they both continued to pretend nothing was wrong even though Michael was increasingly covering up for her. He didn't mind but felt sympathetic when she obviously couldn't read the words on a page or when she called someone she knew by the another name.

Michael stepped into the darkness which his right knee soon discovered was filled with bulky objects. He said, "Ouch" and put his hands in front of him to discern if a path led deeper into the interior. His hip hit the corner of what seemed to be a crate and he repeated, "Ouch."

From behind, Erica asked, "Can you see anything?"

He rubbed his hip and said, "You might ask if I'm okay."

"I know that, or you wouldn't be talking."

Ahead he saw a faint horizontal line of light. He put his hands out again and slowly made his way toward it. As he moved closer, he could barely make out a large wooden door with inset panels. From inside, he heard music, a jazz guitar. He knocked but no answer came. He knocked, louder this time and, after some seconds, the door flew open. Light and music blasted out at him. He stepped back from the glare.

On the other side, a woman in her sixties, with a mane of frizzy gray hair, dressed in a shapeless blue smock, stood with a sheet of proofs in one hand and a cigarette in the other. She looked at him, puzzled. Behind her, a wall of windows looked out on a park and let in a full volume of light from the sky.

"Hi," Michael said. "I'm with Erica. We called?"

She nodded her head in dawning recognition.

"Oh, I'm sorry. I forgot the lights."

She reached around him and flipped a switch. The warehouse behind Michael was illuminated, revealing an ordinary space filled with wooden crates.

"I'm Peggy," she said, reaching out and shaking his hand.

"Michael."

"Where's Erica?"

With the lights on, Erica was making her way through the path between the boxes, keeping one hand tentatively in front of her.

"Peggy? Are you in the smuggling business now?"

Peggy laughed. "No, I'm renting this space from an import/export business. I have an entrance on the park but it's not marked so I gave you the official address. Sorry about the lack of lighting."

She and Erica embraced and looked at each other at arm's length. They both laughed at the changes age had brought.

"Did you ever think we'd end up like this?" Erica asked.

"We used to be the hottest girls at the openings. Maybe we still are." Peggy gave Michael an appraising look. He examined the expanse of the room where Peggy had unframed prints of her photographs arrayed across the interior walls. He could see immediately how good she was, even though he didn't know much about photography. In his painting, he'd been thinking a lot about composition and he could see her work was solid on that level.

As Erica told him, Peggy had an eye and composed her images in depth as well as on the surface so the viewer was drawn in by the deep focus. Her subjects looked into her camera with unguarded expressions, as if they didn't notice the apparatus she carried in her hands. The various people weren't attractive in themselves but the experience etched into the lines and folds of their faces made them beautiful. He was impressed, he had to admit.

Peggy and Erica went over and sat down on a couch under a window looking out to the park where trees and benches had been arranged on various levels of poured concrete. He only partly paid attention to their conversation which consisted mostly of catching up on the whereabouts and, often, the deaths of those they knew from New York and Paris.

Michael walked up and down the room, examining the prints closely and enjoying what he saw. He didn't know if he should say anything to Peggy about her work but when he returned to the couch and sat down next to Erica, Peggy asked him, directly, "So what do you think?"

He blurted out, "They're great!" and blushed. Erica and Peggy laughed, making him blush even more.

"That's what we want to hear, isn't that right, Erica? I like your young man."

Erica smiled, "I suppose he has his uses."

Michael changed the subject by showing Peggy the list of sculptures whose photographs they wanted to include in the book. Most of them were in museums in New York but others were spread across the U.S. and Europe, in San Francisco, Dallas, and Miami, in Brussels, Berlin, and Milan. The publishing company had approved expenses for Peggy to travel plus money above that to compensate for her work.

"I've been in a rut here and this will break me out. Is there any particular approach you want me to take?"

Erica sat up straighter. She looked at Michael but he knew it wasn't for his input.

"Nothing fancy, just what you see. I know what you do and I feel honored you would apply that to my work."

"Erica, we both know who's being honored here. My photos aren't bad but nothing I've done approaches your sculptures. Every woman artist owes you a debt of gratitude."

Erica made a dismissive gesture with her hands.

"I didn't do them for women in particular but I'm glad people sometimes find them inspiring for their own work."

"I'll send you the proofs first before I submit them to the publishing house."

"I'd appreciate that," Erica said. "I don't want them deciding on their own about which ones they want."

Peggy laughed. "How unusual for you to have strong ideas about your work. I seem to remember you dressing down the Director of the Tate in a slightly heated discussion about which gallery he was using for your exhibit."

"A tea-drinking pipsqueak, as I remember."

"Michael, you may have experienced that Erica has a way of royally telling people off."

He shook his head in mock disagreement. "No! I never would have expected that."

Peggy served them coffee. Michael gave her the information about their publisher and who she should contact to make the travel arrangements. The conversation was winding down and Erica's eyes were half-closed as if she were about to nod off into a nap. Michael knew this was a sign they should go. Peggy showed them through the door to the park, opening through a small gate into the Square Leon Serpollet. She told them to turn right to reach the street where they could find a cab stand.

Peggy hugged Erica and turned to Michael. She hugged him as well and whispered, "I'm glad you're with her. She needed this."

"What?" Michael asked.

"To be out in the world. To have something to do. It's worth whatever you cost."

Michael was startled at what sounded like an insult. But Peggy smiled and put her hand on his cheek.

"I mean that in a good way," she said, although Michael had difficulty seeing how it could be regarded in a good way. But before he could ask her more, she was walking back to the house, turning to wave as she went.

Erica took his arm as they walked through the park.

"Isn't she splendid?"

Of course she was, he agreed, but felt very unsettled. He hadn't ever thought of himself as being bought.

61

AWAKE

With Peggy signed on for the project, they decided to take the train to Aix-en-Provence the next morning. After Erica woke up from her necessary nap, they discussed where to go for dinner. Erica wanted to make good on her promise of showing Michael the Café de Flore with its literary and artistic history, where Hemingway, Picasso, Sartre, and Simone de Beauvoir had been patrons. They went out and only had to walk a few blocks along the crowded streets. The air was warm so they sat at the outside tables of the Cafe and watched the evening activity. An accordionist added to the cliche of the scene in a pleasant way by playing "La Vie En Rose." Michael gave him all the change in his pocket which, if he judged by the gleeful twist of the musician's mustache, must have added up to a significant amount.

Every so often, passersby would do a double-take on seeing Erica but even if they recognized her, no one intruded on them. They made a dinner from the limited menu out of a large cheese plate, salads, bread, and two bottles of wine over the course of the evening. The cheese was so good that even though the dish held plenty, and Erica didn't eat much of it, on finishing the first plate, Michael had an immediate impulse to order another so he did. They talked very little as they both felt talked out.

As they sipped the wine, excellent as always, Michael sat back, watching the patrons and passersby. He tried to figure out who was a tourist and who was a local even if he couldn't hear them speak. He speculated that the French were better dressed and more comfortable with themselves but he couldn't be sure. The sophisticated-looking young man with black hair, a brown leather jacket, and tidy jeans, who was smoking a Gauloise and leaning against a lamp post, could have been from Little Rock as far as Michael knew.

While they were waiting for the waiter to notice they needed to pay the bill, a process seemingly obscure in every restaurant they patronized, the owner, who was also the chef, came out from the kitchen and greeted Erica warmly. He said in halting English that he'd been a mere waiter when she'd last been a customer but he always remembered her dignity and grace as well as the breathtaking beauty of her work. Erica glowed at the compliments and thanked him for continuing the century-long tradition of the establishment.

They returned to the hotel and went to bed in their separate rooms. Erica was happily tipsy and kissed Michael on the cheek before retiring. Michael woke up at 2 a.m., partly because of the wine, partly due to jet lag, but primarily because of a desperate sense of being lost. He looked out the window where people were still strolling in the night, mostly couples holding on to each other, returning from their evening activities. Some individual men hurried along the street, perhaps for a late night assignation, Michael speculated, while a few inebriates stumbled on the uneven pavement. He thought of looking in on Erica but didn't want to bring up the possibility of staying in her bed which he did not feel like doing right now, if ever again.

He felt strongly how alone he was on the planet. His parents had been estranged from their families and he knew he had an uncle in Delaware and an aunt in Albany but had never met them. His only contact had been to let them know of his mother's death after finding their names in her address book. He'd received perfunctory sympathy cards without any suggestion for getting together, much less their coming to New York or helping him out. He didn't mind. He accepted being shy and reaching out to others was not usually in his repertoire. Knocking on Erica's door that first day, after falling off the cliff, was the bravest social overture he'd ever made but he had to admit everything had changed because of it.

He pulled a notebook from his suitcase and started to write a few words about Erica's sculptures that he might be able to use for the book but quickly found it painful. He'd been a passable writer in high school and college but didn't believe it was something he excelled in. He wasn't sure what to say about her work. He admired the elements she combined and the audacity of her execution but, beyond that, he didn't know enough about the history of sculpture to put her work into any kind of context.

He thought of the slides of sculptures he'd seen in his Art History classes. Michelangelo's David, his Moses, and the Pieta were the ones that stood out for him, of course. He'd been most drawn to the raw power of those figures, graceful yet assertive in line and execution. He wished idly that he had a body like David's but knew he had no definition to his muscles now he wasn't doing the daily manual labor of the Ranch. He supposed he could work out but wasn't sure how to get started. He could easily buy some weights and use them in the garage but he felt fully occupied in taking care of Erica, preparing the book, and trying to save time for his painting. That was an excuse, of course, but he didn't feel the impetus to take action. Being in shape wasn't going to make any difference in his meeting interesting women. Why was he thinking of random things in the middle of the night? Maybe because he didn't know where he was going or what he was doing.

Their immediate plans were clear: they had train tickets for the morning and a place to go but he didn't know in any larger sense what his life meant or what his purpose was. When he was first with Erica, he had the sense of being on a mission, of trying to shape himself into what he thought an artist must be. Now he wasn't sure what he was doing. He was living well, and traveling, and staying amused but the days seemed empty for all that.

His parents hadn't been religious in any traditional way. For his father, poetry filled the space most people reserved for God. It was the major frustration of his father's life that his own creative powers were weak in comparison to Whitman and Dickinson, Wordsworth and Eliot. Thinking of him made Michael feel tired as that was a major unresolved relationship in his life. (Although had he been in a resolved relationship? Only the trivial ones).

He remembered his father bent over the dining room table, working on his poetry and growling when Michael tried to divert his attention. Michael would sit on the floor and lean back against his father's leg, for as long as his father would let him. The feeling of that pressure from his father's shinbone was still in Michael's spine and was somehow comforting. He moved to the bed, closed his eyes, and glided down, buffeted by occasional thought currents, into sleep.

62

TRAIN

They didn't have breakfast but went directly to the station and bought coffee and croissants from a stand. They boarded the train and traveled for the day down to Aix-en-Provence. The journey was familiar to Erica although now she could only see a glow out the windows but Michael found the ongoing views fascinating, catching a glimpse of Versailles soon after leaving Paris. He thought of the hundreds of years of history experienced by each copse of trees and each ancient house. The various wars must have washed back and forth across this countryside.

He wondered: if he'd been alive back then when the soldiers passed by, could he have hidden himself in the brush, in the forest, along a riverside, avoided the conflict around him? Maybe he would have wanted to participate if he'd been there, fought for one side or another. Hard to imagine as he had no current desire to be a soldier and fight for whatever they'd been fighting for in Vietnam. Thanks to luck or whatever ruling deities were out there, he'd been given a high draft number so he wasn't called up when he left college. He felt no sense of loss at missing the battles of his generation.

However, didn't every place on earth have a similar history of combat and violent death? He thought of what the various parts of the countryside passing by his window might have been like during the time of Nazi occupation, or in the Napoleonic era, or even earlier, under the various kings. He knew that property and military power had been the primary forces across the earth since the beginning of history so assumed there had always been the struggle between rich and poor, with those who were ruthless and wealthy always having the edge.

Michael became sleepy while looking at Erica dozing with her mouth part way open, her breath slightly moving her lips. She was becoming like a cat, sleeping half the time. The countryside gave glimpses of farms and suburban houses and the back sides of row homes. He always fantasized about living in another country and now he supposed he could. They could live in the Midi if they wanted to. But what did he want? Reviving the thought strand from the previous night, he again had to admit he wasn't sure.

What were they going to do in the Midi? He knew Erica wanted to visit the house, with all its memories, at least one more time. He wanted to see where she and Harold had made many of their sculptures, works drastically different, his in grand proportions in marble and steel, hers in intricate boxes and frames containing elements from the natural world. He knew she had works stored there and wanted to see them for himself. Some might be suitable for the book, in which case they would have to arrange for Peggy to visit the house and take photos.

Erica dozed, lulled by the rocking of the train, but always remained, to some extent, aware of what was going on around her.

Or at least so she thought. She'd made this trip hundreds of times when she and Harold were living in France. She remembered the early springs and late autumns when it was cold and gray in Paris but the sun would be blazing down in Provence. On the train, she'd wake from a nap in layers of clothing to a heat that would make her strip down to whatever she wore over her underwear. Harold would be sketching or taking photos and humming to himself, a habit she found increasingly irritating over the years. In the end, as he drank himself to death, the art work stopped and all that remained was the tuneless humming.

They had bought the Provence house together and now it was all hers and therefore Michael's as well. Although she wouldn't be able to benefit much from the visual input the house provided, she was happy to be going back in order to smell the fields and flowers and gusts of salt air from the not so far away sea. She knew her end was coming soon so everything, at least in this moment, seemed precious. She'd forget, of course, from moment to moment, that she was on the edge of abyss and would relapse into an unthinking state of grouchiness until, eventually, some moment of pure sensual experience would cause her to remember the necessity to appreciate, fiercely, all that was flowing around her.

63

PROVENCE

They arrived at the station, a bland tan building, and made their way through the waiting room out to the street where Michael was staggered by the light, pure and rich and yellow. A squat white-haired taxi driver leaned against his cab, smoking a cigar. Several other drivers approached and importuned them but Erica forged ahead toward their elder. He removed the cigar and looked closely at Erica.

"Madame Hanlon? Good to see you again. You remember me? Leon. I drove you and Mr. Harold many times."

He kissed Erica on both cheeks and shook Michael's hand, giving him an appraising look as he threw their luggage into the trunk of the cab. He stubbed out his cigar against the curb and put it in his shirt pocket, already marked by ash from previous smokes. He held the door for Erica and, after they were in, trotted around to climb in the driver's side door. The back seat, covered in ancient leather redolent of cigar smoke and sweat from years of trips, cracked under them as they sat down.

Shoving the taxi into gear, their driver launched into a rambling monologue telling them of the changes in the town, including the adultery and divorce of the Mayor, the shops that had opened and closed, the houses remodeled or sinking into decay. Looking over to Michael, Erica shrugged her shoulders to indicate she had no idea what he was talking about. Driving out of town, they gained altitude as they headed to the foothills of Mont Saint-Victoire.

The driver didn't seem to notice or care if they were listening so Michael occupied himself by looking out the window at stone walls, vineyards, ancient houses, gardens, donkeys and horses grazing, people trudging along the roads. The light was fascinating to him, with a richness he realized Cezanne had done a good job of capturing in his paintings. Michael had only brought a sketchbook and pencils so he wouldn't be able to do much in response to the color.

After steadily gaining altitude on a winding, wooded track, they arrived at the house, a two story stone structure with a balcony on the second level, presumably next to the master bedroom. The roof was of red brick tiles while masses of ivy hung from the stone walls. Small brown birds flew in and out of the leaves. Erica and Michael were greeted enthusiastically at the doorway by the housekeepers, Andre and Natalie, the elderly couple who lived in the village and came up to the house daily to care for it. The couple took turns kissing Erica on both cheeks and formally shaking Michael's hand. Andre ushered them inside and showed Erica how they had repainted the kitchen and repaired some water damage from where the roof tiles had cracked. Natalie reached out and put a hand on Michael's arm as they followed.

"We are very pleased to meet you. Erica needs someone she can rely on. She's brought some other companions to the house but..." She shook her head and made a sour face. Michael had to keep himself from smiling at how stereotypically French she looked, with her halo of frizzy gray hair and sharp vulpine features.

After the brief house tour, Andre returned to the kitchen to help Natalie prepare dinner. Erica and Michael went outside to see the garden and the mountain painted so often by Cezanne. He couldn't believe the natural force of the blunt massif rising above the tree line.

"This is incredible," Michael said, "Reminds me of New Mexico, with more water, of course, but the colors are similar, and the light! I understand Cezanne better now I've seen the actual light. Makes me think he's even more of a genius than I realized."

"I know that reaction." Erica said. "I was only thirty when Harold brought me here for the first time and I couldn't get enough. I'd leave early in the morning on a bike and be away all day, gathering whatever objects I could find that seemed to reflect the light and putting them in saddlebags to take home. I'd be up until late at night trying to assemble the pieces into something that could stand on its own. I'd sleep a few hours and start over again with the dawn. Harold was in his marble phase and he'd be out in the shed carving away at blocks of marble, trying to rival Michelangelo, a foolish ambition, of course, but he did okay with what he had. I'll take you up on the ridge tomorrow where you can see even better."

She turned and walked back to the house. Michael stood in the color and silence, feeling completely free.

That evening, Natalie made dinner for them, a fish cassoulet, and Andre served it up with as much insouciance as any Paris waiter. After dinner, Erica and Michael went out and sat on the porch. The sun had set but the sky was filled with dark clouds, tinged with rose.

For Erica, the colors were diffused in what was left of her eyesight. She felt a vast sadness about being in this house, lovely and familiar yet associated for her with pain. She wanted to explain what had happened here to Michael but was beset with doubt. What difference did it make anyway? Harold was gone and she and Michael were together even though Michael didn't know anything about decades of her life, how she came to be who she was. But who was she anyway? Words, mere sounds, seemed insufficient for the task of conveying her experience. She stood up and put out her hand to Michael who took it and led her to bed.

64

RIDGE

The next morning, Natalie came to the house before they rose and made breakfast. Michael slept in the bedroom next to Erica but they woke up at about the same time and heard each other moving through the wall. In the kitchen, they found Natalie just finishing the second of the perfect omelets she'd concocted. Michael thought he'd never tasted anything so good in his life. The eggs, butter, and milk were of a different order from any he'd had before, bursting with flavor. The coffee was strong and bitter, just as he liked it. The light from the window above the sink filled the room with a golden glow. Natalie chatted with Erica in French. Michael understood little of it but could hear in the tone of Erica's voice that she was relaxed and happy.

After breakfast, Erica told Michael it was time to show him something. They walked out to the walled garden where butterflies and hummingbirds fluttered and streaked across the glowing air. Erica held on to his arm but didn't say anything, just led him by pressures to a gap in the far end of the wall that opened on a trail winding through the trees and brush. After a hundred yards or so, the angle grew steeper and they breathed hard as they lifted their feet to the grade. Reaching a rocky section with only blue sky above it, Erica stepped carefully but confidently from one foothold to the next. Michael wondered if she remembered the contours of the path. Maybe generations of walkers had grooved the steps the way the Anasazi had defined the trails around the mesas.

They reached the crest of the ridge above the house and Michael immediately saw why she'd brought him up there. Mont Saint-Victoire was revealed in its totality directly in front of them, the blunt broad peak standing in stark contrast to the blue. Michael recognized the shape and color from multiple paintings by Cezanne he'd seen at the Museum of Modern Art and in the art books he used to pore over at the New York Public Library. He loved the paintings and he realized that love had its source in this mountain as distilled on canvas by the great artist. The air was cool against his face. He turned to Erica:

"Now I know why you lived here for so long."

She smiled. "Yes, I'd be up here daily, even when the clouds were so thick the mountain could not be seen. Even then I felt its presence. I took this to be the brother of Obsidian, some seven thousand miles away. When life with Harold was at its worst, I could hike up here and find connection with my inspiration back in New Mexico. I don't know where the magic comes from but I know it's here and I trust it with my life."

Just as he had back on the summit of Obsidian, Michael felt the sacred resonance of this place. He was grateful Erica had brought him here and hoped he could be worthy of the beauty. He also felt a darkness moving through him, flowing from a reservoir of grief that felt endless. His father's death when he was twelve and his mother's death seven years later had left him believing that a malevolent hand was ready to smash him at any moment. No matter how well he was doing, whether he was making love or making art, whether sitting in Erica's living room reading to her or standing out in the sun mixing adobe for the walls, even when nothing bad was happening or looming, he was always aware of death coming for him, as indeed it was for everyone. He had no idea how to relieve himself from what he believed to be the core truth of life, that everyone was going to die and that everyone included him.

Erica seemed to sense the darkening of his mood and pointed to the summit. "How would you paint that?"

He shook his head. "I don't know. Anything I'd do would be overshadowed by Cezanne."

She shook her head with exasperation. "To hell with Cezanne! He's dead and you're not. What do you see?"

"Okay, okay. Sheesh. I see the mountain, a jagged shape blunt against the sky. I think I would mix a single color for the slope and use brush strokes to indicate the surface features. As for the sky, I don't see a lot of variation on a day like this so I'd use a single color, blue with maybe a hint of yellow to suggest the glow."

She nodded her head as he spoke. "Just words, of course. Let's walk down to the house where I have a store of supplies. You will come back here alone to paint what you were talking about."

He shook his head. "Erica, you can't just order me to start painting."

"And why not? Isn't that what you want to do?"

"Yeah, of course, but...

"What?"

He stared up at the mountain and felt as tired as if he was trying to climb it internally. "I don't know. I have jet lag and I'm hungry again and..."

She stared up at him with her clouded eyes.

"Tell me!"

He paused, unwilling to confess the banal truth, but finally said, "I don't feel like it."

She shook her head and hands as if trying to ward off a swarm of bees. "Pathetic! Why am I with you if that's all you can come up with when faced with this mountain?"

She turned and strode down the ridge ahead of him. He felt ashamed but recalcitrant, feeling he had to assert even the passive, fearful parts of himself. He followed, staring angrily at her back, hating her for forcing him into this pathetic position yet realizing he'd chosen all of this for himself.

65

GRANTED

The evening was cool and Andre lit a fire after dinner before he left with Natalie in their little Citroen to go down to their house in the village. Michael and Erica sat in armchairs separated by a couch, staring at the fire, each unhappy with the other. Erica was drinking sherry and muttering under her breath to herself. Michael knew she was going to berate him and sat steeling himself for it. A log popping loudly in the fire seemed to be the ignition for her to start.

"What is wrong with you? The whole point of your coming to live with me was to do your work and now you refuse to do it and all you can say is that you don't want to. What does that even mean? Why don't you want to?"

He sat seething with anger but actually didn't know why. Some part of him knew she was right while another more primitive part resisted what she was saying.

"I don't know what's wrong with me. I don't even know why I'm here. I thought I was helping you but that doesn't seem to be enough. Maybe I should just leave, fly back to New York and go to Alaska, do something completely different from life at the Ranch. I have no idea what I'm doing. Maybe you should just let me alone until I find out."

She shook her head. "What's your hesitation? What's holding you back? You know you want to do art. You've said that since the day you arrived. When I was your age, I just did it, no matter whether anyone paid attention or not. Why do you resist when I've given you everything you need to work?"

Dark emotions surged through him, making him want to get up and run out into the night. He was being forced to look at parts of himself usually kept hidden and struggled to find words to express what he was feeling.

"When my mother was in her last days at Sloan-Kettering, I wanted to leave, constantly, but instead I stayed to the end. She'd been reduced to a skeleton and could barely speak. I don't remember what her last coherent words were to me because they must have happened so long before the end. Maybe something insignificant like, 'More ice chips, please.' She might have said something critical I don't remember because she couldn't look at me without wanting to change me into someone who seemed a little more functional in the world."

Michael was sitting forward on the couch, his hands clenching his knees. A bolt of pain burned behind his eyes.

"I sat for days watching her breathing gradually become slower and softer until at 4 a.m. one morning it just stopped. When she left, I was awake in a chair, listening to the Manhattan street noise. Horns were honking, people were shouting, sirens blasted through the streets, all seeming even louder because it was night. I was relieved she didn't have to remain in the body that let her down so much. I sat in the room while the nurses called various people and I had what you might call a vision of every one of us being just like she was. Death is always waiting inside us, ready to show its face at any moment and take over. We're all completely at the mercy of chance. Beauty is all around us but it's indifferent to what we want and how we feel."

Erica moved over to the couch to face him directly and spoke with great force, her pale blue eyes filmed over and watering:

"I know that. Anyone who's aware at all remembers all the time that we're walking on the edge of the grave. That's why we have to create while we're here. I wasn't a parent and you're not likely to be one at the rate you're going so all we have in the world is what we make. You're welcome to give up and live a life without any great purpose but I know the young man who dropped into my life off a cliff was looking for something beyond the latest girl and the daily routine of the pious ranchers you were living with. You wanted the real thing, to make something where nothing was before, and that's what I've given you the freedom to do. Don't worry about my sculptures. We don't have to do this damn book. I'm happy I created all those pieces but the fun was in the process and that's what I miss more than anything. You can do it and I can't and that infuriates me. You're young so you take your strength and vision for granted. I would give anything to have what you have but you want to throw it away. Don't throw it away. That's all I can say."

She sat back on the over-stuffed couch so the pillows folded around her, almost encasing her. She downed the rest of her sherry and reached forward, slamming the glass on the side table so hard Michael was surprised it didn't break. He felt flattened by the force of her will. He knew she was right but didn't think he could rise to her challenge. He felt broken inside, as if whatever creative impetus he'd carried had dissolved away in the darkness he carried inside. The pain twisted even tighter in his skull. He stood up.

"I'm sorry. If you want me to, I'll leave and never see you again. Is that what you want?"

"I don't want you to leave."

"In that case, I'll go to bed."

He left the room without her saying another word.

They stayed at the house for another week but didn't talk about painting again. One day, without telling Erica, Michael went up to the ridge with a sketchpad but found he could only doodle a bit, trying to replicate the distinct line where mountain met sky. It didn't feel like anything he could work on.

He and Erica took walks in the day, but not up to the ridge again, and in the evening talked mostly about the book and what they hoped for it. They planned out the rest of their tour, with Michael reading out loud from guide books while Erica commented on her own experiences in each city. They both knew something had changed between them. They slept apart all night, every night, and that separation continued for the rest of their days together.

They journeyed on through the major cities of Europe, touring Rome, Florence, Pisa, and Venice, continuing on to Vienna and

Berlin. The days passed like a travel documentary, seen late at night after too much to drink, flickering through cities, tourist sites, hotels, and restaurants, each seeming as evanescent as the light rising and falling upon the city streets. They would meet with museum directors and plan out the details of Erica's traveling show with final scheduling to take place in conjunction with the book being published. The directors would try to arrange receptions and parties for Erica but she would always refuse, preferring to return to their hotel rooms in whatever cities they were in.

Michael was overwhelmed in Rome and Florence with too much art and felt discouraged by the great distance from his skill to that of the painters and sculptors whose work he encountered. He loved physical Venice but saw it a noble but dying animal swarmed over and eaten by the ant-like tourists who filled the squares every day. He took to waking there early before dawn and walking the neighborhoods, crossing the bridges, exploring the narrow streets all smelling of the sea and the consequent mold, trying to have a sense of what it must have been like through most of its history until its current end-state.

Erica increasingly stayed behind at whatever hotel they were in, ordering from room service, listening to music on the portable radio he'd bought for her at a flea-market in Rome. Michael felt gloriously alone as he prowled the cities, talking infrequently because he didn't know much French, Italian, or German, sometimes striking up conversations when he heard English being spoken, usually by long-haired young nomads with backpacks.

However, he had a hard time connecting with these seemingly carefree travelers who stayed in hostels and campsites while he and Erica always stayed in one of the most expensive hotels. He would sometimes be offered a hit off a joint but when he'd tried grass back in college, he'd been plagued by incessant racing thoughts revolving around his usual themes of death and shame, so he felt little incentive to join them.

In the evening, he'd return to Erica and tell her of his day, the churches he explored, the art he contemplated, the encounters with shopkeepers and locals and other tourists. She would listen and smile but said little. After a month, they had met all the museum staff they wanted to see and Michael ran out of curiosity so he suggested they fly home, and they did.

They arrived at the house on the Ranch in the middle of the night. Michael woke up at dawn and walked out to the courtyard. Obsidian sat quietly as if the mountain had been waiting for their return. After the crowded streets and intensity of the cities they'd visited, the desert was a return to the bare basics of life: sky, land, air, the river and lake, all stripped down to their essentials. Michael felt himself loosening, taking up more space than he'd let himself have on the trip. He had an urge to go up to the roof and start painting but he still felt a blockage, an unwillingness to commit himself to art, or maybe anything.

66

HEART

November, 1978

She was in her bedroom, lying down although not asleep when he'd last checked. She'd had a series of strokes that left her voice slurred and her gait impaired. Although she was still able to walk, the strokes had devastated her, physically and emotionally. The last one had been the worst and she'd spent weeks in the hospital and a month in an expensive nursing home in Santa Fe. When he finally brought her home, Michael had settled her into her bedroom and taken a long nap himself as he'd spent many hours at her bedside, presiding over her care.

He woke in the middle of the night with a feeling of dread in his chest. He walked in the dark down the gallery and listened at her door. The light inside gleamed through the frame and he could hear her labored breathing. He called to her:

"Erica?"

"Go away," was her reply.

He opened the door and found she was sitting up in bed with the Colt in her lap, turned around toward her and aimed at her heart, both hands clasping it, two thumbs in the trigger guard. The gun rested against her nightgown, the barrel just to the left of her sternum. Her hair hung down her face, framing her nose and the inside edges of her eyes. Michael inhaled rapidly.

"I told you to go away."

She slurred her words and her mouth drooped to the left.

He walked in and sat down in the armchair by her bed.

"You don't have to do this," he said.

"Don't tell me what I should do."

"You heard what the doctor said. You'll get your speech back, maybe slowly. We can still have fun."

"Fun! I can't see and now I can't speak but you talk of fun."

"Maybe it's not much to you but it's fun for me. We still have music and I read you books and we talk about all the fools we have to deal with. Isn't that entertaining?"

"I'm a weight for you. You want to find someone young and be with her."

"Erica, we've been over this. You're not going to deprive me of my job, are you?"

This made the corner of her mouth twitch.

"What a job you have."

"We never did decide on a salary but the extras make it worthwhile. Now give me the gun."

"No. I want it near, just in case."

"This is not negotiable. I'm going to take care of it. That's the price for me staying on."

They looked at each other, Michael directly, Erica through the blur of her vision.

She said, "Sorry," but before the word had finished coming out of her mouth, he jumped onto the bed, yanking the barrel of the gun upward as she pulled the trigger. The explosion filled the room with light and sound. Bits of wood and insulation from the ceiling fell around them.

Michael firmly pried her fingers from the trigger and took the gun from her.

"You should have let me."

Michael could barely hear her.

"I couldn't do that."

"I lose everything."

"This isn't losing," he said. "I don't know what it is. Maybe just living."

She shifted herself down in the bed and turned on her side.

"Let me sleep."

Her hair and the covers around her were sprinkled with debris. Michael thought of trying to clean up but decided to return later. He switched off the light and left the room. He went out to the garage where he removed the remaining bullets from the Colt. Placing the weapon in the vice on the work bench, he twisted the handle until he could hear the barrel crack. He put the bullets in the drawer with the nuts and bolts and threw the Colt into the waste can by the door.

Erica kept a cowboy bedroll, a mattress with sheets and blankets, covered in canvas and held with straps, in a corner of the garage. He took it into Erica's room, undid the buckles, spread it out on the floor by her bed, and slept there. He continued this routine nightly for months until her depression lifted.

67

GOTHAM

January, 1982

With a sudden flare of rose-tipped wings, a pigeon plummeted in the dense air past the window of their suite in the Plaza Hotel. The pollution hung low and brown over the buildings surrounding Central Park. Too many wood fires in the penthouses, Michael thought to himself, not to mention the exhaust from the hordes of cabs on the streets below. In the winter, the air in the city was a steamy chowder almost too thick to breathe.

Erica always insisted on staying at the Plaza despite his protests that the experience was not quite worth the expense (unless one had really loved the Madeleine books as a child). Now the Museum of Modern Art was paying for their suite and room service and Erica accepted their generosity with her usual regal indifference. However, Michael suspected she was nostalgic for the times she'd stayed there with Harold more than half a century before, when Harold was receiving his first commissions and money was flowing (just before the crash of '29) and they were in what they both considered to be love. Michael often had the sense that behind the dimness of her vision she spent the great bulk of her time inwardly evoking the epochs of her history, much more compelling than the ruinous present. He had now been with Erica for more than a decade, a long time for him yet a small portion of her life span.

They had gone together to the Russian Tea Room where she'd ordered her favorite borscht while Michael had unwound from the labors of the day with two Martinis. They'd been in New York for a week so far in order to arrange a show at the Museum. Actually they didn't actually have much to do because the curator was handling everything. Erica and Michael only had to give their approval to the arrangements, although Michael was aware they had managed to make pains of themselves by getting involved in the minutia of the display process. He didn't care how the sculptures were positioned, as long as they weren't too close together, and Erica couldn't see well enough for it to make a difference to her but they both seemed to get some measure of entertainment from throwing their weight around. The Museum had wanted them to be in town for the opening so Erica could be displayed at several gala events for the wealthiest patrons (See the artist! Pony up the dough!)

The book had been a success, justifying the publishing company both in the money they paid Erica and in their significant expenses for Peggy's photographs, considered by critics to be a major asset of the project. Erica didn't want to do any television interviews to generate publicity so Michael arranged for carefully chosen print interviews, along with photos, in the New York Times, Vanity Fair, Time, and Newsweek. On the phone, they talked to the London Times, the Guardian, and Paris Match. For these media occasions, either at the larger house in the village, or in hotels when they were on the road, they would give a performance, gently kidding each other but demonstrating great respect. In fact, they were getting along better together in print than they were in real life where Michael struggled in his role as a combination caregiver, manager, and restless subordinate.

Money came in abundantly from the book and from the shows that were taking up an increasing amount of effort for Michael to arrange. Wealthy collectors were pushing up the price of Erica's work so Michael hired a new financial advisor in order to invest the money in what he hoped was the wisest way.

Despite the increasing hassle of traveling with Erica in her frail state of health, Michael felt it was worth the effort just to get away from New Mexico for awhile, to see cities, to be feted, to break up their routine. Unfortunately, he had to spend a great deal of his time in the role of gatekeeper, fending off the press and avoiding the celebrity-seeking rich who attempted to add them to dinner parties or even worse, weekends at their country estates.

They'd tried going to such events together and Michael knew Erica would invariably sit, glaring and sphinx-like, except for a few gnomic utterances that would, if they were lucky, bear some tenuous connection to the ongoing conversation. Of course, the content of what she said didn't matter to anyone because she had the gift of presence. Just being in a room, dressed severely, casting her eagle's gaze about even though she could barely see shapes, was gratifying enough for her public. He would take the opportunity to chat with the prettiest women in the room and, if he lucked out, arrange a date for later. This wasn't a bad life, he supposed, but he found himself wanting more.

He looked out to the dark trees of Central Park and the trails of footprints winding through the snow. He thought of the dusting of white they'd seen on top of Mesa Montejo and Obsidian the morning they'd left. The ranch became particularly claustrophobic in the winter when no seminars were scheduled. The year round ranch families were then the only residents and the various feuds suppressed during the busy days of summer would produce open conflicts in the cold isolation, providing a provocative but eventually tiresome diversion. He was glad to get away from the place and head out for the multifarious pleasures of New York.

In the course of this particular day, he'd arranged a date, a dinner reservation, and theatre tickets for the evening. Jeremy, a curator from the museum, had agreed to be with Erica who had declared herself uninterested in evening events. The man probably hoped to elicit revealing insights from her to use for a book or an article about her work but Michael knew he was bound to be disappointed. Despite her ongoing speech difficulties, Erica tended to converse in long rambling stories about the early days in Manhattan and Paris as if her youth could be summoned up by incantation but the stories had all been well documented. Moreover, their hotel room didn't contain much for Jeremy to snoop into because all important papers were stored back at the ranch.

Michael looked down at the people foreshortened on the sidewalks as they moved swiftly past each other with only the rare collision. The street lamps and red brake lights created a sinister Christmas bulb effect through the distortion of the glass. The sky to the north was a deep gray with subtle highlights from the mass of city lights in Harlem, Washington Heights, and the Bronx. He was struck by the contrast between the fifth floor walk-up apartment where he was raised down in the Village and the aging luxuries of the Plaza. He wondered what his mother would have made of his current position in the world and his unusual occupation of taking care of Erica. While she was still conscious, before the opiates had drowned her consciousness, his mother had looked at him with pure panic about whether he'd be able to make his way in the world. He had made his way but not by any usual method, certainly not one he could explain to his mother.

68

ILL

He heard Erica stirring in the bedroom. Thank God she was continent again. There had been periods during the previous winter, after her latest stroke, when she'd needed nursing care on a round the clock basis but she was once again ambulatory and able to make it to the bathroom. Despite how close they'd been, he did not want to have to clean her or change her. He did just about everything else but drew the line at interactions they both considered to be too difficult and too intimate. He was also thankful Erica had not again been as depressed as she was after her first cardiac events. A slightly bemused acceptance alternated with minor bursts of irritability.

His routine of rising every morning and painting for hours had ended years before. Her affairs were now his only occupation as he planned out how to maximize the profits from the exhibition and sale of her works. They'd spent a full year writing and designing the coffee table book about her sculpture, an activity Erica welcomed as an opportunity to sum up all she had to say about her way of making art. Michael had been intimately involved in recording her commentary on the pieces and checking the transcripts, believing what she had to say was important for an understanding of her work. The household checkbook became his responsibility and, in due course, he bought himself suits, a good watch, luggage, the various accoutrements befitting the companion of a great artist.

When they were home, he spent little time in the studio or up on the roof, in fact, avoided these locations, preferring to work on their finances, correspondence, or projects. She spent many hours listening to recorded books or music, and dictating long letters on tape to old friends and relatives. Michael had them typed out and mailed but many of the would-be recipients never replied because they had long ago passed into dementia or death. Where she had once been the imperious queen, she was now merely a frail and elderly lady. She was like a beloved aunt for whom he was responsible. When her temper would flare, he'd simply become silent and withhold his attention, a highly effective ploy against someone who needed him so much.

69

RENOWN

On this trip to New York, he'd been overwhelmed by their reception at the Museum. He'd been so busy promoting Erica's work, enjoying both the responsibility and the power, that he hadn't quite realized what a success they'd made of it. This success was partly, maybe primarily, due to the plan he'd worked out to arrange for more exhibitions. He'd learned of a number of petty feuds Erica had carried on over the years, with the Palace Museum in Santa Fe, with many of the wealthy art dealers in Paris, with MOMA itself. Erica had mostly forgotten how the feuds started so Michael went ahead and made the first contacts in years, leading to lucrative arrangements that tended to be profitable in direct relationship to the length of time the feuds had lasted.

He also paid close attention to which of her sculptures were shown and when. He didn't want to create a sudden glut on the market of her work and he'd arranged it quite well, he thought, given how little he knew about the art world. He'd decided from the start that it was important to be selective about what they agreed to, to open shows in cities that were far enough away from each other so as not to compete, to give interviews only to major outlets of the media under certain limited conditions. He and Erica had some powerful bargaining tools for dealing with the press and the art world: they didn't have to make money, they were absolutely indifferent to publicity, and they'd agreed to walk away from any deal at any time if it didn't suit them exactly. Paradoxically, they made massive profits with this stance and gained a substantial amount of media attention.

The contrast between New York City in the fall of 1982 and rural New Mexico couldn't have been more extreme yet he enjoyed the tightly packed abundance of urban life, its intricacy and speed. Erica, of course, had lived here in the city in her early days with Harold when he was making monumental sculptures for the skyscrapers that were going up, before he decided he wanted to do his own work and not what was dictated to him by commissions. Although Erica was primarily an artist of the natural world, she'd found a powerful subject in the booming city around her.

Erica's sculptures from this period formed their own section of the museum show and Michael had been fascinated to see them all together. During the past week, he'd come to appreciate her ability to capture the emotional resonance of a place in a way that went beyond realism. Her desert works, with their light colors and surreal juxtapositions, seemed to him to express perfectly the openness, the strangeness, and the spirituality of the high mesa country. In the city sculptures, by contrast, she'd evoked in gleaming steel the brooding and oppressive bulk, the demonic hilarity of Gotham.

As far as he was concerned, the blind and absent-minded woman in the bedroom behind him had been, at one time anyway, if not a genius, then at the very least, an artist. He had been using that as a justification for not painting his own works anymore, that he was just fumbling, not anywhere close to her greatness.

70

DATE

Michael paced around the room, feeling suddenly encumbered by the ornate and delicate furnishings. He couldn't wait to get out and become part of the energy on the streets, think about something other than Erica and her work. He simmered with anger at himself for letting his own practice of painting ebb away. He didn't believe he would ever have been great but he could have built up a body of work all his own. Instead, he lived on what he'd found in her shadow. Their confrontation in Provence had made him aware of the depth of her disappointment in him but her health problems and consequent depression had become the primary concerns and they never talked anymore about whether he was painting.

He thought of his date for the evening, a woman named Karen who was an administrator at the Museum. He'd been attracted immediately by her slim figure and air of cosmopolitan chic and they'd started talking while the show was being set up. She asked what he was doing for fun in the city and he replied that he just wanted an evening on the town. She responded that she'd be happy to go along with him. She was tall and angular, a chain-smoking Barnard graduate with a degree in Art History, the quintessential arts person in New York. They chatted about the artists showing at various galleries and what their works were selling for. He played the laconic cowboy who didn't know much about the arts scene (but knew what he liked) and she played the world-weary aesthete who found him to be a refreshing change.

He hoped the evening would end up in her bed but he wouldn't be hugely disappointed if it didn't. He'd managed to initiate a few relationships over the past years but felt that his own life, so tied to Erica's, was ebbing away with her. He still wanted to create and to be in love, but these things did not seem possible right now. He tolerated the dark emotions running through him as the living remnants of his childhood.

Once in the past decade, during an earlier visit to the East Coast, he'd visited his mother's grave in the far reaches of Queens, a plot he'd paid for with the modest insurance settlement, with enough left over to help him travel west to the Ranch. In a vast city cemetery, her small headstone was almost overgrown by grass that was missed by the mowers. He'd cleared off the front of the stone and sat cross-legged in front of it, the skyline of Manhattan in the background, a soft rain watering the acres of dead people, seeds whose flowering was purely theoretical. He knew what he owed his mother but didn't feel close to her. She'd devoted her life to raising him but they had always looked at each other with mutual bewilderment.

The only person he seemed to be close to was the old woman in the next room. Surrounded by millions of people engaged in a myriad of activities, she was the only one with a connection to him.

71

GO

He went over and knocked on her door. He heard her sharp, "Yes?" and went in. She was lying in bed on her back with her hands folded, eyes closed, in the stiff funereal pose she'd slept in ever since he'd known her. He walked over and sat on the bed.

"Erica?"

No answer.

"Are you awake?"

"That's a funny question. What if I said no?"

"Then you'd be asleep."

She laughed. He was glad she was lucid for the moment as that was becoming less often the case. He missed the days when they could tease each other like brother and sister, before the fog of confusion had infiltrated her brain.

"Were you able to sleep at all?" he asked.

"I was listening to sounds: engines and horns and that electric hum underneath everything. It's pretty much the same as when I lived here in the thirties. Most of all I love to hear trains everywhere, the clash of couplings as the cars start to move, whistles blowing, engines slowly gaining speed."

"I haven't heard any trains."

"I have. Maybe I was hearing them from under Grand Central Station or from way out in New Jersey. The Hudson can carry sounds right across the water, all kinds of sounds, dogs barking, even people coughing."

"That's interesting."

"I know you don't believe me but it's true."

"Of course I believe you."

"I always know when you're humoring the old woman. But go ahead. I'd rather be humored than ignored."

He smoothed out the covers on the bed around her.

"And when do I ignore you?"

"You're always ignoring me."

"Bullshit."

"A touch of the coarse to divert my attention. I'm glad I'm thinking clearly right now because I haven't always been present in recent days. I've been wanting to say things to you and sometimes I thought I had but later I knew I hadn't. Sometimes the words formed in my head but my mouth wouldn't work to say them."

"You don't have to say anything."

"Don't worry. I won't tell you how I feel about you but I will say I'm sorry things turned out this way. I was completely selfish and my only excuse is that I couldn't help myself."

"Maybe you are out of it. This isn't making too much sense."

"Don't condescend to me!"

She barked this out at him with the assertive energy she used to have. He sat up straighter and thought of how to get out of there.

"I know I'm dying and you know it, too. My body might hang on for awhile but the self that used to do all the art work has almost faded away."

"Erica, you're doing fine. Maybe you're a little tired but your mind is clear."

"I'm going to ignore that because it's so *clearly* untrue."

She pulled herself up to a sitting position, stuffing the pillows behind her back. She turned her chin toward him.

"Would you let me touch your face?"

Michael sighed but moved over closer to her. Her long fingers moved up, grabbed his chin, and played gently across his features, smoothing his face out from his nose to his ears.

"I want to let you go. When I don't come back anymore from these spells, find a good nursing home and put me away. I should have cut you loose before you were caught up in the Erica Hanlon industry, something I always avoided myself. That was my mistake, to keep you as my assistant, to let you stop painting."

"Everything that's happened has been of my own free will. You didn't make any mistakes."

He began to get up to leave. She reached over and grabbed his arm to prevent his departure.

"It's not too late. You can still do your painting. You don't have to set up these shows and write the catalogue notes and date these silly girls. Of course, I know about that, and realize it's something you have to do. Better, though, that you find someone you can trust, and live with, and have children by."

Michael stood up, sharply pulling his arm away from her, and walked over to the windows. The view was to the east looking toward Queens and Long Island, revealing lengthy angles of complex structures between the closer buildings and bridges. Beyond, clouds hung low over the length of land stretching out to the Atlantic. He thrust his hands in his pockets and marched back and forth between the two windows as he spoke.

"The problem is I don't believe I've ever had what you've had. Caring for your work is not a bad life. At least I respect what you've done and believe it should go out to the world."

Erica spread her fingers on the comforter. As the room grew deeper in shadow, the lights from outside seemed more insistent.

"You don't yet know about yourself. You don't know what you're capable of because you haven't really tried. We're different people. My work is not your work so you can't compare. All I know is that I'm about to end my life while yours hasn't really started. Most of what I have goes to you and a little to the scheming relatives to keep them off your trail. You won't have to work after I'm gone and my only request is that you keep painting, with or without a teacher. Just keep daubing paint on canvas."

He looked out at the staccato parades of light moving through the streets and felt completely empty, as if he'd been drained of anything to call his own.

"I don't feel very inspired. We all have dreams but few people are able to fulfill them. You're one of the few who's done it, who's gone your own way."

"You sound like a publicist now. It wasn't like that. I didn't know for sure where I was going. All I had was the work and I kept working even though it wasn't clear where it would take me. When I was teaching school in the woods of Maine or when I was waitressing in Greenwich Village, and stealing time to make sculptures, do you think I knew all this would come about, that I'd become this institution, this word in people's mouths? No. I was just as confused as you are but I've always held on to one thing. Do you want to know the secret? The awful mysterious truth that everyone wants to know? The secret I've told you about before but you didn't listen?"

He stared at her. She hadn't talked so much in years.

"The secret is that the work is all that matters, not what people say to you about it, and not what it brings you, except if it allows you to do more work. The young always have fantasies that their art will make them rich and win prizes and attract lovers, but those things turn out to be ashes blowing across the desert. All you really have is the work, so you wake up and do it every day, whether you want to or not, whether the checks roll in or not, and you engage with what you're looking at, the nature that's in front of you, whether you're facing the most beautiful mesa or the dullest rock. That piece of reality is your window to the divine, and that's all I can say about it in words. I don't know how it works if you're a writer or a musician or whatever the hell else there is to do in the arts these days, but I do know about what I've done for seven decades, and I know the work is the way in to the center of everything. Do you hear what I'm saying?"

He didn't reply, just stood looking down at the floor, a vast thickness inside his head. She continued:

"I can't tell right now which of your many silences this is. Is this the silence when you're in the room but you're not listening, or is it your silence when I'm getting through to you but you're still not listening, or could be it possibly be the silence when you actually are listening?"

Silence.

He cleared his throat, went to the window and put his hand on the latch, feeling the cold metal. Below were the same smeared lights and dark human ants as before. Had a star ever propelled its light into this room? Had a baby ever cried? Had someone died? Of course, at one point, everything had happened, perhaps even a plague of locusts, because time and its ongoing reality held out the possibility for anything. Everything.

"Yeah," he said finally.

"And what does 'yeah' mean?" She supported herself on one elbow in bed to look at him.

"You're right. I can feel it. I do need to work. This is just a sideshow, isn't it?"

"It's been a good sideshow. We've been able to see some sights and meet some people but it didn't mean very much, did it?"

"No, not really."

"So maybe you needed to get it out of your system."

"Maybe."

"Let's go back. The desert is always waiting."

"We have to stay for the opening."

"No, we don't. We don't have to do anything. We could say I was sick, or we could pretend to have a fight with one of these curators, or we could just say nothing and leave. That would certainly add to my mystique, wouldn't it?"

"I like the just leaving idea, except I'd be the one who would have to deal with all the nasty phone calls and correspondence."

"So you still care what people think about you."

"That's true. I must care or I wouldn't worry about the things I worry about."

"So let's go."

"We only have four days until the opening and they're paying for all this."

"As if I give a fig that they are. The luxury of the Plaza doesn't mean much to a blind woman. The only thing I'm grateful for here is that we're up high enough that the exhaust smell is minimal. Otherwise we might as well be at a motel in New Jersey."

"That's what I've always thought."

"I miss Obsidian."

72

FAR

Michael thought about her proposal as he looked out at the lurid red sky over Queens. He couldn't see any negative financial repercussions to going. Their stock in the collecting world wouldn't go down any. People expected artists to be eccentric. This was the same place that showed Pollack, Rothko, and Warhol, not to mention Van Gogh, bless his tortured soul. Michael wondered if he wanted to stay because he hoped to get laid while they were in town? Maybe. But he was held back by something even sillier, the fact he'd arranged everything and had allowed his ego to become entwined in the success of the exhibition.

His modest skill at organizing shows was the only career accomplishment of his life and he didn't want to throw it away just because he had some dream about art. Erica was right, he was sure of it, that the work was all that counted but he still felt the need to make himself known in the world, even though any renown he achieved was always based on his relationship with her. It didn't make sense, of course, but there it was.

He turned to her.

"I'd like to stay for this one last show, and then we can go back."

"You're afraid."

"That's not really it but whatever."

"We can stay if you want. Why don't you come and sit beside me?"

"I have to go out. I have an appointment."

"She won't be ready on time. You know that."

He looked at her. He always assumed these days that she didn't know anything about what was going on but repeatedly she proved him wrong. He went over and sat beside her on the bed. She put her hand on his forearm, this time in a friendly fashion.

"You've done a good job," she said.

"You think so?"

"Oh, yes, I do indeed. Before you came along I went through assistants like they were toilet paper, an inelegant comparison, I admit, but an apt one because that's how I used them. You never let me shit on you, did you?"

He laughed. "No, I guess I didn't."

"You've done a good job promoting my work but now it's time to do yours."

"After the opening."

"As you know, I believe one should follow through on what one's begun. You were painting before you began to manage my affairs so don't let it go."

"I have to get ready now."

She pulled his hand to her and kissed the back of it. He didn't shrink away but he didn't move closer as he would have before. She seemed to read his thoughts.

"I'd ask for a real kiss but that might be going too far."

"I was just thinking that those days have passed."

"I know. I won't insist."

He leaned over and patted her shoulder. She pushed him away.

"Just leave," she said abruptly.

"I'll look in on you when I come home. Are you going to get up when Jeremy comes?"

"I suppose. I'll have to think of more lies to tell him about my career. If he really is writing a book about me, it will be funny to find all my tall tales in it."

"I wouldn't mind seeing his ego trimmed."

"I'm sure you'll have fun."

"I'll try."

"Goodnight, Michael."

"Goodnight, Erica."

He left the room.

73

BREAKING

Later that night, after Jeremy, who fancied himself an expert in her work at the Museum, finished pestering her with boring questions and finally departed, after she clumsily made her ablutions in the unfamiliar bathroom and put herself to bed, she lay awake, tired but with her mind as restless as a hungry coyote. Something about being back in New York made her agitated, caused an ache in her heart as it hid, fearful, deep in her chest cave. The surgeons had pierced it and put in bits of plastic but it was still her own, still the engine for her blood and creativity.

She thought of the early days when she was going to art school in the Village and had first fallen under Harold's influence as he sculpted her nude form into great marble slabs to be displayed to pedestrians in the lobbies and passageways of the city. She remembered how safe New York felt in the early twenties, how she'd walk by herself without fear all around the West Side, Central Park, and Midtown. Now in 1982 she could sense the desperate poor and the agitated hustlers all around when she and Michael made their way through the streets. Voices emerged from alleys and rose up from sidewalks, supplicating for cash. The poor had always been in the city, of course but somehow had never seemed this urgent.

They'd given her medications for pain after her cardiac events and the pills reminded her she'd smoked opium in Paris in the thirties, because Harold thought it would be fun. She didn't see what the attraction was in that dreamy blunting of the senses. She liked to see clearly and to work with awareness. Opiates were just barriers in the way of making art. Life provided enough obstacles without any added assistance.

So here she was in New York City sixty years later, with no focus whatsoever. She knew she was going to die soon, no doubt about that. She could feel her internal systems breaking down, the blood more reluctant every day to push its way through her flesh but she didn't feel any sadness about the inevitable conclusion to this process. She had done just about everything she'd wanted to do except for having a baby. At least through Michael, she had one link to life ongoing, but only one because she didn't much care for her few actual relatives who remained alive.

With her strokes, heart by-passes, and suicidal depression, death had hovered close but she knew nothing about what the ending would be. Maybe it was indeed nothing: annihilation, the unthinkable, the void. She couldn't go back to her childhood in the Dutch Reformed Church for answers because she didn't believe in its harsh mythology. If an eternity of torment was the price for making love, she was doomed but she couldn't see the Universe or the One or the great Whatever as so lacking in a sense of humor. Sex was hilarious, for the most part, and she had laughed a lot in her life. All she really wanted from the afterlife was to somehow keep doing art and her fantasy was that after her death she'd once again be able to see and keep working. She imagined a heaven set up as an artist's colony with a population of one, herself, not wanting to be jostled by all the other paint-stained strivers.

74

SEE

She'd always known in her life as a sculptor that she'd been a mere apprentice to the real artist: the divine presence in nature. Someone was constantly making art of the highest quality everywhere, all the time, and what she did in her work was respond to that busy non-body. Responding had actually been easy once she learned to trust herself. That was part of what she was trying to tell Michael but hadn't been able to get across, something about trusting himself. But that wasn't quite it either. She wanted to tell him about a way of standing, as she'd stood facing the world from whatever vantage point she'd had, taking in aspects of reality to recombine into something else, a stance approaching nature as her equal, albeit an equal possessing infinite beauty.

Or maybe she wanted to convey a way of seeing, seeing what was really in front of her. This, she thought, she had tried to teach him, and he seemed to have started learning although now she wasn't sure the lesson had stuck. One had to let the eyes function without interference from thought or memory or anticipation. If you could just see in this undistilled way, you were already halfway toward making something good.

One could learn technique but maybe it was more a way of being in the world that mattered. She had known something about that. She had never been so filled with fear that she couldn't go forward. Even when she'd been intimidated, as a student, or as Harold's consort, or by being on her own, she had always chosen to go her own way and that was what had mattered in the end. She had never really loved anyone more than herself because she feared having to follow somebody else's way instead of her own.

So here she was, lying blind and physically weak on a soft bed in an expensive hotel in New York City. This was what her life had come down to. She was alone, as she always was, and that was okay. Although the passion with Michael had ended, their connection survived and meant far more to her than the sex, although that had been a wonderful surprise at the end of her life. She cared for Michael and, perversely enough, she cared for him like a son.

They had ended up together, and that was an anomaly, certainly by New Mexico's standards, if not by standards everywhere. She'd never worried about what her neighbors thought although, given their reactions, they definitely seemed to find the relationship offensive. The mindless disapproval obviously bothered Michael but, because she had gone her own way for most of her life, she was used to isolation and opprobrium. She knew compromise might buy her some momentary peace but being relentless in doing what she wanted was the only strategy that had ever made her happy. This ferocity of intent was what she had not been able to teach Michael, to her sorrow and to his detriment.

75

INHERIT

The noises of the city drifted up to her: the low thrum of car engines, the intermittent punctuation of horns, the flutter of wings as pigeons settled and resettled on the ledges of the ornate building. She noticed another sound vibrating deep within her bones. Maybe it emanated from the trains she'd described to Michael, or the subway, or the collective resonance of all the machinery on this island, but the sound seemed very intimate, vibrating inside her bones. Maybe she was hearing the movement of Being inside her.

As she grew older, she seemed to edge ever closer to the bare essence of what it meant to be alive. This essence, this reality, was within her skin, and must live inside everyone if it lived at all. She could feel it as a constant awareness underlying all her thoughts, an awareness with which she was only intermittently in touch. This moment held the rustle of the sheets on her skin, the scratch of the pillow edging against her cheek, the rise and fall of the breath inside the brittle frame of her rib cage, the pulsar of pain inside her heart. What was at the root of these sensations?

She was definitely moving closer to whatever it was and she felt the fear receding. She'd experienced a great deal of pain in her body for a long time so the pain itself didn't scare her anymore although she was looking forward to its cessation. What she really wanted was to leave something positive for Michael. He was the one who had sacrificed because she had manipulated his innate weakness against him. Now she wanted him to discover his own path and not just snuffle around hers. That he should find his way was important to her but she knew she couldn't force him, or anyone, for that matter, to be courageous. She could point him in the direction but it was one of those things that was only possible from within, not from without.

From another perspective, it really didn't matter anyway. Either he would find his way or he wouldn't. Despite all the agonizing choices, she intuited something fated about each life's path. But she cared about him, and what happened to him, and that was the truth of it. She had indulged herself by connecting with him and their liaison had stirred up a vast reservoir of feelings.

In her will, she had left him most of her money but she struggled with intermittent regrets about that choice. Maybe she should have left him just the house at the Ranch and enough money to survive on but not enough to squander. Maybe instead of giving him money, she should have opened an account at an art supply store with an unlimited balance. However, if he acquired a cocaine habit or some other pernicious influence (such as a predatory female), he could still sell his supplies cheap and waste resources that way. But he didn't seem to have an addictive personality, despite his evening drinks. His problem was that he was highly dependent on her despite thinking of himself as such a free spirit.

His inheritance had all been arranged with her attorney on one of the rare occasions when she'd managed to leave Michael at the movies for a couple of hours in Santa Fe. He often complained he couldn't get any time away from her but the reverse was true as well. She had never in her life had anyone around as much as Michael was around. She didn't know what would happen to him when she no longer needed care. He could use her money to destroy himself if he wanted to, but even poverty was no barrier to that, nor was a middle-class income. In truth, she wanted to indulge him, based on her memory of their passion. The details of sex were not the crucial element. What she held close was the intimate warmth with him that had dissolved into her bones and redeemed the last decade.

76

GAS

As these thoughts drifted through her mind, she felt a heaviness expanding outward from her chest to her arms and legs and head. She wanted to escape from the confinement of her blind aged body, which brought her the claustrophobic image of Prometheus bound to the rock. What she hoped for from an afterlife was to be freed from the chains on the barren rock that was now her life. She imagined the popping of the tiny balloon of her individual ego leading to the escape of its air into the eternal gas surrounding it. She laughed at this thought of the eternal gas, not a very respectful image for the divine but being respectful was never the strongest element of her personality.

She wasn't afraid of pure annihilation, if that's what had to happen. She just wanted release from the paradoxical burden of losing her art while becoming a celebrity, a supposedly important person who could no longer function. She feared the dark and narrow, the possibility her present blindness would extend into infinity, imposed upon her agonized awareness. But, of course, she didn't know anything about what waited for her. The world, if any, beyond this brief flash of light of her awareness was the great mystery.

From somewhere down the hall came the whirring of the elevators, vertically penetrating the vast rambling box of the hotel, carrying guests to and from the myriad experiences of their rooms. A service cart creaked as it passed down the hall. The heating vent sighed to itself. The darkness around her head held colors, swirling flickers of pigment dancing before her eyes, and that was a relief. Her vision all day long was of various degrees of deep gray so the colors of falling asleep were especially compelling.

She also saw little men, as she often did, hypnagogic figures dancing, gremlin-like, through the room around her. She welcomed them and they bowed and saluted her with flourishes. She laughed at them and they laughed right back, supporting huge bellies with their hands. The only distinct creatures she ever saw anymore, outside of her memories and dreams, were these strange figures at the very edge of her consciousness. As the impending sleep settled down into her marrow, they faded away.

77

CASEMENT

Just as she was about to fall deeply asleep, her mind conjured up a piece of music heard long ago, a skirl of bagpipes in the Edinburgh castle. Funny she should remember that because it wasn't a remarkable or even a pleasant trip. She and Harold had become bored during a stay in London, something about a commission not working out, so they bought tickets for the Night Scotsman and headed north. Instead of sleeping, they argued for hours in the dark in their compartment where they tried to share a single berth. The rocking of the train repeatedly jostled them into one another, increasing their mutual irritation. She could no longer remember what it was all about except that as soon as one of them fell asleep, the other would wake up the sleeper to continue the fight. They were exhausted the next morning when they arrived in the drafty booming station. They checked in to a noisy and ordinary hotel nearby and slept for a few fitful hours. Bleary-eyed and disoriented, they went to a café for tea and watched through the window as the rain poured down.

In the afternoon, after they spent some exhausted hours wandering in their trench coats through used book stores, the rain receded to a fine mist so they dutifully trudged along the mile of ridge between the palace and the castle. She forgot what they called the walk, the Magic Mile, maybe? The Royal Mile? Probably. After they entered the castle, they heard a bagpipe echoing through the stone corridors and vaults. She remembered feeling tired and irritated and wishing she were with someone else. She walked away from him to a window and looked through the narrow aperture down upon the red tile roofs and congested traffic of the city. She was thinking something at the time, some banal thought about the minimal importance of a single life set against the billions of people in the world.

Now here it was, the reason this had come up. She had thought in that musty chamber of how important a single life would be if it were her child's life, if she could have a child. She turned and stared at Harold who was frowning over some densely typed pamphlet. He liked to show off his knowledge of history by criticizing trivial details presented as fact to tourists. She looked at him and realized he would never want more children so she would have to trick him in order to become pregnant, and she wouldn't do that.

In that moment, she knew she was never going to have a baby and that loss filled her with grief and fear. She didn't want to cry but the tears fell anyway. The chilly air flowing through the window pulled at her blouse, trying to draw her forward to jump, to end the pain and any possibility of joy by plummeting to the cobblestones below. To resist the temptation, she raked the back of her hand along the rough stone edge of the window casement until it drew blood. She turned, supporting the bloody right hand with her left, and brought it up to Harold as if it were a crippled bird she'd found on the street.

She laughed to think of herself then, so young and so emotional. Harold became solicitous, as she'd wanted, but to her embarrassment directed anger at a bewildered guard, yelling about the unsafe conditions. Harold insisted she see a doctor who turned out to be a grimy old man smelling of cigars who slapped on a dash of antiseptic, topped it off with a bandage and, after receiving his payment, pointed out they could have performed this simple bit of treatment for themselves at a druggist, precipitating another bellow from Harold. The sound of bagpipes was associated for her with that moment when she felt the loss of potential for creating new life. She returned from that lost day in Scotland to the hotel room and the self she'd been carrying for eight decades over the surface of the planet. She realized she'd attempted to compensate for the loss she felt that day by creating in another realm that sometimes sufficed.

78

PARK

These emotions going back so long ago woke her up and agitated her. She fantasized about putting on her clothes, walking down the hall to the elevator and pressing the button, pretending for the sake of any passersby that she had the ability to see. Downstairs, she'd march through the lobby she remembered clearly from her decades of patronage to the establishment, trusting no new impediments had been placed in the twenty years since the last time she could see clearly. She'd find her way out by following the rush of air and traffic noise from the brass revolving doors. She'd go through them and free herself to the New York night, gliding down the stairs, her hand lightly brushing the railing. A left turn would lead to the corner with its traffic light. At the curb, she'd listen for the sounds of passing engines, breathe in the exhaust as if it were perfume, and step out to cross the street when, aided by the decreased traffic at this late hour, she'd sense the cars had stopped.

On the other side, cobblestones were embedded in the sidewalks so she'd have to be careful about where she stepped in order not to turn an ankle. Straight ahead, at some distance she couldn't quite visualize, would be the stone wall marking the edge of Central Park. She'd place her hand on the rough surface, a distant relation of the stone wall on which she'd cut herself in Edinburgh. Keeping her fingers lightly on the stone, she'd walk to the entrance of the park and down the stairs into a darkness so deep it would brush against her skin.

She'd pretend to be a stroller in the city out for air after a late night. She didn't know what she'd encounter there, a mugging, perhaps, or a rough embrace, or simply a walk in the dark, the shadows rushing to greet the corresponding shadows in her eyes. She'd wander through the night, her hands held up lightly in front of her, her feet following the contour of the pavement, and go where she was led, just as she'd done throughout her life.

This imagined walk in the night felt like a preview of where she would soon be going. An image from somewhere in Nabokov's writings came to her: she'd soon step out of the room where she'd lived her life, a room full of lovely and delightful and terrifying things but a room whose doors and windows were always sealed. She'd spent all of her days in that room, constructing art and judgments, worrying and making love, resisting and giving in, interacting with her fellow inhabitants of the room, but at her final breath the sealed door would finally open and she'd step outside to see what the real world held.

And then what joy she would have (she hoped), like being on the rocky coast of Maine in Acadia National Park where her family camped when she was a little girl. She remembered waking up in the canvas tent just as the night sky turned toward blue. As her parents and brother and sister slept, she quietly dressed herself, putting on sneakers before pulling a rough sweater knitted by her mother over her blue pajamas. Shivering in the cold of dawn, she ran down the path to the bluff above the ocean to watch the sun come up. Just as the first rim of light appeared, a gold spread across the waters, richer than any color she'd ever seen, before or since. The surface of the waters became precious beyond any earthly measuring and the power of the sun bursting into the atmosphere evoked the power of being that keeps this infinitely intricate show going on, new in every moment. Even as a child, she knew while she stood there, alone on the sea cliff, that she would have to do something in life to speak back to this golden presence.

79

THREE

And now physically in the room in New York City, she found she was in three places at once. She was wandering blindly through Central Park, risking whatever the darkness wanted to do to her, unable to see the towers of the wealthy rising above. She was standing as a girl back on that cliff in Acadia looking out at the brilliance of the rising sun, and she was also lying flat on her back in the Plaza, wrapped in silk sheets, her heart reducing by the moment the amount of blood pumping through it.

She was held, as she had always been, by imagination, by memory, and by what passed for reality. Her current decaying form held both the darkness and the light, the old blind woman with her creativity at an end and the young girl with infinite possibility facing the rise of day. She knew these seemingly disparate selves would soon unite somehow, the darkness leading her back to the light, just as the light had led her to this darkness.

A storm began to rush through her, its clouds moving fast to obliterate the moon, the winds ripping away her thoughts, the rain slapping straight into her face. She knew she should let go and submit. Best to die rather than lie here and imagine Michael having sex with that museum woman who was probably even bonier than she was. She laughed. She still had enough juice inside her to become jealous but it didn't matter anymore. All would soon be taken away. The storm that had blown her into life was going to blow her out again. Her struggles and pleasures and griefs and joys would be flung away in a tornado of piñon nuts whirled up from the sand to be scattered throughout the desert. A fine mesh was being thrown over her nerve endings, preventing them from sending any messages requiring her to cry out.

She heard music coming from somewhere. The intricate patterns reminded her of Bach's Goldberg variations but she couldn't tell if the notes were arising inside her brain or from somewhere in the hotel. She remembered going to a concert hall in Marseilles with Harold and making their way through the rustling crowd to their seats. The rug beneath them was a dirty maroon littered with bits of peanut shell and the curtains were greasy gilt but they opened to reveal an orchestra whose music was so beautiful she wanted it to last forever. Bach definitely wasn't playing at the time. Maybe it was something piercing and romantic like Tchaikovsky's violin concerto but she wasn't sure. She remembered holding Harold's hand and feeling how heavy and dry it was, like a block of wood, while her own was so fidgety and sweaty.

80

MOUNTAIN

Scarlet sparks flared across her vision as if the rods and cones in her retinas were being unnaturally stimulated. She remembered one summer when she climbed Obsidian with a few artist friends visiting from back east. The afternoon was as hot as a kiln while they made the ascent. When they reached the summit, they were exhausted and barely had the energy to crawl into the shade behind some bushes where they fell asleep only to wake and find themselves completely surrounded by the deep red of a sunset so intense it looked like the world had finally decided to end itself in fire.

And what did that have to do with anything? She didn't know. She just enjoyed thinking of that endless view from the top of her mountain, the rising cool of the evening air in stark contrast to the flaming clouds all around them. She remembered as well the stars bending down to sear her dreaming forehead as she slept in her sleeping bag on the summit that night.

She thought of the apocalyptic storm she and Michael danced through, and she remembered the various sculptures she'd made, of every material she could think of, based on all the sensory impressions she'd had about that peak. Obsidian was the home of the Gods and it was her mountain as well, her own private world she'd created by being the single person who had looked at it with the greatest intensity. Now she was about to enter the realm of the Gods and she would finally know (or not, as the case might be) just what was going on.

She became aware of sharp repetitive pains in her chest and down her left arm even as she struggled to remain separate from the protests of her body breaking down. The problem (and it was a big one) was that she could feel herself imploding, a grinding, chaotic, nasty feeling, not at all peaceful, although peace existed within her. Some part of her sat on a hillside watching the city of her body being pillaged and burned. She felt some regret about the city, having grown up there and lived within its confines for so long, but she was far more interested in other matters, in the infinite sky above the flaming buildings, the ocean throwing waves at the shore, the vast countryside spread across the earth beyond.

In her head was a panoply of color, a pressured music, a sinuous flow of images from memory. All she wanted to do was lie back and watch the show inside her mind. Although the living would never believe it, she was coming to the belief that dying was much worse for everyone around than it was for the person dying. In her case, she didn't mind, or maybe not very much. In truth, she was ambivalent, but she was curious and wondered what it would be like, who she would meet, whether she would be conscious at all.

81

FACE

She'd always had the intimation that nature was merely a shadow of the excellence that lay beyond. She found that any small segment of nature was far superior to the best of her own art work. She remembered Michael had read her an article about an installation piece by an artist who'd made a structure with an opening in its roof. You took a seat along the edge of the room, a seat angled back so you could look up at a framed segment of sky. To her this sounded like the ultimate work of art. Her life had been aimed at attempting to make something even remotely as beautiful as the sky above her. Certain people said she'd succeeded but she didn't think so. In death she would pass into nature, and thereby become an integral part of the art she'd always wanted to create.

But she also was afraid that instead of being absorbed into beauty, she'd be swallowed up by darkness and pain. This fear was present even though she knew with all her intellect and believed with the fierce conviction of her soul that something fine was in and beyond this reality, something vastly powerful whose face was veiled by nature. Soon she would see that face but she didn't have any questions to ask when they finally met. She didn't want any special favors. What she'd always wanted was the big picture, the ultimate perspective on everything going on, along with all that had been, all that would be. Was she asking too much? Well, yes, of course she was. But only a cosmic perspective would provide adequate recompense for the enormous burden, the heartrending ecstasy, the proliferating sorrows of living a life.

A line of painful incandescence throbbed inside her chest. She couldn't think anymore or understand why she was here, who she had been. All she knew was that she was present and tired and waiting to go home to a place she'd never visited. An odd saying popped in her mind, from some spiritual reading she'd done long ago: "The one who brought me here has to take me home."

She wanted her mother to come and take her in her arms and carry her to bed. She remembered the old farm house where they'd lived when she was little and how the windows would freeze in lovely patterns. How cold it would be when she first climbed into bed and scissored her legs rapidly to warm up the sheets.

82

CAT

And she remembered a cat named Felix at the farm, a huge ungainly thing with unkempt hair who would waddle around the place coexisting peacefully with the dogs and livestock, as well as the rats and raccoons. She would curl up with Felix beside the fire on winter nights and the two of them would stare into the shifting shapes for hours as she whispered into his ears all she would do with her life. When Felix became so sick he could barely walk, peeing wherever he lay on the floor, her father talked at dinner about putting him down the next day. She cried for a long time, tears splashing on her mashed potatoes, until her father told her abruptly to stop it or he'd smack her.

She later sat down with Felix by the fire and told him he was about to be killed and how much she loved him and how he was free to leave if he so desired. Some hours later, before she went to bed, Felix stood painfully, limped to the door, and cried to go outside, something he hadn't done for weeks. She opened the door and Felix disappeared in the night, never to be seen again.

Too bad, she thought, that she herself couldn't go that way, simply walk off into the desert, her beloved red hills, and die out there without all this pointless commotion. Too bad it had to happen in this expensive hotel in a huge brutal city with no one who loved her nearby. No one, especially herself, should have to die. An option should exist whereby one could simply transfer to another body and go on, to make more art, to make more love, to use the wisdom so painfully accumulated. But she also felt grateful she'd been given so much, that astonishing amounts of the world had passed by her and through her.

She had been given the greatest gift a human could receive, the intimation of what it was like to be the central creative force at the center of all. Her sculptures, as imperfect as they were, at least indicated her vision that this world was constantly being created, that creation hadn't been a one time event back on the Bible's third day, or at the Big Bang, or when the earth finally cooled enough to support the first stirrings of life.

Creation was happening now, instantly, without a doubt, as she struggled to suck breath into her crushed chest. Right now she could feel that someone or something was bringing her decaying body and its dying heart out of nothing into this very moment, even though she was about to return to nothing.

83

FLIGHT

Birds dipping their wings outside, plaster beneath paint, rain slanting against the frozen invisibility of windows, these were miracles as potent as water into wine, Lazarus from the tomb, the resurrection itself, because in each moment the dying world was being brought back to life by some loving will. What kept everything from flying off into its component molecules and atoms and quarks and charms? Whatever it was, she had followed it faithfully, even in her darkest moments, even in her despair, even in the wasted time (and she had wasted less than most people), but especially in her art and in the loves she indulged, and in her awareness as she took in, every day, the world around her with its movements of sky and clouds and water and desert.

And now her time had come at last. She felt a vast tearing at her center followed by a whirlwind of commotion. She hoped no one tried to save her because she didn't want to stay. She wanted to go now, to change, to step outside the room. Huge locks were being unfastened from their hasps. A sound like all the orchestras in the world playing all of Beethoven's pieces simultaneously filled her mind. Everything was vibrating as particles of matter surged around her in kaleidoscopic patterns. Her atoms began to shake so intensely that they separated out, tearing apart the very fiber of her being. She was going now and all was lost, all was found, all was disintegrating. All was love in its most devastating and unthinkable manifestation.

84

ALONE

On his return from New York, Michael found a German news crew in front of the Chamisa house, using it for background while a striking blond woman spoke intently into her microphone. He heard the words, "Erica Hanlon" in the midst of bursts of Deutsch. A camera on a boom had been lifted above the wall to send images of the house out across the globe. As he unlocked the gate, the woman dashed toward Michael, her hair bouncing in a solid mass as she ran. He thought for a moment of allowing himself to be interviewed, distracted as he was by the reflections from her head and the Teutonic prominence of her bosom. Instead, he abruptly waved her off and drove through the gate, stepping out to close it on the crew who grabbed a few seconds of footage. Michael hoped they enjoyed looking at his face in Hamburg.

After taking his and Erica's luggage inside, he sat in the living room and looked out to the garden, a study in cactus, sage, and desert rose. He'd been alone in the house before, of course, when Erica was in the hospital for her various procedures over the past years. When released, she spent most of her hours in the bedroom, cared for by the nurses he hired to come up in shifts from San Juan and Santa Fe. He read to her and brought her the gossip from the

Ranch and the village. As reclusive as they both were, they always shared an interest in the follies of their neighbors.

Now he sat on the couch watching the dust motes, stirred up by his arrival and floating in the strong light, as visible as snow. During the flight, he'd made a list of the various things he had to do, the people to call and letters to write. The most important task was to take Erica's ashes to the top of Obsidian but he didn't feel in any hurry to do that. After the brief service at the funeral home in Manhattan, he stayed as her casket was conveyed into the furnace. Outside, he watched the white smoke rise to join the vapors of the city sky. He missed her now but not as she'd been for the past several years. He missed the woman he'd first met on the day of his precipitous descent from the mesa.

He didn't know anything about an after-life but hoped that somehow, somewhere, she was in a place where her eyes could see clearly, where the landscape was as intricate and as lovely as the earth around her houses at the Ranch and in Provence. He remembered her striding ahead of him on the trails in their early days together, moving relentlessly through the terrain she knew better than anyone and he thought of all the hours he spent breathlessly trying to keep up. His current sadness, standing on the shoulders of all his other sorrow, threatened to overwhelm him. He stood up suddenly, propelling himself to open the windows, stow the suitcases, air out the house.

85

AVOID

Later that day, Jed Mills called first and came by, having to shoulder his way through the news crews. He called out at the gate until Michael came to unfasten the lock and let him in. Jed sat down in the living room, stretched out his legs, and crossed his cowboy boots at the ankles. He took out his pipe, played with it, and put new tobacco inside the bowl but didn't light it, presumably out of respect for Erica's strict rule forbidding smoking inside the house. Michael didn't know if he cared about it or not.

Jed made several opening gambits about the weather (hot), the grasslands (sparse and dry), the summer college staff (more religious than rowdy this past year). He said the media people were out at the ranch wandering around, looking for the other house where Erica Hanlon lived but he'd run them off. Jed told him the stories on the network news had ended up being about thirty seconds long, each with a brief shot of the walls in front of the Chamisa house followed by images of Erica's sculptures.

He tamped down the tobacco into the bowl of his pipe with his thumb and said with transparent nonchalance, "So, how are you doing?" Michael thought of when Jed had asked him something similar when he'd first arrived at Erica's house and was up on the roof. He decided once again to take the path of least resistance and least involvement.

"Fine," he said.

The answering machines at both houses quickly accumulated messages until they ran out of tape. He didn't bother to erase them. The phones rang almost continuously so he disconnected them and only plugged them in again when he wanted to make a call out. To avoid being disturbed, he'd leave the house just before dawn and find back roads to take him miles into the National Forest. He'd park the truck and hike along the top of a ridge or along the edge of a mesa, moving all day to exhaust himself. He'd only stop to eat the lunch he'd prepared in the kitchen the night before. He wouldn't return to the house at the Ranch until the sun had gone down. Lupe would leave his dinner in the refrigerator to be warmed up, usually with a friendly note.

86

WILL

Erica left a very specific will. She allotted relatively modest amounts to each of her five American relatives. Michael was given control of her assets in the seven figure range, her three houses, and the rights to her sculptures. Erica's attorney handled the distribution of the funds. He told Michael the relatives weren't happy and talked about breaking the will but couldn't find any leverage to bring that about.

Her nephew from Maine, who hadn't seen Erica for twenty years, hired a private investigator and instructed him to interview various disgruntled locals. They portrayed Michael as a Svengali angling for her money but when the P.I. talked to Lupe and asked if Erica had been in her right mind at the end, Lupe just laughed. She said Erica had always done things her own way and the will was just the final example. Nevertheless, the relatives and their lawyers continued on.

Michael didn't care much about what he received and talked to the attorney about letting them have it all. The lawyer, an aging Brahmin with an office in Santa Fe, was shocked by his indifference and argued that Michael was the only one who could continue Erica's legacy. Michael shrugged because he didn't know what the legacy would be now that Erica was gone but he agreed not to give up.

After a year, a settlement was reached. Michael would receive the houses at the Ranch and in the village, about half the available cash (still in the seven figure range), and publishing rights to the book he and Erica had made, along with any other forthcoming publications. The sculptures would be managed by a non-profit foundation, to be directed by Jeremy, the curator from MOMA, who happily resigned from the Museum for this new position. The other assets, including the house in Provence, were divided up among the relatives Erica had no use for during her life. Michael felt he had more than enough.

In that year, the media people and the curious and her relatives all stopped bothering him and the world turned its attention to the the succession of better stories that followed Erica's departure. After months of doing very little aside from the basics of existence, he decided the time had come to climb Obsidian and settle Erica into her rest.

He prepared his backpack on a Sunday night in early October, figuring he was least likely to encounter others by going up on a Monday morning. Erica's ashes were in a ceramic urn with a screw-on lid. He took it down from a shelf in the living room and looked inside. Small chunks of white bone poked from a clot of ash in a plastic bag, closed off with a twisty. Hefting the bag, he found it only weighed a few pounds. None of it seemed to have much to do with the Erica he knew but this was all that was left. Outside, clouds made for a starless night but he hoped the sky would be clear by the time the sun came up.

He thought of the night of her death, when he returned from his date in Manhattan, feeling dissatisfied because the woman from the Museum made it clear early on that nothing would happen between them. By contrast, as soon as he opened the door of their suite, he knew something had indeed happened inside. The silence struck him as having a quality of waiting, to see how he was going to react. He knocked on Erica's door and, when she didn't answer, let himself in. She lay in the middle of the bed, her hands folded just below her sternum, the covers turned down neatly across her abdomen. Her face was stern, with maybe a hint of an ironic smile at the corners of her mouth. He'd seen her sleep in this position many times before but knew immediately that no one was home. The flesh and bones were there but Erica was gone. Now, weeks later, her physical presence had been reduced to this small pile of rubble that was up to him to cast away.

Because of the weekend, Lupe hadn't come so he made himself dinner of a sandwich and canned tomato soup and went to bed feeling satisfied but not full. He woke up several times in the night, thinking he heard something moving outside the adobe walls but he didn't have the impetus to go out and look. He listened for awhile to coyotes howling on the flats before falling back into sleep. Given how tired he'd been, he was surprised to be awake again at five. But he actually felt like getting up. The danger of this post-Erica phase of his life was that he didn't really have anything to do. On some mornings, he'd only wake up when he heard the sound of Lupe turning the lock of the front door at ten a.m. However, on this particular morning, he once again had something specific to propel him out of bed.

87

ASHES

With night bulging at the windows, he stood in the light of the single bulb in the kitchen, feeling groggy and confused. He made a pot of cowboy coffee, throwing in cold water to settle the grounds. He drank some and put the rest in a thermos. What else did he need to pack? Food. He reached in the fridge, grabbed cheese and ham, took apples and oranges from the bowl on the kitchen table, added half a loaf of bread from the box on the counter, more than enough to keep him alive for a day. He jammed it all in his pack and shook his head to clear his thoughts. He picked up the truck keys from the counter and opened the front door. He stood for a moment and breathed in the aromas of the desert and the night, cool and fragrant in his nose. He was glad to be heading out on a trip, but to do what?

Her ashes. He left the door open and returned to the living room where he grabbed the urn and put it in his pack, moving things around so the fruit wouldn't get crushed. He realized he hadn't brought water. He retrieved the canteens from under the sink as the night air followed him into the kitchen from the front door. What else had he forgotten? Lots of things. He stood for a moment and tried to think of anything else he might need. Compass? No, that was in his pack and, besides, the way to the top was pretty clear. He didn't see how he could get lost, unless he went astray in the trees going down to the truck but he didn't think so. Even if he missed the clearing, he'd have to cross the road at some point and would be able to make his way back to where he parked. Extra clothes? The weather could change but he always had a slicker in his pack and could bivouac if need be. Something else was missing but whatever it was merged into everything else he'd lost.

Driving in the dark was a pleasure as he banked into turns and glided through the mesas without another car in sight. As Aretha Franklin played on the 8 track, singing "Spirit In The Dark," he let his mind wander over all he might do in the coming days. He could stop by the Ranch of the Spirits and reconnect with people there, maybe take Val up on her offer to come by her house for dinner. She'd called several times and left messages with Lupe but he hadn't called back. If he wanted to, he could track down Sheila, wherever she was, and try to meet up with her again. But did he want to? He was a fool with women, that much was sure, and now he was a fool of some substance but didn't want anyone who'd be attracted by Erica's money.

The roads to the mountain were enclosed in cloud and the autumn sun had not yet risen. He didn't feel the excitement he'd experienced on his first approach with Erica but he wanted to be on top of the mountain again. After the turn from the highway, few details could be seen in the landscape, just the dirt road unrolling up the slope, the tree trunks leaning toward him. The terrain looked so different in the mist he wasn't sure of the turnings but did recognize a boulder, shaped like an Easter Island head, marking the trail for the ascent. He pushed the truck up the steep hill, the engine roaring in first gear, and found himself in the clearing where they'd stopped before.

He remembered Erica smoothing the suntan lotion on his nose and the shiver he'd felt at her touch. Thinking of their nights together, he didn't regret anything. He needed someone and she needed him. She'd actually given him more pleasure than any of the women he'd been with before or after. Maybe the forbidden nature of their encounters added to the excitement but she'd been skilled at drawing him out. When he gave himself over to her, and didn't let his mind ruin the experience, he entered a realm of pure erotic impulse. She'd been an artist in more than one area.

88

FOG

He stepped out of the truck, grabbed his backpack, and began the ascent. The clouds were hanging in thick slabs around him, a fog so thick he could feel it coiling around his head and brushing against his hands. The steep grade taxed his lungs and he stopped whenever he felt tired. There was no hurry. Once again, no one on the planet knew or cared about his location. Erica's ashes were his only connection to the human race. He'd never been so alone and yet he didn't feel bad about this fact. Being alone was his usual condition and Erica's death had not changed that part of his reality.

When he reached the chimney leading to the top, he took several swigs from his canteen and began climbing. He remembered looking up at Erica as she swung herself easily from rock to rock. She'd been in her seventies then but in better shape than he was. He looked out behind him but where there'd been a panorama of ridges and peaks on their previous ascent, now he saw only fog, thick, brooding, so close he couldn't imagine the distance beyond, as if he were climbing inside a chimney.

He concentrated on what there was to see, the texture of the rock, lichen spotting the surfaces, his hands reaching up repeatedly like a cat's paws scratching a post, but even what was close was obscured by strands of mist passing in front of his eyes. He hoped it was fog and not the beginnings of the macular degeneration that had drained Erica's creative spirit.

89

SPIRAL

Reaching the top was anti-climactic, a last pull over the rocks and he was bent over, panting hard on the trail across the short length of peak. The clouds hung all around him. No wind moved the vapors. The sun must have risen by now but produced only a dull glow emanating from every direction, a faint luminescence seeping through the clouds. He took a long drink from his canteen and sat on the ground next to a rock he seemed to remember from being up there with Erica. Closing his eyes, he listened to a faint sibilance as if he could hear the thick particles of fog brushing against the rock of the summit. The sound of a passing car engine drifted up from the far off highway. Somewhere in northern New Mexico, in a feat of long-distance ventriloquism, a rooster crowed.

He put the backpack between his feet and opened it wide. The urn required wiggling to pry it from inside, past the food, the poncho, and the miscellany. He held it in his lap, the surface warm, not, he considered, from the lingering effects of cremation but from the sweat on his back. The clouds showed no sign of dissipating. He had nothing else scheduled for the day or, indeed, for any other day so maybe he should just stay there on top until the sky displayed some of the beauty they'd seen on their first ascent. He sat cross-legged, listening to his breath and letting thoughts of Erica rise and fall in his mind, Erica in the day and Erica in the night. After an hour of this contemplation, and a sore rear from sitting on the small rocks, he realized the weather gave no sign of clearing. Aesthetics weren't really the purpose of this trip. Erica wanted her remains to be part of this isolated immensity and the co-mingling would happen whether or not the sun was shining. He had an intuition she didn't need for the external factors to be perfect before she returned to what she loved.

The lid of the urn was stuck and took some effort to pry off. When he did free it, the lid popped up in the air and almost went over the edge of the peak before he grabbed it back. He pulled out the plastic bag and again hefted the weight of it in his palm. It seemed so light for the force of who she was. Of course, her matter was now almost completely turned into energy and was loose in the world. All he held was the residue from the vibrancy of her being.

He undid the plastic tie holding the bag shut and looked at the contents. He couldn't help but think of the phrase "ashes to ashes" although that never made sense to him because people didn't originate in ash but in various degrees of living liquidity. The air was still so the remains weren't likely to blow back on him. Standing over the edge of the precipice, he remembered dancing with Erica in the storm rising up to surround them on that same spot.

Holding the bag open with his right hand, he used his left to push the ashes out over the drop. The chunks of bone fell right away and he could hear them clatter against the side of the peak but the ashes themselves hung in the air directly in front of him, buoyed up by the fog. The remains of Erica's physical presence moved through the air in a slow spiral, turning on some internal axis in the cloud. He sat down and watched the gray of the ash float in the mist that was slightly tan, as if the grit from the desert below had been gathered up into the air.

In the ashes, he thought he saw his mother's face for a moment, dissolving into Erica's face, and eventually into the face of another woman, someone who looked familiar yet he couldn't identify, maybe someone not yet in his life. The faces shifted through various expressions as the particles revolved, suggesting outrage and fear and pain and grief but ending in an enigmatic smile. Slowly, what was left of Erica spread out so he could no longer distinguish between ash and cloud.

90

REPAIR

Over the following weeks, he kept to a routine at the house on the Ranch, catching up on some repairs and patching adobe he'd been neglecting. Lupe continued her long-established rituals of cleaning during the week and leaving dinner for him. Jed Mills made it a point to stop by every so often and chat in his terse way about what was going on at the Ranch but didn't put any pressure on Michael to donate or help out or do anything. Michael thought maybe when summer came again, he would occasionally stop for meals at the dining hall in order to involve himself in the abundance of intricate life gathered every week at the Ranch.

He had the stirrings of desire to meet some of the young, and not so young, women who would be arriving there weekly but he couldn't imagine how he would go about starting a relationship, given the weirdness of his life and the fact that most of his potential partners would only be at the ranch temporarily. But maybe, eventually, he'd find somebody to share this with, whatever "this" was.

91

BLUE

November, 1983

Six weeks after the scattering of ashes, he stood on top of the house looking out at Obsidian, a view he'd taken in a thousand times. In the cold shadows, he carefully set up the easel, anchoring it with sandbags to prevent the desert winds from rising up suddenly and blowing it away. Opening the paints, he took a deep, carcinogenic sniff from the box. He laid the silver tubes out on the small table he'd set up next to the easel. The tar paper at his feet was cracking. A new roof would have to be put on fairly soon although it would probably hold until spring. Soon he felt the sun lifting above the mesas behind him, sending its strong light directly onto his back. The edges of his shadow glowed white on the surface of the canvas before him. The entire basin was now flooding with color and texture, almost too intense for his eyes to take in. He picked up a brush and ran a finger through the fine bristles as he peered out on the expanse, trying to discover a way into its infinite detail. A raven flew straight out from the mesa and past his shoulder, so close he could feel the air move from its wings before it soared slowly down toward the river.

On his left, he could hear the sounds of heavy equipment at the ranch. Jed always started some construction project in the off-season to improve the facilities. Erica had always liked Jed and his wife but never cared for the rest of the church people and what she called their worshipping ways. Michael didn't mind them because, after all, they had given him his start in the Southwest. He'd already recorded in his will that after he died, the house and whatever remained of the money would go to the Ranch.

In front of him, the passing cars and trucks made soft sounds drifting up from the highway. His only reservation about the house was that it wasn't as quiet as he would have liked but he had to admit the thin noises wafting across the desert had a good effect in reminding him he wasn't alone in the world. He now had the resources to move further out if he wanted, buy land and build somewhere in the mountains, if he could find the right parcel. In fact, he had the money to live wherever in the world he desired, could easily move to Europe, for instance, but he didn't want to leave, especially with Erica dead.

Her ghost seemed to inhabit everything in and around the house but she was much easier to deal with as a spirit than as a living being. Her ghost was friendly where she herself had been prickly, supportive where she'd been confrontational, erotic without being sexual.

The brush rested lightly between his fingers, poised like a pen, ready for him to engage in his first real act of the day. He stopped before committing, however (no use rushing into things), and took a sip of coffee. He'd recently acquired an electric coffee maker to replace the ancient and battered metal pot Erica had kept for decades but he missed the coppery tang the coffee used to have. In his usual spirit of procrastination, he tried to think of some chores he might do but none came to mind.

He took a deep breath, inhaling the remaining coolness of the morning, the dryness of the desert, the tang of sage. Standing on top of the house, he was the tallest being between the mesa cliffs and the green hills on the far side of the valley. No matter what he went through in life, it all came down to this, rising in the morning, preparing to do some work, not knowing what the day would bring. Would he paint something extraordinary or just another muddy botch? Right now, and maybe always, that didn't matter.

He put the coffee down and flexed his wrist, sore from misjudging a handhold during the climb down from Obsidian. He picked up Erica's old Bowie knife to dab colors on the short plank he used for a palette. In the mixing, he wanted to re-create the textures and hues of those hills far away, adding in the reflections from the clouds above him and from the lake below him. He tried to include some of Erica's vibrant energy along with his own dark complexity. Pausing for a moment, he looked at what had been brought together by the knife. He dipped the brush in what might be sky and lifted it to the canvas.

Acknowledgements

As always, thanks to my family for being here for me, and to my friends for being there for me. Thanks to Nicole Davis, Sulo Turner, Linda Dunn, and Linda Lyon for their close readings and excellent suggestions that helped me rein in this wayward story. Engaging with a long manuscript these days is definitely a labor of love. A special thanks to the Washington State Ferry system for providing me with a floating office for writing over the past sixteen years. My appreciation goes out to Chris Peters for once again designing a cover I can live with.

And finally, I want to express my appreciation for all my fellow writers who put words together for non-utilitarian purposes, both those who receive recognition and those who never do. I'm reminded of Mark Twain's story, *Captain Stormfield's Visit To Heaven* in which people are rewarded in the next life not just for what they did on earth but for what they might have done, if given the chance. "That tailor Billings, from Tennessee, wrote poetry that Homer and Shakespeare couldn't begin to come up to; but nobody would print it, nobody read it but his neighbors, an ignorant lot, and they laughed at it." The pay-off is that in heaven he's honored as one of the greats: the ultimate scribbler's fantasy.